All my life I've been dreaming up stories. My mum said when I was little I used to make all the My Little Pony figurines talk to each other and even fall in love. Later, it was Barbie and Ken. In my teens, I played matchmaker with my friends at school. When I wasn't creating imaginary scenarios, I had my nose stuck in books, reading across genres and there was one thing I loved more than the escapism—the fact a story could touch me so deeply, like I was experiencing everything along with my characters. I knew from early on this was something I wanted to do for others. Fast forward a few years and the dream almost got lost in real life, but I still couldn't shake it completely.

Now I write sizzling romance with the hope of making my readers' hearts race as if they are falling in love for the first time.

You can follow me on Twitter @AimeeDuffyx.

PRAISE FOR AIMÉE DUFFY

'The perfect, girly summer read'
Reviewed the Book

'Action packed and fun'
Shaun the Book Addict

'Sexy, fun and as hot as the summer sun'
The Book Geek Wears Pajamas

'A great summer read!'
Lost to Books

'Sensual, sexy, heart stopping'
Contemporary Romance Reviews

The Summer Flings Travel Club

AIMÉE DUFFY

A division of HarperCollins*Publishers*
www.harpercollins.co.uk

Harper*Impulse* an imprint of
HarperCollins*Publishers*
1 London Bridge Street
London SE1 9GF

www.harpercollins.co.uk

A Paperback Original 2016

First published in Great Britain in ebook format by Harper*Impulse* 2016

A catalogue record for this book
is available from the British Library

ISBN: 9780008182410

This novel is entirely a work of fiction.
The names, characters and incidents portrayed in it are
the work of the author's imagination. Any resemblance to
actual persons, living or dead, events or localities is
entirely coincidental.

Set in Minion by Palimpsest Book Production Ltd, Falkirk, Stirlingshire

Printed and bound in Great Britain

MIX
Paper from
responsible sources
FSC° C007454

FSC™ is a non-profit international organisation established to promote
the responsible management of the world's forests. Products carrying the
FSC label are independently certified to assure consumers that they come
from forests that are managed to meet the social, economic and
ecological needs of present and future generations,
and other controlled sources.

Find out more about HarperCollins and the environment at
www.harpercollins.co.uk/green

For the ninja, super-graphic-girl and queen Catco. I couldn't have done this without the support of you 'special' ladies.

LA

Chapter One

'*This* is where we're staying?'

Ciara Bree gaped for so long her eyes watered and stung. When they had first talked about a round the world trip, back when they had spent those endless days in their college library at Oxford, she'd never expected this.

Glamping in some fancy static caravan rigged out for the three of them, yes. Maybe even the odd budget hotel or hostel – something that would be affordable with the cash she'd managed to save from her part-time uni job. But this... A mathematics and statistics graduate from Wicklow didn't have words for this.

Her bestie, Elle Muir, sauntered towards the white mini-mansion, right smack at the bottom of Hollywood Hill. 'My granddad said we could crash at his houses during our trip, as long as we promise not to break anything. No point wasting precious shopping credit when we can have this for free.'

'C'mon Ciara!' Her other best friend, Gem, shoved her shoulder, but she must have still been in shock because her legs refused to budge. They'd never been poor growing up, and her da had always given her everything she wanted – and some things she didn't, like tuition fees to Oxford. She'd known Gem and Elle came from families so rich the Crown Jewels would be their Mas' idea of day jewellery, but she'd never met them in the flesh and it was much easier to believe her two best friends liked to exaggerate. After all, like her, they were super smart. Only difference was, when she'd gone to Oxford, she was The Ultimate Geek and they were more Geek Chic.

With a laugh, her friend said, 'It's not like we're staying over there. You can pick your chin off the floor now.'

Following Gem's outstretched arm, towards a mini-version of the White House, Ciara saw the comparison. They were staying in what looked to be the garage of the super-mansion she had first seen – though this garage still came with a huge drive, palm trees and exotic-looking flowers galore. But… feck. Their temporary home had her flustered, or maybe that was the midday Californian sun made stronger since it reflected off the bright walls.

Ciara just shook her head. 'I'll never roll my eyes at you again when you go on and on about this stuff.'

Gem pulled back her bright red hair into a ponytail then swiped a coat of sweat off her forehead. 'I want to have a dip in the pool to cool off before the jet lag kicks in. You coming?'

Nodding, she followed wordlessly into the house to be shocked anew. If the outside had her chin dropping the inside would have her tongue rolling down to meet it. Chic, shiny floors covered what she assumed was the entrance vestibule, though this was much bigger than her dorm room. Bigger than five, probably. A massive, spiral staircase was situated opposite the door and artwork that looked suspiciously like originals instead of knock offs hung strategically on the walls. Ciara was scared to breathe for fear of steaming up the shiny floor or staining the pristine walls, and feck! She still had her shoes on!

'Let's turn this duty free bottle of tequila into something strong and icy before we hit the pool.' Elle held up the airport bag with a grin.

'Ooo iced margaritas?' Gem asked.

At Elle's nod they rolled their suitcases through the swanky house. Ciara worried that her Tesco special bag was spoiling the look of the whole place just by being there.

The kitchen was bigger than her whole house, complete with shiny chrome accessories, a kitchen bar and small dining table – not to mention the integrated appliances and even crushed ice maker. It did make Elle's job of filling a massive jug with ice much easier, but everything seemed so foreign, like she was watching an episode of MTV Cribs not getting ready for her first stop on a crazy round the world trip.

'Should we take our bags up first?' she asked, having visions of jet lag kicking in when she was poolside and falling into a margarita induced coma.

'No way. I say we dig around them for a bikini then chill at the pool for a while,' Elle replied.

Gem agreed, unzipping her bag and picking out one of goodness knew how many two pieces, all still with the tags on. Ciara did the same. After all, she was as unlikely to win a fight with Elle as she was able to pick up a car and swing it over her head.

They took turns in the laundry room getting poolside ready and slapping on the SPF 30, then Elle led them through another hall.

'Does that belong to one of you?' She asked, toeing a bag out her way with her flip flop.

The sports bag was so full it almost burst the seams. 'No,' Ciara said at the same time Gem did.

'Hmm,' Elle scowled at the bag like it was filled with manure, then shrugged. 'The housekeeper must have left it.'

Ciara slipped her sunglasses on the second they were outside. Elle and Gem insisted panda eyes was never a good look but since the weather back home was overcast eighty percent of the year, bright sunlight generally fried her retinas. And if she wanted to stay awake instead of lying out here all day frazzling, she needed to keep her eyes open.

It wasn't too hard to manage since she was hit with another dose of the OMGs. The pool area was about the size of a holiday complex, with a stone terrace, terracotta furniture and the comfiest sun loungers she'd ever had the pleasure of lying on.

'Drink up girls. The Adventures of Muir, Bree and Howard have begun!' Elle filled up their glasses.

Gem pouted. 'I still prefer Geeks on Tour.'

'Nonsense. We're too chic to be geeks, right Ciara?' Elle said.

They might be, but all she'd ever been was a geek as far as her schoolmates were concerned. Instead of taking sides, she shrugged and chugged down some of the drink. Her eyes watered and she made a vow to make the next round or that margarita coma might come sooner than she'd feared.

'It's really, really, scorching here,' she said to change the subject. Sticky lotion aside, her whole body was melting.

'It's great isn't it?' Elle said, chugging down more of her drink.

Against her better judgement, she did the same but the ice didn't help cool her off. Since they'd left the wonderfully air conditioned house, the lack of a breeze and sun beating down was a little too much for her.

'Feck it,' she said, finishing the last of her drink and getting up.

'Don't wuss out on us already, Ciara. We've got hours and hours of tanning time left,' Gem said.

'Then I'm going to have hours and hours of cooling off to do.' The tequila had already created a tiny, giddy buzz and the thought that she was in California, LA, hell *Hollywood,* kicked in.

That's all it took to get over the shock of Elle's grandfather's house, the heat, the worry she might pass out on the sun lounger and frazzle – after all crazy girlie holidays were about having fun and not worrying about the little things. So she kicked off her flip flops, removed her sunglasses, took a run for it, and jumped into the pool.

The water was lovely, not cold, more like a warm bath that

6

had been left for a bit to cool down. She swam from one end half way to the other before she broke the surface grinning.

Gem and Elle were already up, giggling at her change of attitude – she had to admit she'd been a bit of a moody cow so far. In her defence, the never ending plane journey had made her so restless and the cabin caged her in. Sitting for a few hours was her limit before the boredom had made her stir crazy... not even the inflight entertainment could distract her.

'Good to see the tequila's kicked in,' Gem said, jumping in too.

Elle didn't, instead she stayed on the side and pulled her long, blonde hair to the top of her head, twisting it into a bun. What was worrying was the look on her face that said she was a girl with a plan. A plan Ciara wasn't going to like.

'I have an idea, since we're just having a pool day...'

Yup, the wicked glint in her azure eyes definitely meant Ciara was going to hate her friend's idea.

Elle dashed back into the house and Ciara threw an anxious glance at Gem who rolled her eyes and started swimming like a pro. Sighing, she floated at the deep end, trying not to worry about what mad thing Elle had come up with now.

She was in LA with her two best friends, she needed to relax. Or learn how to. She'd always had studying and classes, even during the holidays. It might help a little if she stopped worrying over having no clue about her future career, or much else. But she was determined she wasn't going to think about that until she had to. No point in making herself miserable and ruining this trip.

Soon, Elle returned with two huge poles wrapped together by what looked like a net under her arm, clutching a bottle of tequila. After ditching the bottle she came to the pool and started to unravel the two poles.

'Ciara grab this one and stick it in the hole at the other side. Gem, there should be a ball in that shed,' Elle commanded.

Ciara did as asked, giving into Elle's bossy streak because it made life so much easier and she knew Elle didn't mean anything bad by it. That was who she was, and why her granddad was going to train her to be CEO of their family business. Elle wasn't all designer and class, she had authority and command too.

The net that stretched across the middle of the pool reminded her of *90210* volleyball games on the beach. She'd never played and didn't expect to be very good since she had as much coordination as a faulty compass. Maybe the tequila was the prize rather than the punishment.

Gem returned from the shed with a massive, blown up ball which made her relax a little. Hitting something that huge should be easy, even for her.

'Okay, tequila volleyball,' Elle said. She'd found a whistle somewhere and blew it once, then put the string it was on around her neck. 'One on one, you can only hit the ball with your fists and no bouncing off the water or the sides. If it hits the surface, you lose a point.'

'First to five?' Gem asked, sliding back into the pool.

'Yes, and I play the winner,' Elle announced.

'What does the winner get?' she asked, hoping it was a shot of the tequila.

Elle smiled. 'Bragging rights. The loser of each point gets a shot of this.' She held up the bottle.

Half an hour of losing and she'd be legless.

Elle blew the whistle, one sharp, shrill sound. 'Go!'

Gem threw the ball in the air and wacked it with her fist. Ciara tried to run forward but the resistance in the water made it feel like she was wading through sludge. Determined she wasn't going to lose, she dove forward, hands clenched together and hit the ball as hard as she could before she face planted into the pool.

She righted herself in time to see Gem fall back into the water and watch the ball hit home on the other side of the net. She laughed, relieved not to be the first to hit the shots.

Elle took the bottle over as Gem coughed up water. 'Open up and swallow as you go.'

'You said one shot, not half the bottle,' Gem protested.

Elle pulled an expression that on anyone else could be mistaken for innocent but on her looked too suspicious. 'A shot is all you're getting, honest.'

'Give me the bottle then.' Gem wasn't fooled.

'My game, my rules. The ref gets to hold the bottle.'

Ciara giggled quietly, knowing there was no way Gem was going to win.

'Open up,' Elle said, tipping the open bottle above Gem's head.

'Elle, give me the bloody thing. You'll drown me in tequila.'

Blue, puppy dog eyes no man could resist followed. 'Don't you trust me?'

'No one who knows you does, Elly.'

The voice did not belong to any of them and the girls all whirled around.

A man walked into the garden – a very tall, very hot and sweaty man with nothing on but trainers and a pair of shorts. Dark eyes, hair and a slight day old growth on his jaw that made Ciara feel dizzy wondering how it would feel against her face, her neck, her...

And how could she miss those abs? Better definition than the polo players at uni, no contest, and those little dips disappearing under his shorts at each side made her finger tips itch to reach out and touch...

For the second time that day she was imitating a fly catcher.

Elle stormed across the terracotta tiles to get in the man's face. 'Don't you dare think you're staying here! Granddad said we could have this place for a few days.'

The hottie didn't shrivel away from the heat of Elle's fury like anyone else would have, but his frown and the way his jaw hardened made her wonder if he had a temper of his own.

'I'm not going anywhere except for a shower.' He shoved by her and headed for the house.

Ciara had never seen Elle's temples throb like they were about to burst before, but she guessed there was a first thing for everything. Elle took off after him, shouting 'Pack up and get out, I mean it!'

Ciara made her way to the edge of the pool, about to go after them but Gem grabbed her arm.

'Don't, seriously. You don't want to end up in the middle of a fight between them.'

'Who is he?' Elle had never mentioned a brother. Maybe an ex?

Gem's eyes got that gooey way they did when she nattered on about Aidan Price, superstar actor extraordinaire. 'He's Zack Muir, Elle's hotter, older cousin.'

Ciara didn't want to look at why that made her relax a smidgen. After all, he didn't spare her a second glance and even if he had, she wouldn't *do* anything with him. Tempting as it might be. She wasn't a stayer, just like her ma. She got bored too easily.

Sighing, she thought about the way he looked drenched in sweat with all that delicious muscle on display and reckoned it would take a long, long time before she got bored of someone like him.

The voices upstairs were too muffled to make out the words the Muirs were throwing at each other – Elle's voice was high pitched, ringing through the patio doors while Zack's rough and sexy tone didn't carry. Maybe Elle was giving him a monologue stream of abuse.

'Back to the game, sans tequila?' Ciara asked.

Gem glanced up at the French doors lining the upper floor of the mansion. The sound of a door slamming shut was followed by a shriek.

'Good idea. The splashing might drown out the crazy,' Gem said.

It didn't take long for Elle to come back, but it did take a while for her to lose her temper. They made another jug of iced margaritas. By the way Elle sucked down half the jug, she was either cooling down or heating up for round two. It was better for everyone if they could calm Elle down before she went catatonic, and since Gem seemed more interested in drying off with a magazine in hand it looked like it was up to her.

'Elle, this house is huge. We can all squeeze in fine.' And have rooms and rooms to spare.

Elle slipped off her *Ray Bans* again, no doubt to avoid reverse panda-eye. 'That's not the point. I just don't want him to ruin LA for us with his moping. We have houses all over, why did he come here?'

He was moping? Ciara wanted to ask what had happened but this was about cheering Elle up, not grilling her about her gorgeous, mopey cousin. 'He's not going to ruin anything. We're just cranky and jet lagged. A good long sleep and a cuppa in the morning and we'll tackle Rodeo Drive.'

That earned her a grin and she thanked the stars the worst seemed over for now.

'You're right, we'll just carry on like he isn't here. He spends all his bloody time running and working out anyway. I don't know why our granddad even keeps him on the books.'

Ciara nodded. She could pretend he wasn't there if it meant there'd be no more screaming matches.

'We have more important things to worry about,' Gem chimed in. 'Like what we're wearing to Aiden's premiere.'

Taking a sip of the cocktail was much, much safer than laughing at the way Gem spoke about the Hollywood star like she knew him – sometimes like she was dating him. And that's all it took for Elle and Gem to have a marathon chat about what cut of gown they were going to keep an eye out for tomorrow, argue about the pros of *Gucci* against *Marc Jacobs* and Ciara decided it was time to clear out and heft her suitcase up god knew how many stairs before she was too shattered.

'Which one will I take?' she asked Elle.

'Any. Most are the same and no doubt that shit has taken the master suite,' Elle said with a scowl.

11

Ciara cleared out of the way before her friend erupted again.

As she roamed through the mini-mansion, suitcase in toe, she tried not to feel crappy about the dress she'd picked up in *River Island* for the premiere. She'd love to get glammed up and drip with designer gear and accessories but that wasn't going to happen with the limited savings she had for the trip – the flights alone had ripped off a huge chunk.

But she was in LA, on the first part of her journey before she had to go home and face the fact she had no job, a lot of university debt, and no clue what she wanted to do with her life. In the grand scheme of things, worrying about a high street dress was ridiculous. She shoved everything from her mind and focused on the tasks at hand.

One, pull a possibly vital muscle by dragging her hundred pound suitcase up the stairs – what had she packed in it again? Cement? She didn't want to imagine how flushed her pale skin was after, or whether her face looked like she'd pressed it into a puddle – especially since the hottie she wasn't supposed to be thinking about was in the house somewhere.

Two, find a room that didn't look like it had been taken by the gorgeous, sweaty hunk she shouldn't wonder about. This was trickier. Every door she opened looked the same. Pale décor, silky looking sheets instead of a duvet, and mini balconies facing down the hill, showcasing the city below. Surreal.

There wasn't so much as a rickety floor board in the house so when she heard someone clear their throat behind her she about jumped out of her flip flops. Turning, she prayed again that her face didn't look like she'd sputtered her way round the London Marathon five minutes before.

'Can I help you?' Zack Muir asked.

Thank goodness he was fully dressed this time. She didn't think she'd be able to force words out if he was still sweaty and half naked.

'I don't know what– what's up here.' Keeping her mouth shut

and staring at him like an eejit would have been better than what came out. Instead of Maths she should have studied English. Or taken a course in how to behave around gorgeous men she couldn't have.

He cocked an eyebrow. 'What's what?'

'You know, which room's taken? Elle said you have the master suite.'

Great, now her palms were as sticky as her face. So much for everything the girls had taught her about flirting. She was sweating buckets and getting tongue tied over a man who looked at her like he thought she was about to clear out with all his cash.

Zack closed his eyes and shook his head. 'That's Elly all over. She shoots her mouth off without checking the facts. They're all empty. I'm in my room downstairs. Take your pick.'

'Okay, thanks.' Ciara turned before she said something that would paint her cheeks scarlet, caught her toe beneath the cement filled case and took a not-so-graceful nosedive into the floor, cursing like a trucker all the way.

Luckily she caught herself before she cracked her skull but she'd never live the shame of this one down. With her bikini covered bum – hopefully cellulite free – in the air and Zack now on his knees at her side, she'd be quite happy to have knocked herself a good one so she didn't have to face him.

'Shit, are you okay?' he asked, pulling her off the floor so she was kneeling behind the case, not sprawled across it. At her nod, he smiled. 'I didn't understand half of what you said but I'm guessing it was pretty creative.'

Her face burned, adding more humiliation to this scenario. 'I'm glad you didn't, it wasn't very polite. Sorry.'

Zack didn't seem appalled, thank god. He pulled her to her feet. 'So where in Ireland did you grow up?' he asked.

A quick glance at the bikini top to make sure the triangles were still in place – check – and she felt a tiny bit better. 'Blessington. Not too far from Dublin.'

'I've never been, but keep meaning to. The accent is adorable.'

There goes the flame again, heating her face all the way to her scalp. 'It's a great city.'

Time to move away from him before she tripped up and fell through one of the windows or something worse. Pulling up the case, she turned to go but Zack lifted the whole thing off the floor like it didn't weigh more than she did.

He lifted an eyebrow. 'Compared to Elle and her mum, you definitely travel light.'

'Thanks,' Ciara said, not sure what else to stay.

Following him down the corridor she tried her best to keep her eyes level with his shoulders. But they were wide and strong looking, and this really wasn't going to help keep her mind off him like she'd promised she would.

At the end of the corridor next to yet another set of stairs, he opened the door and led her in. This suite didn't look the same as the others. It had too much space, a walk in wardrobe she'd never be able to fill with all the clothes she'd owned from birth to now and what looked like a massive ensuite.

This had to be the master bedroom, and since Zack had lain her suitcase on a bed big enough to sleep ten people, she guessed he was giving it to her.

'I can't take this,' she protested.

'Why not? Elle thinks I'm here anyway.' He headed for the door but she blocked the way.

'I'd rather not fight with Elle. I'll just take another.'

He grinned and his eyes glowed, honey-like and melting. 'Relax, Ireland. My cousin's bark is worse than her bite.'

'*Ciara*, not Ireland and I'm not coming into my friend's house and taking the best room from her.' If he wanted to fight with Elle he could go right ahead but she wasn't being piggy in the middle.

She grabbed the case, pulled it off the bed and narrowly avoided crushing her toe.

'Give me that,' he said, not as friendly as he'd seemed before. 'Go pick a room before my poor arms break.'

She reckoned it would take a lot more than her luggage to bend those biceps but didn't point that out. She found a room quickly and let him place the case on a more reasonably sized bed.

Before he left, he said, 'Enjoy LA, Ireland. And don't let Elle bully you.'

Her eyes narrowed at the empty doorway for a second but she couldn't stay annoyed for long. She kind of liked that he'd given her a nickname.

And she decided to take the first part of his advice. These were her last eight weeks without worries so she was going to make the most of it if it killed her.

Chapter Two

Gem let out a low, star struck squee. 'Don't look now, but Shakira's behind you!'

Ciara turned anyway, pretending to dig something out of her bag and saw the same thing Gem did. A woman with a mass of gorgeous blonde hair ordering a smoothie at the outdoor café they'd taken a break at. And there was no mistaking who it was – those hips didn't lie.

'I *love* LA,' Elle said. 'There's pretty and celebrity everywhere.'

There definitely was. Elle and Gem had dragged her around the designer shops all afternoon and they'd spotted movie stars, an opera singer and the host of a reality TV show. But the high was mixed with anxiety when Elle got an outfit that probably cost more than her house back home and Gem's wasn't far off. Part of her wished her friends hadn't scored tickets to the premiere later, but when would she ever get the chance to go to something this amazing again?

'You know, you can get a new outfit too, Ciara,' Gem said, waving her father's plastic Amex around. It was as tempting as the double fudge and raspberry sundae they wouldn't let her order (they had dresses to squeeze into later, after all). 'I don't have a limit.'

'I told you, I don't want to spend your money,' she insisted, again.

They didn't understand, since technically neither had paid their bills ever. One of the only things that frustrated her about her friends was that they hadn't a clue how much money was worth – and how hard it was for the normal people in the world to get it.

They didn't get how tempting it was to ditch her morals and let them get her the prettiest dress, shoes, handbag and jewels in all of LA, either.

But they got the important stuff. The first night she met them she was studying in the library at uni and it had hit her hard that she was really alone. At school she'd always gone home to her da and been able to tell him about her day but all bets were off in England. That's when Gem and Elle had found her.

She'd escaped to a quiet corner in the library when the water-works started. They'd cheered her up, comforted her and made her feel like she had other people in her life who cared. People she could rely on.

They'd grown so close over the years they even knew her worst fears and insecurities – mainly that she'd end up like her ma.

But, more importantly, they knew how much she hated charity.

'Okay, so if you don't want to hit our plastic, but you're miser-able about having nothing—'

'I'm not miserable and I do have something,' she said, cutting Elle off.

'That's why you've been all smiles since we left Gucci?' Gem asked.

'Is this pick on Ciara day?' She wasn't budging, or spending enough to buy her da a house for one party. It was madness. Wasn't it?

Elle relaxed back into her chair with a calculating gleam that kept Ciara sharp, despite her wavering. After sipping on her ice tea, Elle said, 'Okay, so you rent. You can afford that, surely.'

'Rent?' she asked.

Gem clapped her hands. '*Yes*! Why didn't I think of that?'

'Because I'm trained to see every angle and you're trained to see whatever's in front of you,' Elle suggested.

Before a fight erupted about business management verses biological science, Ciara jumped in quickly, 'How do I do that?'

'Exactly how Shakira does it!' Gem said too loudly. Ciara hoped the woman was out of earshot. 'You don't think they really buy all those red carpet dresses to wear once, do you?'

Ciara did, and also thought it was a bit of a waste when you could do so much more with the money, but she didn't say that to her friends either. They wouldn't get it. She was just the poorest point in their triangle who always dressed plain and had such a thick accent when she got worked up that it was hard for anyone to understand her. But she *was* pretty and funny at times too, so the other girls had taken her under their wings, styled her hair and taught her about make-up and boys.

More than that though, they'd been there for her when she needed them. More than she could say for her ma who'd walked out on her without saying goodbye.

'Which shops do that?' she asked.

Elle slipped her *Ray Bans* off and leaned over the table. 'We flash this, and we're good to go anywhere.'

The little rectangle of plastic was black, no doubt limitless in its spending potential but she couldn't take money from her friends. It was bad enough her da had worked fourteen hour days to send her to Oxford and she was done owing people she cared about.

'Elle—'

'Before you start, this is just to wave at the sales assistants so we have their undivided attention. You can give me back the dollars if it makes you feel better.'

It definitely did.

Elle hadn't been kidding. The second she flashed the black

credit card at the *Louis Vuitton* counter she had three sales assistants eager to give her anything she desired. Ciara had even wondered if they'd go out to get her lunch if she asked, but according to Gem and Elle they wouldn't be eating anything after three in the afternoon so they could look slim and sexy tonight, and by the time they'd got to the shop it was closer to four.

And after she'd been brought a zillion dresses, stripped and dressed in the middle of the biggest dressing room she'd seen surrounded by her friends, sales people and far too many mirrors, they'd picked the perfect dress – or so Elle and Gem said. Personally, she liked it. It had a high neckline and focused more on the simple slit all the way up her thigh, almost to the right of her belly button. Knickers would be out, but the deep blue looked great with her dark blonde hair, which the sales assistants said had to be put up.

Gem agreed, planning the perfect style all the way home and now it was 6pm they had mere hours to get ready (which according to Elle, was not enough time). While her friends hectically showered, buffed, fake tanned and buffed again, Ciara snuck off to the kitchen to find something to ease the grumbling in her stomach. She didn't care if she burst out the dress, she just wanted the starvation pains gone.

Jackpot. There was cheese, like honest to god full fat cheddar cheese and a loaf of British, thick cut bread. Heaven. Firing the grill up she hunted for a knife and got to work shredding thin slices of cheddar, hoping Gem and Elle didn't catch her fatty carb on carb pig out.

When one side of the bread was nice and toasted, she flipped it over, layered on the cheese and slipped it back under the grill.

'So you won't steal a room but you'll steal food?'

She whirled around, her hand over her heart to stop the thumping – like that would work. Ciara just hoped it was shock and a little bit fear rather than think Zack brought this reaction out in her.

19

Then something clicked. Elle had barely nibbled on a carrot stick since they'd arrived – there was no way she'd eat bread and cheese when they were hitting the beach in a few days. She dived for the tray, whipping it out before the lovely, orange stuff even managed to bubble.

'This is yours, isn't it? Sorry.' She switched off the grill, thinking it was a bit late since she'd already wasted his food.

He sauntered over to the tray and poked at the cheese on top of the bread.

'It doesn't look done.' Zack then switched on the grill and shoved it in. 'You don't have to apologise for being human. I'll bet Elle has you all on a fast for your party tonight.'

Ciara smiled. He knew his cousin well. She wondered why Elle never talked about him. 'I'm rubbish at diets. I like food too much.'

He nodded. 'I can tell.'

'Did you just call me fat?' she asked, shocked that he wasn't more polite. And she certainly was *not*.

Zack laughed and squeezed her hip. 'No, you've got curves and that's not a bad thing at all. Sexy, but not bad.'

Instead of fawning over the fact he found her sexy, sputtering incompetently because he'd touched her, she checked the grill to see the cheese starting to bubble. Her poor, empty stomach groaned at the delicious smell.

'I was referring to your choice in snack. You've got good taste. But let me show you how to make it even better.' He opened the cupboard door, pulled out some Worcester sauce and handed it to her.

'I didn't think you'd have this here!' Ciara pulled the tray out, splatted a few drops on top and then shoved it back in. 'Amazing.'

'Enjoy it, and tonight,' Zack said, then turned to leave.

'Don't you want a slice? It's your food, after all.' Her stomach growled out a protest at the threat of having to share, but she didn't want him to go.

He grinned. Her heart started to race.

'Sounds like you need it more. Oh, I almost forgot.' Zack pulled a piece of paper from his pocket and handed it over.

Ciara opened it and her lips parted on a gasp. 'Is this your number?'

'I know how Elle can be. If things get too wild or out of hand tonight phone me and I'll pick you all up.'

Oh, so it wasn't just *for her*. He was worried about his cousin. 'And Ciara?'

'Yes,' she answered, trying not to hope.

'Your grilled cheese is burning.'

With more make-up, hairspray and designer clothes/accessories than she'd ever had, she made her way down stairs five minutes before the taxi was due. Elle wasn't anywhere to be seen, but Gem was in the kitchen making short work of a glass of pinot grigio.

'You're going to be smashed before we get there,' Ciara pointed out.

'It's for Dutch courage. C, you won't mind if I can't come on the rest of the trip, will you?' Gem asked.

'What's happened?' she asked, thinking about hugging her friend but not wanting to mess up the pretty, fire red ringlets or the dress that cost an arm and a leg.

'Oh, nothing yet.' Gem grinned. 'But if Aiden asks me to stay I'll have no choice.'

She refrained from rolling her eyes, but said with mock outrage, 'What happened to chicks before dicks?'

'Some dicks can't be resisted.'

This time she did roll her eyes.

'Not a conversation I want to hear.' Zack. His deep voice made her shiver, and feel a bit more aware of her underwearless state.

'Depends what kind of dick you want to be,' Gem replied, smooth as silk.

Why couldn't she be like that?

21

He laughed at Gem and reached over to ruffle her hair. It was the wrong thing to try on a girl who'd just spend three hours perfecting those ringlets. He was met with a scowl that put the shits in her, never mind poor Zack.

'So you're that kind of dick,' Gem said, 100% serious.

Ciara wondered if she'd have to referee an argument, but Zack just laughed. 'Gemma, you should take a leaf out of your pal Ireland's book and chill out a bit. Looks aren't everything.'

'So earlier you called me fat and now you're calling me ugly?' Ciara demanded, stung by his comment.

'Girls,' he mumbled shaking his head. Then he came closer, put his hands on her shoulders and turned her all the way around, too slowly. 'I like what it hides, better than what it shows.'

He winked at her, then turned back to Gem. 'You better drag Elle away from the mirror or you'll be here all night.'

With that he was gone. His clean cut, slightly expensive scent still lingered, making her feel a bit dizzy.

'Should I go up for her?' she asked, when Gem just stared.

'Oh. My. God. Elle's hot cousin is totally into you.' Gem's voice was just a whisper, but her cheeks flamed when she thought of him hearing.

'Get real, Gem. He's way out of my league.' And then some. But there *had* been a little flirting, hadn't there? He did say her curves were sexy, her accent was adorable then sort of complimented her tonight. She got a glass out the cupboard and poured a mouthful of wine to distract herself.

'You didn't see the way he checked out your arse. I swear. He's probably away to relieve himself with that image ingrained into his retinas.'

Ciara wrinkled her nose, but really. The thought of Zack on his bed, all naked and pleasuring himself to visions of *her* arse wasn't off putting at all.

'Don't give me that, you'd totally nail him.' Gem just wasn't going to quit.

'I wouldn't, actually. If he was a random guy we met in a bar, I'd probably go back to his place but Zack is Elle's cousin.'

Gem poured another drink. 'Cousin, not brother and anyway it shouldn't matter. We're here for another day. Why not spend the night with him? You might learn something.'

'I know plenty,' she protested, smiling. 'But it feels... weird.'

'What does?' Elle asked.

They both turned and, though Ciara was used to being outshone by Elle's elegant, snow princess beauty, this time she was stunned. The dress Elle picked hugged her all the way to mid-thigh, where it broke off into strappy things that had studs on the ends. She looked like she should be walking down the red carpet with the other stars of the show, not arriving five minutes early to be escorted in the side entrance.

'Zack's got the hots for Ciara, and she wants him too.'

She was going to kill Gem.

'Eww,' Elle said. 'Zack's disgusting.'

Since Elle then rushed them to the door, Ciara didn't think there would be any repercussions for lusting after her cousin. And during the limo ride they sipped champagne, listened to Rita Ora, reassured Elle that leaving her phone at home because it was out of charge was not the same as being without her liver, and debated over which of the actors would show up stag (of course Gem *knew* Aiden would). There was no mention of Zack, no change in the way Elle spoke to her and Ciara decided to forget Gem's slip up, friend's cousins she shouldn't be thinking about and enjoy the fuzzy effects of the bubbly.

'How fun would it be to show up late and walk down the red carpet? I bet E! would dig our dresses.' Elle sighed.

'I think we should stick to the plan. I don't want to spend the night in jail,' Ciara said, more because the thought of being on the red carpet with all the attention and flashing lights filled her with icy dread.

Gem and Elle grinned at each other, no doubt finding it funny because she was the only one out of the three of them that couldn't afford the bail fee. 'I mean it. I don't want to repeat Easter Break.'

They burst into giggles, no doubt remembering the donkeys they 'borrowed' in Brighton to get back to the hotel instead of walking the extra half mile to the taxi rank in high heels.

'Easter break was tame compared to what I have planned this summer. Relax, Ciara. We've just finished university after studying for the best part of our lives. We're due some fun before we start real life,' Elle said, reassuringly.

Ciara didn't disagree. If only she could just go with the flow and stop worrying about the future.

***

'Wait for it,' Gem said to Elle.

Ciara would bet the rest of her savings on this latest scheme falling flat on its face but Elle and Gem were too determined to move onto the after party to be talked round.

'Okay, go.'

Gem and Elle linked arms with her and pushed their way through the crowds of superstars to the weakest link – a group of supporting actors with minor roles. They were young, their eyes gaped when they saw the three of them and Ciara tried to hold her face in an expression Elle had assured her was sexy.

'You were amazing,' Elle purred in the oldest guy's ear – though he couldn't have been older than 19, 20 at a push. 'Much better than that Aiden what's-his-face. Sexier too.'

'You girls English?' the low-grade actor said. 'That's hot.'

And that was Ciara's cue to keep her mouth shut. She didn't have that well-bread, smouldering, Lady of the Manor thing going. She nodded with Gem.

'We are, and we wondered if you three wanted to join us for a drink? Maybe go to a club?' Elle asked, just like they'd planned.

'Can't,' the gangly, younger looking guy said. His face was

clearly plastered in make-up, giving a baked bean effect. Better than showing off the red spots, but not by much. 'We're heading to the after party but you girls are welcome to come with.'

Looked like Ciara would have been down her last few grand. She should never underestimate the power of Elle throwing off sex kitten vibes. They were escorted to another, bigger limo with lots more champagne. She didn't have to worry about speaking in front of them. The guys only cared what Elle had to say anyway, and Gem seemed more interested in necking the Crystal at record breaking speed.

Her mind drifted to Zack, wondering if he was out in the city picking up gorgeous girl after gorgeous girl, just like these three actors were out to do.

But her mind was soon distracted when they got to Nobu in West Hollywood where the party was hosted. It was flashy, the outside was surrounded by paps and everyone who was anyone in the spotlight was there. Suddenly she was supremely grateful for her designer getup, and even more grateful that Elle had thought of a way to get it.

Everyone at the party dripped in designer tags, cracking hair-styles and accessories that made her drool a little. Gem scanned the crowd the second the poor escorts had slipped drinks into their hands and she couldn't help feel sorry for them. Elle had her eye on a rock star, but her face fell when she saw him grinding against a bleached blonde.

The boys fawned over her, oblivious to her disappointment but Ciara wasn't. She took her hand and squeezed hard. Then the three young actors noticed her.

'Hey, if you two are bi you up for a threesome?' one of them asked.

'*What?*' Elle asked, her hurt being replaced by her fiery temper. 'Who do you think you are, asking us that?'

'Lady, we're stars. We don't have time for teasing sluts who won't put out.'

Ciara had a flash of what would happen next, but she wasn't quick enough to stop her friend. The contents of her champagne flute soared through the air, splatting the middle boy and dripping down his – was that colour really gold or shiny beige? – shirt.

His face turned red and she got the feeling Elle had only just started, so she grabbed her and pulled her into the crowd. Gem didn't follow, but Ciara didn't have time to worry about that. Gem was the more laidback of the two and could look after herself.

She got Elle into the bathroom and the other girl whirled on her. 'Can you believe the nerve of that Z list loser!'

'If he tells security we'll be thrown out. Deep breaths, Elle. Come on.'

Elle squeezed her eyes shut and did as she was told – for once. 'You're right. We need to get out there and have fun. Who cares if some vagina starved tween gives us shit?'

Ciara released the breath she'd been holding. 'Exactly.'

'Let's go have fun!' Elle, seemingly having done a one-eighty, linked arms with her and dragged her to the bar.

Pink champagne this time, and lots of chat with a few starlets who were not so down with the drinking – you couldn't be too careful with the press waiting outside to snap every slip-up. Ciara was glad that would never be something she had to worry about.

A while later, she scanned the swarm of people there. 'I wonder where Gem's gone?'

Elle laughed. 'Find a hot actor and you'll find her.'

She pointed across the room to where Gem was standing close to Aiden Price, chatting away and grinning. Gem might not be coming with them after all. But then she leaned forward in what felt like slow motion, grabbed Aiden by his shirt collar and dragged him down for a kiss. He stiffened for a second, then seemed to get into it, and Ciara just had enough time to sigh in relief, before Gem clearly decided to live up to her YOLO motto and took it a step too far.

26

She wrapped herself around the actor like he was her personal get-off toy, grinding against him, right there in the middle of the room. Heads whipped round to stare and gossip. What made it all worse, Aiden was pushing her away but he couldn't extract himself from her hold.

Shit.

Two security guards managed to do what Aiden couldn't and ripped Gem right off him. Ciara shared a WTF glance with Elle before they were both putting their stilettos to work, scampering after Gem who was being carted off by two huge, scary looking men in uniform.

When she spied an unattended magnum of Moet on a table, she shared a quick glance with Elle, swiped up the bottle and they both burst into giggles.

Chapter Three

'He was so amazing,' Gem said, swaying a little until she grabbed onto the bar of the cell.

Police cell. They'd only gone and gotten bloody arrested. Again! Elle giggled. 'So worth it then?'

'Am I the only sane one here?' Ciara asked.

The champagne buzz had quickly died when they'd tried to stop security from calling the cops – and holding a bottle of the restaurant's Moet didn't help convince the man she was an upstanding citizen. They'd been asked for their invitations, to which Elle had told them the actors had invited them but of course that just made matters worse as the guy she'd doused in champagne told security the 'crazy British girls' had attacked them.

Now they were all locked up for the night, until they 'sobered up' but Ciara was feeling far from giddy. Unlike her friends.

'I'd kiss him again and again, even if it meant having to pee in front of my friends,' Gem said, making her way to the stand alone loo in their cell.

'Eww,' Elle complained. 'Can't you wait till we get home? There are pervy looking cops in here.'

Gem ignored her and went on with her business. They stood in front of her to shield her modesty, though Gem was too far

28

gone in an Aidan Price induced fantasy fuelled by too much bubbly to notice.

'How are we going to get home, Elle? It's not like we can grab a cab. We've been locked up!' It felt silly to have to state the obvious, but really. One of them had to at least try and be a bit responsible.

Gem flushed, then had her second good idea for the day – just a pity she'd won the eejit award in between. 'Call Zack. He'd bail us out.'

Elle said, 'I don't know the number by heart and my phone's at home.'

'I have his number,' Ciara admitted and both of them turned to stare at her with wide eyes. She held up her hands. 'I didn't ask for it, he just scribbled it down in case we got into trouble.'

'I'll bet he did,' Elle frowned. 'But this does spell trouble, so bugger it. Let's ask for our phone call.'

It took a lot of sweet talk to persuade the cops to let them get Zack's number out of her bag, and then she was dialling with shaking fingers, not sure if she'd rather he was asleep already. This had to be one of those worst firsts she kept hearing about. How many people could say the first time they phoned their crush it was to ask for a bail out instead of a date?

When Zack answered, her hands started shaking.

'Zack, it's Ciara.'

'Are you okay? Is Elle?' he asked, sounding a little bit sleepy and a lot confused.

'We're all fine, sort of. Shit.' How did she ask someone she barely knew to get them out of prison?

'Ciara, what's going on? You're worrying me.'

Taking a deep breath, she blurted everything out, apologising every chance she got.

He listened all the way through her convoluted confession, never interrupting her and when she finished, there was a pause before he said, 'Give me an hour.'

The line went dead. Her heart melted. He'd just dropped everything in the middle of the night to rescue them from this Hell hole.

But then she realised something worse. She was starting to feel things for Zack. Real honest to god warmth and then some.

She really was in trouble now.

Zack didn't speak much in the car, but she supposed anyone would be fecked off at having to bail out three idiots in the early hours of the morning, then help two of the said idiots up to their rooms. Gem had long since passed out and Zack had to carry her up. Elle was dead on her feet but able to walk, so Ciara managed to get her into bed.

When her friend was tucked in, she tried to sneak along the corridor unseen but he was leaning against her room door with his arms folded and what looked like a frown marring his pretty face in the dim light. Shit, why couldn't Elle be awake for this? She'd never wimp out of an argument with anyone.

'I'm sorry we woke you,' she said. It was the best she could think of.

He sighed. 'When those two were little I took so much shit for them that our granddad threatened to send me to boarding school. I thought that would end when they grew up.'

'We thought it would be fun to gatecrash a celeb party,' she defended

'And you all got carried away?' he asked, his expression too cynical.

She scowled at him. 'Something like that.'

Zack lifted an eyebrow. 'So stealing a bottle from the restaurant, assaulting an actor and pouring a drink over another was all in the name of fun?'

She gritted her teeth and sucked in a breath. It didn't help with the irritation bubbling beneath their skin. 'Exactly.'

There was no way she was going to apologise for getting carried away. Nobu, Aiden and the Z listers were not going to press charges so really, there was no harm done.

'I only came because you were in trouble, Ciara. A night in the cells would be a good reality check for them. Although now I think that might be the case for you too.'

She didn't know whether to be outraged or insanely pleased that he cared enough to rescue her.

Zack didn't allow her time to think. He came close, far too close until her chest was flush against his. 'But I'm glad I didn't leave you there.'

Her breath caught in her throat and the attraction she'd felt today seemed magnified in the hall. They were alone, or as good as. He smelled spicy, delicious and a lot like he'd been in bed for hours and hours. The buzz that thrummed between them had the same kind of affect as the champagne had on Gem earlier with Aidan Price, and she wanted to wrap her arms around Zack and use him for her own pleasure.

She had to tilt her head to keep eye contact. Even with just the moonlight from the massive windows at either end of the hall, she could see him and he was too gorgeous. And, mad as it might be, she was just pleased that he'd helped them out for her.

'Are you going to kiss me now?' she asked.

Maybe it was the intense look in his eyes drawing out delicious anticipation, or maybe the champagne had blasted her patience and inhibitions, but she couldn't hold the question in. Or regret asking him.

'Do you never wait for a man to make the first move?' he asked, stroking her cheek with his finger.

Little jolts zapped from his touch, all the way under her skin and shivered down to her belly. She wanted more. She *needed* more.

And why couldn't she have more? She'd spent so long worrying about this trip, what happened after, her future. She'd already

31

missed out on having fun. And she'd miss out on having him if she let it continue.

No more.

'Life's too short.' And she was only here two more nights. Whatever the reason for not asking him sooner had fled her mind, if there ever was one. Right now it was just him and her, about to kiss – she was sure.

'Some things are worth taking your time over.'

His breath swept her face, warm, tickly and far too teasing. His finger outlined her lips, making her breath hitch a little and her stomach flip.

'Maybe,' she whispered in the darkness. 'But not things with a time limit.'

Instead of waiting, she pushed high on her tiptoes and pressed her lips against his. Zack didn't pull away or admonish her for the assault. He pulled her flush against him, taking control of the kiss until her blood hummed and her knees got a little bendy.

He opened the door, dragging her into her room and still not taking those taunting lips off hers. When she parted her lips his tongue breached her mouth and she did the same to him, eager to taste. And it still wasn't enough.

Ciara wanted to feel that defined body against hers, without the silky dress or his cotton shirt in the way. But the only problem was she didn't want to stop kissing him either. He was definitely a hottie and lacked the washing machine technique she'd been treated to more than once by the guys from uni.

With the two warring urges – getting him naked and refusing to stop kissing him for a second – strong, she fisted her hands in his hair, ground her hips into his erection and let out a frustrated groan.

Zack made the decision for her, pulling away with a smouldering grin. 'We need to get naked for the rest to work.'

Ciara went straight for his belt, ignoring his chuckle. He whipped the shirt off then helped her shove his jeans down, pausing to remove a foil package from his pocket. She grabbed his dick, thrilling at the thickness of it and growing more and more impatient to have it inside her. He groaned, the sound vibrating through her right to the spot between her thighs that ached for him.

He must have been impatient too, because he whipped her dress over her head, forcing her to let go of him. But that was better. Now they were naked and she raked her hands all over his torso, feeling every line of muscle beneath the tanned skin and wanting more and more.

Zack kissed her again. She barely heard the tear as he suited up for round one of many, or so she hoped. When she was sure he was ready, she dragged him back onto the bed, aligning her hips to give him easy entry and he took the offer.

This wasn't slow and delicate or short and furious either. They fucked their way to the top of the bed, got twisted up against the headboard but that didn't stop either of them. So many new sensations flooded through her that she wondered if she'd been slipped something at the party or maybe it was just Zack.

By the time her second orgasm built and exploded, he followed her over the edge with a few jerks that had her head hanging off the side of the bed.

He kissed down her throat, making her shiver with mini after-shocks and relighting the heat in her lower belly.

'I know one more thing about you,' he said.

She jerked up, instantly on the defence. 'What, that I'm a slut?'

He laughed, kissing her frown. 'No, definitely not that. I was going to say impatient.'

All the blood had rushed to her head anyway, so the blush came swift. She was getting paranoia around this man. 'Waiting isn't one of my best qualities.'

She didn't think she'd ever get used to his smile. It was so far from mopey that she wondered if Elle had been exaggerating.

'Round two we're doing my way,' he insisted.

Since the mad rush to rip off his clothes and have him any which way had ebbed, she could allow him that. 'Deal.'

***

It took her a while the next day for all the details of the night before to come back. She remembered the movie, then the party and shit, they'd been bloody arrested! She sat up so fast she swayed a little. When the room stopped tilting, she looked down at herself. Her very, very naked self.

Fuckity fuck.

The rest of the night, and the early hours, came back in a startlingly erotic and overly sensory flash, making her blush. What had she been *thinking*? Jumping into bed with Elle's cousin was like a normal, more put together person jumping into bed with her best friend's brother. She couldn't start anything with him, she'd never been able to hold down a boyfriend before and her ma was exactly the same.

The saving grace was that Zack wasn't here. He obviously wasn't making a big deal out of it – just a night of fun with one of his cousin's friends. The relief lasted about five seconds before the slice of pain to kick in. Despite knowing last night shouldn't have happened, she was pissed off that he could just drop her like a cheap hooker.

Gem could add him to another dick list – the fuck 'em and leave 'em one.

Ciara got out of bed and made her way to the bathroom. She braved glancing in the mirror. It wasn't pretty. Her make-up was a streaky, dried sweaty mess and her hair would be better suited to a scarecrow. No wonder he'd left!

By the time she looked more human and was ready to go to the kitchen in search of coffee, the smell of steamy, ground bean goodness registered before Zack did. He brought in a tray topped with two cups of black and a little jug of cream and sugar. She couldn't be bothered dressing it up, instead took a huge gulp and ignored the burn in her mouth/throat.

'I doubt the others will surface for a while,' he said, with an undertone that hinted at more mind blowing funny business.

Though happy he'd come back, and with coffee, she worried he might think there was more to last night than just… God, even she'd read into more. What was it about him that screwed with her head? She didn't even know him!

'Zack, about last night…'

His grin was just like it had been last night, or this morning, when she'd told him she didn't scream ever during sex and he'd proved her wrong by going down on her for almost an hour until she felt raw and exposed and the orgasm was so intense she couldn't *not* scream.

Ruthlessly, she pushed the memory away and pressed on, refusing to be distracted by the thrum in her blood that insisted she take him up on his offer. Right *Now*. 'I'm not looking for a relationship, or to get involved with someone I know. I'm not a stayer.'

He just stared at her with amusement glittering in his eyes. That wasn't the least bit insulting, she thought wryly.

'So what I'm trying to say was that last night was a mistake. I'm sorry.'

'You really believe that, don't you?' he asked, placing the tray down then putting her coffee on it. 'You really think that last night was a one off.'

He grabbed her hips, pulling her closer and her heart took off full speed. 'It was. It has to be.' She tried to reply firmly.

His lips brushed her ear and she shivered. 'You're wrong. Last night wasn't a mistake, and this isn't over – it's just on hold until you realise that.'

She was about to protest but he kissed her first and she was gone as thoroughly as she had been the night before.

He pulled away, far too soon. 'When you figure it out, you have my number.'

Ciara watched him walk away, trying to fight with her body's urge to chase him, *her* urge to chase him. She stumbled to the hall, but he was already out of sight. Before she could take off after him, Gem's door opened.

Her friend looked scarier than she had. 'Want to come in here? I have coffee.'

'Gimme,' Gem said, crossing the hall with her arms stretched out like a zombie.

She was thankful for the distraction and time she'd have to give herself a good mental talking to.

***

They spent their last full day at the pool topping up their tan, going over what the hell happened last night with Gem and eventually laughing a little about their run in with the law. It was so the Easter holidays all over again, except this time their lucky escape came quicker.

Though she knew being with Zack had bad idea written all over it, she couldn't get him out of her head. When Gem asked what he was doing there anyway, her ears perked up waiting for Elle to answer.

'Far as I know, he wants to do some freelance work as well as working on the company properties but I don't know why he came here. It's not like the buildings are his style. He prefers older, run down places with renovation potential,' she said with a shrug.

'Eh?' Gem asked.

'Oh, he went back to university to study architecture a few years ago. Zack doesn't have what it takes to run the business.' Elle laughed.

Ciara wanted to defend him, which was ridiculous. It had nothing to do with her, she had no clue why he'd switched to architecture – or whether he would have made a good CEO. She had no clue about him at all.

Except that he could reduce her to a screaming, begging, hussy who couldn't get enough. But she doubted that little bit of info would be much of a defence for his business skills.

Then Zack appeared at the edge of the garden. He must have been jogging because he was shirtless and sweaty again. She had no idea where he got the energy but was sort of glad he had it, otherwise last night wouldn't have been half as fun.

'How are the heads today?' he asked.

Elle answered, 'Fine, darling cousin. Now run along.'

'Thank you for last night,' Gem said earnestly. 'That was my fault completely.'

Zack grinned at her. 'So I heard.'

Wasn't he even going to acknowledge her? She tried not to show how miffed she was and picked up a magazine.

'Any plans tonight?' he asked, glancing in her direction and she made a point of lifting the magazine higher. 'I'm not on call again, am I?'

'No, Zack. You can run off and do what you like. We're having dinner later then an early night. Our flight leaves first thing,' Elle said.

'Probably best you have a boring night. I think you've had enough excitement to last you a while,' he quipped.

She ground her teeth and tried hard to ignore him. It was so obvious he was having a dig at her.

'We're saving our energy for Miami, right girls,' Elle said.

We nodded.

'And *you're* not invited, by the way,' she continued.

'Since LA's a bit further than an hour drive to Miami's local police station, you better be careful,' he said, then took off for the house. 'Have fun.'

Elle rolled her eyes. 'He's so annoying, but he does have a point. We'll need to dial down the crazy in Miami. There will be no one to bail us out.'

Gem and Elle kept talking but Ciara didn't hear a word. She

was too busy telling herself that one night with Zack was all she was allowed.

It was for the best.

Even she wasn't convinced.

Miami

Chapter Four

It didn't take Ciara long to figure out why Elle had starved herself for days. On the way from Miami International Airport to yet another of the Muirs' properties, she was treated to more styles of bikini than she'd ever seen.

And the women who wore them were thin and toned enough to be models.

The guys, on the other hand, were mostly huge, muscled up and tanned to the point she couldn't tell what nationality they were. But they were very pretty to look at.

'Tomorrow we're hitting the beach,' Gem said, her gaze glued to a group of guys that reminded Ciara of the rugby players back home, only less rough and more buff. 'I've got rebounding to do.'

Ciara bit her lip to stop the giggle waiting to burst out. Elle wasn't as subtle and her laugh had Gem whipping her head around.

'What's so funny?' Gem demanded.

Elle pulled it together. 'Come on, Gem. Hollywood megastar Aiden Price was never yours so you can't rebound.'

Gem lifted her chin. 'Rejection still hurts and what better way to get over him than with one of those guys.'

Elle smiled. 'I'm not saying it's a bad idea. I think a few nights with a guy like that would be fun. What do you think, Ciara?'

They both turned to her with scrutinising eyes. Her face flamed. She knew she should say yes, why not, let's go grab one or something like that. But the words refused to come. Images of Zack flooded her mind instead. He wasn't as ripped as those men on the beach, but he had definition that made her drool and she could still feel his skin under her finger tips just from remembering their night in LA.

'I think she'd prefer someone a little darker haired. Maybe a man who likes to strip his shirt off and get all sweaty while pushing those thick, muscly thighs to the limit,' Gem said with a sly grin.

The blood in Ciara's cheeks burned so hot she was sure it would evaporate.

'Who? *Zack*?' Elle said, her mouth gaping. 'Aw Ciara he's... *ewww*.'

He was anything but, though she wasn't about to tell his cousin just how hot and amazing in bed he was.

'To you, maybe,' Gem said. 'But we don't share his blood – thank God. We can perv all we like.'

Elle sighed. 'You two have no taste.'

Actually, he was the most delicious thing Ciara had ever tasted. Again, not something she wanted to share with Elle. Despite what Zack said, their night together was a mistake – okay not quite. She'd wanted him more than she'd wanted anything and didn't regret taking it. But it was definitely a one-time thing. There was no way she could start something with Zack when she couldn't guarantee she'd be able to stick around, and with her track record and her ma's, the odds weren't good.

And to make sure she wouldn't be tempted for a second round, she left his number in her room back in LA.

'We're here,' Elle said as the taxi pulled into the grounds of a massive beach condo with its own private pool.

She thought that after the shock of the previous mini-White

House at the bottom of Hollywood Hill she'd be used to luxury by now, or at least learn to stop gaping. But Elle's granddad's beach house was like something out of the movies. One wall was completely glass and she could see right inside to the open plan kitchen and lounge area.

Outside, there were padded sun loungers galore, an Olympic sized swimming pool and a sitting area with rustic style chimneas dotted all over. This was definitely a house for pool parties that went on to the early hours. She wondered if she'd get any sleep at all before they left for Europe.

'Come on girls, I want to start getting ready for tonight. Miami here we come!' Elle said, climbing out of the taxi at record speed.

Ciara wondered if she should warn someone before Elle got loose.

Their pub crawl – or bar bounce or whatever Gem called it – took them to hot, sweaty places full to the brim of surfers. Ciara was gutted when she didn't get to hear at least one 'cowabunga dude' but stereotyping surfers on her favourite mutant turtle was probably way off.

Or maybe the assortment of cocktails they'd picked up in each bar was going to her head.

It wasn't all bad. In the one bar they'd found with air conditioning, Elle had fluttered her eyelashes and gotten them table service, which meant they didn't have to brave the crowds of perspiration to get a drink.

When the young bartender brought them the next round, he handed Elle a sheet. 'For you, angel.'

Ciara grinned. 'You seem to be attracting a lot of tweens on this holiday.'

'Shut up!' Elle said. 'Anyway it's not his number.'

'Lemme see.' Gem grabbed the piece of laminated paper. The excited glint in her eyes had Ciara on edge.

'We're so entering!' Gem said.

43

'My thoughts exactly,' Elle agreed.

Oh no, what had they planned this time. 'Entering what?'

Gem slapped the sheet down in front of Ciara.

Her first reaction was to laugh. They couldn't be serious, a drinking game? They'd get ploughed by the regulars. But then she saw the grand prize being offered to the group still standing. A limited edition *Gucci* beach bag – masterfully structured, the most beautiful thing she'd seen with baby pink leather. And it was practical too. But that meant...

'We're entering,' Elle said. 'I want that bag.'

Ciara quickly scanned the rules. Everyone in the group entering had to buy a massive – and it really was massive – jug of either mojito or Caipirinha. The first table to finish and still be standing would get the bag – and possibly alcohol poisoning.

'I'll get a mix and we can share,' Gem said, leaping off her chair.

'Wait,' Ciara grabbed her arm. 'Have you two lost it completely?'

'Dear Ciara,' Elle said on a sigh. '*Gucci* is calling. And anyway, we're newly ex students and we have an Irish girl on our side. This will be a walk in the park!'

'Or a trip to the emergency room to have our stomachs pumped,' she argued.

Gem shook free. 'Don't be silly. Plus the rest of the group gets a $1,000 gift card to spend in the *Aventura Mall*. Even you can't say no to that! If we win, you get to keep the voucher and Elle and I can share the bag. Deal?'

Ciara bit her lip. Bloomingdales was in that mall. The most expensive thing she'd owned had come from a high street store back home. And her friends were right, she could hold her booze. But they'd been on the cocktails for a while now and a glance around at all the new people walking in, looking fresh and ready to go, didn't help convince her this was a good idea.

'You're not allowed to think about this,' Elle said. 'Gem, go enter us before Ciara comes up with an excuse to get out of it.'

Her friend's azure eyes were steely now, and Ciara knew there was no point in arguing. Elle pulled out her phone, tapped the screen a few times and then handed it to her. It was a list of *all* the lovely, lovely shops in the mall, with the lovely, lovely clothes just waiting for her to pick them.

It wasn't like she'd be able to afford something that wasn't on sale without the voucher. If they won this competition, she could spend and spend and spend without the guilt. Which is exactly what Elle had been thinking, handing her the worst kind of temptation.

'Fine, I'm in. But if I end up with liver failure I'm holding you responsible,' she said.

Chapter Five

'Right guys, you know the rules. Drink up as fast as you can and the first group back to the bar with their empty pitchers wins,' the bartender said.

The crowed rumbled their excitement, while Ciara stood over the tallest, fattest jug she'd ever seen. The colours were pretty, and she hoped the limes diluted some of the rum, but the sheer size of the thing scared her.

Almost everyone had to stand up to get to the straws.

The queue for the bathroom was going to be tremendous after this. If she even made it that far. Which was very unlikely.

Gem and Elle didn't look as put off as she was. Elle's refusal to quit had got her far in uni, but this was something else entirely. Gem no doubt had her eyes on the prize, and she did love winning.

Maybe that would work. Keeping focused on the prize.

'Quick, before we start we need something to remember this by!' Elle pulled out her phone again and set it up for a picture. 'Stand behind the glasses and strike a pose. Come on, Ciara. Smile.'

The phone flashed, making her eyes go all spotty for a second.

'Get me, Gem!' she handed over the phone and Gem snapped another.

'I'm Instagraming these. Go Team Elle!'

Ciara rolled her eyes while Gem's narrowed. Trust Elle to take over.

'Ready, set, go!' the bartender boomed.

Ciara did, putting the straw to her mouth and trying a steady suction while breathing through her nose. She doubted anyone could keep guzzling the freezing drinks all the way to the bottom and reckoned her strategy had a 6:2 chance of winning – considering she could handle however many units of alcohol it was packed with.

Gem had taken the guzzle approach, stopping to gasp occasionally and then get stuck back in.

Elle was keeping it steady too, but at a faster pace than Ciara. In fact, she was way behind when she glanced around the room.

She sucked up mouthful upon mouthful, trying to catch up then a searing pain stabbed behind her right eye. 'Ow, brain freeze.'

'I'll knock your brain into next week if you don't hurry up. Drink through it!' Elle commanded.

Ciara forced herself to keep going, but the stabbing in her temple didn't ease up. Someone retched and she looked over to see a ripped guy with bleach blond hair sucking in lung fulls of air, no doubt to stop from being sick. He didn't succeed and she shut her eyes so his gut load of cocktail making a reappearance didn't encourage hers to.

'Done,' Gem slurred, then giggled. 'Oh dear, I'm drunk.'

Ciara felt like the floor was swaying beneath her feet and she opened her eyes before the dizzy, sick feeling kicked in. She was neck and neck with Elle and they didn't have much to go.

'Quick, just pick it up. It's not heavy now,' Gem said.

Elle did, but Ciara's jug didn't seem to shift much off the table.

'Come on, Ciara. Think of those vouchers.' Gem grabbed the bottom, then helped her tip it up.

After a deep breath, she chugged the remainder of the glass

as fast as she could, not caring about the unladylike affects that would no doubt follow. Not caring about much at all anymore as a warm, giddy feeling soared through her.

She finished up within seconds of Elle and they shared a grin.

'That shit's finished too,' Elle said, pointing to another table.

He was, and the women he was with were finishing up as they watched. 'Don't we have to get these jugs to the bar?'

The other group noticed they weren't alone in their victory and picked up the jugs.

'Run!' Elle said.

They did, kind of. Staggered would be a more apt description. But the other group didn't seem unsteady on their feet at all as they rounded tables.

Ciara bumped into a girl who hadn't finished yet and managed a convoluted apology while she got back her balance.

'Move it!' Elle screamed.

Ciara scampered to catch up. They reached out with the jugs, ready to throw them on the bar. The bartender's eyes were wide and he shuffled back to the wall of spirits as they approached.

Team Persistent were neck and neck with them now, and since the girls were fast Ciara knew they were going to lose.

'That bag's *mine* lady. Back off,' Elle said to the other group.

'In your dreams,' she replied.

Ciara slammed her jug down on the bar, and a loud smash splintered her ears. She blinked at her glass – still fully intact. Both Gem and Elle were beside her, with their jugs on the bar too, without so much as a scratch but her friends were looking behind her with their mouths gaping.

Ciara spun around and staggered a little. A woman from the other group had dropped the jug. Glass was scattered all over the wooden floor, shining like little diamonds in the light. At least the woman wasn't hurt, but by the way her eyes narrowed she wasn't happy.

'So, guess you bitches won by default,' the woman said.

Gem laughed. 'It's not our fault you've got butter fingers.'

'I'd say the best bitches won,' Elle added.

Ciara squeezed her eyes shut, but changed her mind the second the room started spinning.

'Come on girls, time to go.' She had visions of getting into a cat fight there was no way she'd win. Especially now the alcohol seemed to be doing its job.

'After our victory pic,' Elle slurred, pulling the phone out of her pocket and pulling them close. Ciara didn't see the flash and dreaded how she looked in the picture but before she could ask to see it Elle had already launched it into social media land.

'I think I'm going to be sick,' Gem said.

'Fresh air will help,' Ciara hoped.

They collected their prizes and Elle took the bag since she didn't want Gem throwing up on it. Somehow the air only increased the horrible, dizzy feeling and Ciara wished she'd ignored Elle's advice to starve herself earlier. She was definitely getting something more substantial than a salad when she got back.

***

'I don't even care that I'm tempted to be sick in it, this was so worth it,' Elle said, hugging the new bag to her chest.

Ciara ignored her, pulling her body through the massive pool. Gem was on the patio near Elle, perfecting her morning yoga routine.

She'd already done twenty lengths before breakfast, but not to burn off all the calories from her mammoth cocktail. This was so not about keeping fit.

Last night after they'd gotten back, she'd raided the fridge and found it lacking so had ordered a pizza. The others had gone to bed, saying they were not eating that many carbs when they had a beach day coming up.

While she'd stuffed her face, her mind had gone back to LA, her first night with Zack and something had happened that she never thought possible. She'd gone and completely lost her sanity.

She'd pretended he was there with her, sharing the pizza and was telling her about himself. He'd told her he wanted to study architecture because he was passionate about sculpture and that he worked out because it took his mind off everything.

And worse, she'd started talking to herself in reply to the imaginary questions!

Though she knew her conversation with him was an alcohol induced fantasy, she hoped to find some truth in it so she tried tearing through the pool doing as many laps as possible. It was helping a little. The burn in her muscles and the rolling feeling in her stomach were stealing most of her concentration.

'You know, Ciara if you hadn't stuffed yourself with pizza last night you wouldn't need to make that horrible splashing sound just now,' Gem said.

'It is a bit too loud for my fuzzy head,' Elle agreed.

When she reached the end of the pool, she climbed out. Giving up was much better than being moaned at and they weren't the only ones who felt a bit light headed. 'I'm bored waiting for you two to decide it's time to hit the beach, that's all.'

'Holidays are meant for relaxing, not always being on the go. We'll have lots of time for partying tonight,' Elle said.

That's not what she'd meant. They were in Miami, somewhere she'd never been and probably never would again. She wanted to explore every inch of the city, not just the shops, bars and clubs. All this sitting around was going to drive her even more insane.

Her expression must show how unimpressed she was by partying because Gem said, 'Grab a magazine and get some sun, Ciara. We'll leave soon, promise.'

She gave in, crossing to one of the sun loungers in the shade and lay face down, leaving the magazines on the table. If they were planning a party tonight she really should get some sleep first.

***

It took an hour for Elle and Gem to find the perfect spot and unpack. They were now lying on loungers close enough to the sea to catch the breeze but not too far from the refreshment stands so they wouldn't have far to hike for an iced tea. Elle had flirted with a guy so he would move the loungers away from the masses of tourists for them.

Then they unpacked the sun lotions, the mini fold up table so nothing got all sandy and a few windbreakers for privacy more than protection from the wind. Ciara didn't care about any of that stuff, not with a view like the one they had. The ocean was beautifully blue and so clear she could see the golden sand beneath. People were windsurfing and there were even speedboats and jet skis cruising across the expanse of the water.

She wondered how much it would cost to have a go, but then what fun would it be by herself? Elle and Gem were settled back and ready for a serious bronzing session. She slipped off her flip flops. There was no way she was coming all the way here and not having at least a paddle in the ocean. Unlike Gem and Elle, she wasn't worried about her bikini being wrecked in the salt water – it had only cost a twentieth of the price of theirs.

'I'm going for a dip,' she said.

Gem rolled her eyes. 'Just watching you is all the exercise I need.'

'I like to keep busy,' she said.

Elle laughed. 'What are you going to do now you don't have all that studying? Even in Brighton over Easter you didn't relax one bit. All you did was cram and cram and cram. It's good to clear your mind and chill out sometimes.'

'Until we got arrested,' Gem corrected.

Ciara shook her head. She'd never even had a telling off from her teachers until she'd met Gem and Elle. Now she had a trip to jail on her record, both sides of the Atlantic.

Ciara headed straight for the ocean.

'I'll have lots of time to chill out when I'm old,' she said over her shoulder, not willing to share that keeping busy was her way of avoiding thinking too much about what she would do when this holiday was over.

She was exactly like her ma. She got bored too easily and couldn't imagine a career that would hold her attention. Maths and statistics had been a challenge and she liked it because almost everything could be calculated or worked out by formulas.

People were different, beyond the chemistry that made them up. There were all different emotions and behaviours she couldn't understand – her ma leaving was at the top of the list. Because even though she had her mother's attention span, she couldn't bring herself to leave her da alone forever. She'd go back to Ireland and keep close because he was all she had and he'd never given up on her. He'd worked himself half to death to send her to university, and she owed him more than she could ever repay.

But the rest of it – the job, a potential husband and kids? She couldn't be sure she wouldn't leave them someday. She hadn't spoken to her mum since and so she'd never know what triggered the behaviour – in Ciara's mind it just wouldn't be fair to lead someone along for years, start a life with them and then just walk away without a word. Like mother like daughter.

It wasn't something she'd want to do, but without knowing the catalyst for her mother's decision, how could she be sure?

As she reached the water with her mood lower than it had been in a while, Ciara pushed the thoughts away and decided a walk along the edge of the sea would take her mind off everything. After all, Miami really was beautiful. It would be a shame to not see as much as she could.

**

An hour later she returned with achy legs and Gem made a trip to the refreshment stands to get them all iced drinks. She sipped at her iced tea, wishing Gem had fulfilled her request of a 'sweet' one but she was too thirsty to care.

Elle perked up when a trio of guys started throwing what looked like a brown rugby ball not far from them.

'There's a good place to start rebounding, Gem,' Elle said.

Gem slipped her sunglasses down her nose. 'You're not wrong. I don't usually go for blonds but with those muscles I could make an exception.'

Ciara could definitely appreciate the muscles as they kept throwing the ball, harder each time until they got closer.

'And look, poor things are trying to be subtle about picking us up,' Elle grinned. 'Should we show them how it's done, girls?'

'I'm in,' Gem said, jumping up. 'What angle are we working?'

'Hmm, English girls wanting to learn the American way to play rugby.' Elle suggested.

Ciara laughed. 'American football is brutal, Elle. I don't think it will be your thing.'

'We're not actually going to *play*. But I wouldn't mind one of them holding me from behind and showing me how to throw the thing.'

'Me either,' Gem added.

'So what you're really saying is you're using the excuse of throwing a ball for foreplay?' Ciara asked, still stumped that after all these years she had a lot to learn when it came to this stuff. She'd dated a little and hooked up with guys at uni but they'd been more about relieving exam stress than anything serious. And it hadn't taken much to stumble across a man willing to have sex with her. The only thing was they'd never understood why she didn't want more than that. Elle and Gem never had that hassle as far as she knew.

'Exactly,' Elle said, then ditched her *Ray Bans* on the table. 'Come on!'

Brandon, Matt and Rye were very helpful when it came to teaching them how to throw a ball, but her coach was a little too touchy feely for her liking. After all, they'd only just bloody met!

'And you stand like this,' Matt said, pulling her hips back into his groin so her bum got a feel of exactly what his long shorts were hiding.

The only thing that stopped her from being completely mortified was that he wasn't fully erect, but she was sure after all the touching to manoeuvre her that he was well on his way.

Elle had dropped the act of wanting to learn and had unleashed her inner flirt. Brandon was falling hook, line and sinker and he was putty in her friend's expertly manicured fingers. Gem hadn't wasted any time either, and had perched on Rye's lap on the sand, already giving him a game of tonsil tennis.

'Just open your legs a bit more, Ciara,' Matt urged.

She certainly was not! Pulling away, she turned to him, trying to keep her irritation from showing. She wasn't about to dry hump him on the bloody beach. But then she couldn't be too mad at him for assuming she was easy, since she suspected Gem was well on her way to getting Rye past semi-hard.

'I don't think I'm getting it,' she admitted.

'Me either,' Elle said. 'You know, we're staying on the beach not far from here. Why don't we go back there, get cleaned up and have a few drinks by the pool?'

Everyone seemed to be into that idea, especially Gem and Rye who looked like they wanted to rip each other's clothes off right there and get down and dirty in the sand.

They made it back much faster than they'd taken this morning – having three strong men to muscle around their things was the only good thing about inviting them back to the house.

Elle had a shower first, so it was up to her to entertain Brandon and Matt – Gem was doing a good job of entertaining Rye in the pool.

Brandon was nice, asking lots of questions about their experience at university and even asking what Elle's favourite food was. Ciara was sure he was going to at least ask her on a date before he dragged her into bed.

Matt was a different story. He kept interrupting, telling her he was going to be a model and that he'd just had a portfolio made of all his best shots, but now he'd gotten better definition in his abs and biceps (both of which he insisted she touched), he needed to save for more.

'Really, that's grand,' she answered, but might as well have been talking to herself.

Brandon's smile was apologetic.

Elle appeared a little while later and Ciara decided it was time to leave Elle with the superficial pain in the arse. But he caught her arm.

'How about I come let you wash my back?' Matt asked.

How about you let go of my wrist before I have to chew through my elbow to escape? 'Maybe another time.'

'Later, for sure babe.' His eyes smouldered and it so wasn't sexy.

Not like Zack's that night. Not even a little.

She took her time getting showered and dressed, even applying make-up but not to attract Matt, just to kill time. She was sure he was too hot for himself to notice – she was probably just another girl to fuck for his pleasure.

By the time she'd grabbed a bottle of beer and returned to the poolside, they were all at the dining table and she stopped the cringe from showing on her face. The only seat left was next to the pretty boy she was hoping had gone off to find some other girl to satisfy his needs.

No such luck.

'Hey Keera, I've saved you a seat,' Matt said.

She gritted her teeth and sat down. 'Ciara, not Keera.'

'Huh. Well, here's to an awesome night,' he said, clinking his beer bottle with hers and winking.

It was going to be anything but.

When Gem disappeared for a shower, she wasn't alone. Rye followed her still sporting the tent in his shorts that must be becoming painful now. Elle noticed and grabbed the remote and switched the music on inside the house to drown out anything they didn't need to hear.

Brandon was still being really nice, asking everything about Elle and letting her prattle on and on about her life. He seemed more and more into her as the day went on.

On the flip side, Matt told Ciara everything about his. Everything. Even without her asking. And she had to zone out after a while, forcing a smile and nodding between gulps of beer.

Rye returned alone, looking flushed with his hair still damp and a self-satisfied smile on his face. She looked for Gem, but she wasn't far behind, grinning wider than she'd done in a while. She didn't use the other chair, just slipped straight onto Rye's lap.

At least someone was having fun.

Matt took her hand off the table and held it in two of his. 'You don't seem into this.'

He sounded surprised. She had to bite her lip before she asked if he was kidding. Instead she shrugged. 'It's been a long day.'

He moved closer until she could smell the beer on his breath. Eww. 'It could be a long night too, if you want.'

She leaned back and tried to remove her hand from his clasp but it was useless. 'Let's take it as it comes.'

She heard the metal gate slam shut, even over the sound of the music blasting out the glass sliding doors and turned around. Zack stood just inside the garden with a holdall slung over his shoulder, scowling at her and Matt. Everyone turned to look and she used Matt's distraction to free herself.

The music cut off and Elle shouted, 'What are you doing here, Zack?'

Elle's eyes were blue fire, but Ciara was having a different reaction. A more visceral one. Her heart took off full speed and she struggled to get breath into her lungs. He was mad, that was easy to see. But even beneath the crazy attraction she felt just seeing him, she couldn't find guilt. Yet.

'Let's do this inside, Elle,' Zack said, storming past her to the house.

Elle's pulse beat at her temples, then she stormed in after him and shut the glass door so hard it vibrated.

'We should have brought popcorn,' Gem said, then giggled.

The guys looked confused, but the glass was soundproof so they couldn't hear Elle shrieking at Zack like she had back in LA. They could see her face turn red though, and could see Zack pull something up on his phone and show it to her as he shouted right back.

Oh God, the photos Elle had taken. She'd forgotten to check them. No doubt they were awful.

'Who's this clown?' Matt asked.

If a lump the size of a golf ball hadn't formed in her throat, she'd have treated him to a number of insults that would be sure to put a chip in his continental ego.

Gem was more polite. 'Elle's cousin. This is their family's condo.'

Just then Elle came out of the house, sliding the door shut in Zack's frown. 'Sorry, my cousin is staying here too. How about we go out for dinner and a few drinks?'

Both Gem and Elle had changed into sun dresses while she'd chucked on a pair of shorts and a vest. 'Let me put something else on.'

'You look okay, babe,' Matt said.

She didn't take his stellar compliment well. Not now Zack thought she really was a slut, jumping from his bed straight into the arms of pretty boy. 'I'll feel better if I wear something else.'

'Well hurry up. I need to get away from him,' Elle said.

Ciara jogged across the terrace and slid the door open. She couldn't see Zack anywhere and didn't know whether she was disappointed by that. Probably better she didn't have to face him now, after what he'd seen outside.

She darted into her room, pulled a baby pink summer dress off the hanger and slipped on a pair of gemmed flip flops. Her hair had gone wavy after letting it dry naturally earlier which made her look like a hippy but there was no time to do anything with it. Elle would come in and drag her out if she wasted time with straightening irons.

Poking her head out of the door she saw the hall was clear, so made for the exit. Her flip flops slapped against the marble tiles and she cussed the Muirs for their expensive tastes. What happened to a good old fitted carpet?

Zack was waiting for her in the kitchen, his arms folded across a chest she remembered with too much detail. 'So you're bedding that poser tonight?'

The anger that swiftly burned through her wasn't at the insult to Matt, it was the fact he thought she was easy. 'Not that it's any of your business, but no. We just met.'

It was the wrong thing to say. She'd jumped into bed with Zack not long after they'd met too. Talk about leaving herself open to insults!

Zack smiled, then crossed the room. He tilted her chin and the anger evaporated under his touch. It was like his fingers sent little currents into her skin, sweeping down to tremble in her belly.

'Maybe it isn't my business.' He slid both hands up the side of her face and into her hair. Her eyes rolled back as he massaged her scalp. 'I promise you this, Ireland. If you stay with me I'll make sure you have a hundred times more fun than you would with him. I'll even show you what I can do with a tub of Ben & Jerry's and my tongue.'

How could a girl refuse an offer like that? Why would she even consider refusing? She was lost in his eyes, his slightly spicy aftershave and the way he was touching her made her whole body tingle.

'Ciara hurry up!' Elle shouted from the garden. 'The taxi's here.'

Her friend's voice snapped her back to her senses and she pulled away with a boat load of regret. Zack's jaw ground hard and she whispered an apology before she bolted to the door. He was too much temptation and the last thing she wanted to do was to hurt her friend's family by leading him on. It was better he was disappointed now than years down the line when it was too late.

Chapter Six

At Elle's suggestion, they hit a bar on the beach so she could top up her tan. Ciara lost hope that dinner was on the cards the second Gem and Elle said they weren't very hungry and more cocktails were served.

She was too busy remembering the way Zack looked when she left to care too much about what Matt was saying, but tried to at least look like she was paying attention. He took a swig of a creamy looking cocktail that left a white moustache on his smooth upper lip.

Smiling, she picked up the napkin and wiped it off imagining his horror at looking anything other than perfect.

'So does this mean you're back with me?' he asked.

Maybe he wasn't completely self-involved and had noticed her lack of interest. She forced a polite smile. 'Sorry.'

'No problem, babe. I know how you can make it up to me.'

His wicked grin was the only warning she got before her mouth was assaulted by his. Matt wasn't gentle about his seduction – or patient. His tongue filled her mouth before she had a chance to slap him away for his assumption.

She shoved his chest hard, till he had to grab the table for support. 'Are you mad? What made you think I wanted to kiss you?'

Elle and Gem were gaping at her but she was too miffed to care. Matt had crossed the line. She hadn't given him a hint that she wanted him. In fact, she'd been ignoring him all night!

'Well you're friends seem happy having a holiday fling, I figured you would too,' he said with a shrug.

'A fling?' she said through her teeth, but then the anger ebbed. *A fling.* Of course! Why hadn't she thought of that?

'Cia, there's nothing wrong with a bit of fun once in a while,' Gem added. 'You're young, you're single. Why not?'

Elle smiled and nodded. Brandon frowned at Elle. Hmm, he didn't look happy about *just* being a fling.

Would Zack be happy? It would be the perfect solution to all that temptation.

Something fun for both of them with a time limit to stop things spiralling out of control. They were leaving for Europe soon, why not enjoy a few days with someone she actually wanted. Ciara picked up her sex on the beach and downed half before she turned to Matt.

'You're gorgeous and I bet you can have any woman in here you want. But you're not for me, I'm sorry.'

Gem smirked. 'The man for you probably has a private investigator following us and making sure we don't get into any trouble.'

'Define trouble,' Rye said, squeezing her closer – if that were possible.

'Ugh, Ciara. Really?' Elle asked.

Her cheeks flamed and she nodded.

Elle sighed. 'Well, Matt. Looks like we'll have to find you some company.'

Matt didn't seem too put out by Ciara's rejection. Then it clicked and she blinked. Had Elle really given her the 'all clear' to go seduce her cousin?

Gem giggled and since Ciara couldn't see Rye's hands, she didn't ask why. 'Have fun, C. Don't wait up for us.'

'Have a good night guys.'

'We will,' they said, giggling.

***

The taxi journey took forever during rush hour but the jitters in her stomach made it feel like no time at all. She hadn't even planned what she was going to say when the car pulled up at the condo and she was handing the driver a note, telling him to keep the change.

Her legs were unsteady as she made her way up the path to the pool. She wondered if he was still there since the place was tidy and all traces of their afternoon beers were cleaned up. But when she slid the doors open the sound of a familiar English band filled her ears. She hadn't pegged Zack as an Arctic Monkeys fan, though she didn't really know much about him did she?

Maybe she shouldn't. Weren't flings supposed to be on a need to know basis? She wished she'd asked Gem and Elle.

She wandered through the house. The lounge, kitchen, gym and every bedroom she walked past were empty. Then she stopped outside a closed door and reached for the handle.

The thought of finding him with someone else had her snatching her hand back like the thing was on fire. This was a really, really bad idea. The cocktail she'd drained before she left the bar was weaker than the one Gem had bought her last night and she could use some courage about now.

Then the door opened. Zack stood there in nothing but a towel and a few drops of water around his shoulders from his still wet hair. His eyes widened for a second, then narrowed suspiciously. 'What's up, Ireland?'

He had to raise his voice over the music, but that made him sound angrier than before.

'Can we talk?' When he just frowned, she tried a little begging. 'Please?'

He came out of the room, nodding for her to go ahead of him

and when they reached the kitchen he picked the remote off the breakfast bar, switched off the music and then took a seat. 'You wanted to talk?'

She stood at the opposite side, fidgeting with a loose gem on her purse.

'Is your offer still open?' she asked, unable to meet his eyes.

'That depends,' he said and she couldn't keep her gaze off him any longer. He was back to folding his arms. 'Who was that poser you were with?'

She told him everything in a rush, the football game, the way he was too into himself and how he bored her to tears, then came the hard bit. 'He suggested something that I never thought of, actually. He thought I was looking for a... holiday fling.'

'And you weren't?' Zack asked, still not relaxing his rigid pose.

Time for brutal honesty. 'No. Not with him, anyway.'

He put his elbows on the table, leaning forward with a slight grin. She relaxed a bit now that he had. Had he'd been jealous of Matt?

'With me?' he asked.

Nerves made her mouth go a million miles a minute. 'Well, I said what happened in LA was a mistake and it wasn't, not really because I wanted it but I was scared I'd get in too deep and end up hurting you and you're my best friend's cousin and she'd hate me forever but I never thought of a fling, you know, something with a time limit so now I thought I'd see if it's something you wanted.'

He surprised her by laughing. 'I barely understood that, you know.'

Her cheeks burned.

'But I got the gist. So, you want a short term thing with a time limit?'

Ciara nodded. 'We're leaving for Paris in a few days which isn't as easy to get to as Miami.' Then she blurted out a question without thinking. 'Why are you here?'

His jaw set. 'I saw the pictures Elle put up on Instagram. You looked smashed, Ciara. I was worried you would all get into trouble again.'

She squeezed her eyes shut and hid her face with her hands. 'Oh god, I knew they'd be bad.'

He was in front of her then, pulling her hands away. His grin just made her face get hotter. 'Hey, everyone has been smashed at some point in their lives. Don't worry about it. Anyway, I can see you got home unharmed.'

'We're big girls you know. We can look after ourselves,' she insisted, using irritation to hide the mortification.

'Definitely grown up,' he agreed, placing his hands on her hips and sliding them up to rest just below her breasts. She trembled, wishing the cotton dress wasn't in the way. 'But not big, not at all.'

She smiled, remembering when she thought he called her fat.

'And I'd like to be with you while you're here. I have a condition though,' he said.

Frowning, she asked, 'What condition?'

'If I only have you for a few days, then I want all the perks of a fling.'

She agreed straight away, happy for them to start having all those perks right now.

***

'Some perk,' she grumbled as Zack muscled a moped out of the massive garage.

She assumed he'd drag her straight to his bedroom since he was half naked already, but as soon as she'd agreed he'd kissed her nose, told her to wait there and then returned from his room fully dressed, saying he was taking her out.

'Dates are perks,' he said, climbing onto the moped and handing her a helmet.

'Where's your helmet?' If she was wearing something so hideous, she wasn't doing it solo.

'My head's hard, just ask Elle.'

She smiled a little, but still… 'Unlike Elle, I can't afford the bail money if you get busted.'

Zack laughed. 'I won't, I have the right medical insurance policy to get away with it, but you don't.'

She frowned at the lumpy thing in her hands, knowing she was going to look like the biggest eejit ever.

'Here.' He took the thing and slid it onto her head. 'Even better.'

'Now that you can't see my face. Ha. Ha.' she said, not impressed with the joke. Ignoring his innocent, would-I-say-that grin, she climbed on the little bike behind him. 'Why a moped?'

'It's easy to get through traffic this way and you can see the city better. You ready?'

She wrapped her arms around his waist, hugging him tightly and feeling the outline of his thighs between hers. This part wasn't bad at all, actually. He couldn't see her and she could feel every lean muscle through his cotton tee-shirt. *Every single one.*

Zack patted her knee. 'Take it easy, Ireland or I'll end up wrapping us round a palm tree.'

Oh, maybe stroking him like her fingers were starved for him wasn't the best thing for his concentration. She clasped her hands over his abs and resisted the temptation to outline the ridges with her fingertips. He chuckled and the sound vibrated through her, making the spot between her legs ache.

'Let's go before I drag you back into the house,' he said.

She wasn't adverse to him dragging her back, but they were off before she could tell him that. Nothing about the speed was scary at all, and she didn't have much of an excuse for clinging to his back as tight as she did, but his smell was fabulous and she couldn't get enough. It was better than the sights around them. After all palm trees and bars couldn't compare to Zack.

She was blissfully unaware of anything until Zack said, 'Look, we're in South Beach.'

The sun was descending and the hotels were lit up in different colours of neon lights. They weren't the fancy sky scrapers she'd seen from the beach, this was more old fashioned, but somehow prettier to look at. 'Wow.'

'The buildings here are mostly art deco. At night they're illuminated and completely transform,' he said, sounding more excited than she'd ever heard him.

'It's beautiful,' she agreed, glad she got the chance to see this before they left.

They kept going and this time Ciara paid attention to the scenery. Miami seemed to come alive at night and was packed with more people than were on the beach during the day. A while later they were passing through Ocean Drive with even more lit up clubs, restaurants and hotels, but they all looked more modern than they had in South Beach.

'See, much more to Miami than the posers you find on the beach,' he said, turning again and taking them away from the pretty restaurants.

After god knew how long, she reckoned she'd seen most of the city and her stomach started to rumble. She hadn't eaten anything since breakfast and wondered if Zack would mind if she devoured a three course meal in front of him.

He must have heard or felt her stomach growl because he said, 'Just a little further and we'll stop for dinner, okay?'

She nodded against his back and closed her eyes again, just listening to his heart beat and inhaling his delicious aftershave. It worked, taking her mind off the hunger but built up a different kind. She couldn't imagine what he had planned when they got back. More fast and furious? Or would they start slow this time, giving her the chance to savour every inch of his body before she enjoyed him thoroughly?

She was so caught up in the fantasies that she jumped when he said, 'Look, Ireland. We're here.'

She opened her eyes in time to see a sign welcoming them to Little Havana, USA. It was like they'd driven into another city altogether. The buildings were flat roofed and reminded her of Southern America. Since most shops and take-aways she could see had Spanish names, she guessed she wasn't far off.

'What is this place?' she asked, then noticed a wall covered in graffiti. The paintings were cool but the word 'Cuba' confused her. She was pants at geography but not so much that she could believe they'd gotten that far already.

'This is Miami's slice of Cuba. I know a restaurant here that serves the best seafood I've ever tasted. You up for it?'

'Any food would be good right about now. But I do love seafood.'

'I knew you had good taste.'

She hugged him tighter but kept her eyes peeled wide so she didn't miss a single thing.

***

After a daring calamari appetiser which was out of this world, their main courses arrived. Ciara avoided the lobster even though she wanted to try it, because she was going to pay for half of the meal. It was the least she could do after he had shown her the sights.

That didn't stop Zack from getting it though and it looked much better than the jumbo shrimps she ordered.

'I can't believe you didn't go with the lobster,' he said, using a strange looking device to crack through the massive thing's shell.

'I wouldn't have known what to do with it,' she admitted.

His mouth tilted up at one side and her heart thumped. God, he really was gorgeous.

'It's easy, see.'

As he cracked his way into the tail she didn't think it looked easy at all. She stuck to decapitating her shrimp and was pleased to at least find them the best ones she'd ever eaten. Zack used his fingers to strip back the shell and the movements transfixed her to the point she forgot how starving she was.

He put a chunk of the meat in his mouth then groaned. She watched him chew, her body heating with every clench of his jaw and his eyes were full of pure bliss. God, even watching him was erotic!

'You have to try this,' he said, picking up a piece of meat and holding it close to her mouth.

She was sure this moment had the potential for some sexy move she'd seen in movies, but of course she wasn't that graceful when she opened her mouth and closed her lips over his fingers. She did suck a little though, just to get some of the juices off his digits and he groaned again, a deeper sound that made her cheeks flush.

He was right, the meat was delicious – better than anything she'd tasted. Taking her time, she chewed and savoured, never wanting it to end.

'Good?' he asked, his voice rougher than before.

'The best.'

'Let's go half and half,' he said. She frowned, not sure what he meant. Zack smiled. 'We'll share, like this.'

He swapped a couple of her shrimp for way more than half of his lobster and she was about to protest when he distracted her with a question.

'How long are you traveling with my lunatic cousin?'

'She's not a lunatic,' Ciara scolded, but relaxed when he laughed. 'Not *all* the time, anyway. We've got about six weeks left.'

'And then go home, get a job?' he asked.

If only it was that easy. 'Something like that. What about you? Why are you in the states? I thought the company was based in London.'

'It is, but I needed a break. I've been redesigning the offices since I got my degree anyway, but our granddad needs someone to take over. He wants me and Elle to do it together,' he said.

'What about your parents?' She knew Elle's dad had died when she was young and her granddad had taken them in, but she didn't know anything about Zack – she hadn't even known he existed!

'I lost them both a long time ago, in the same car accident that killed my uncle, Elle's dad.' He picked at a shrimp, not meeting her eyes.

She squeezed his wrist. 'I'm sorry, that must have been hard.'

'It was rough, but my granddad took me in too.' Then he smiled, but it looked strained around the edges. 'Growing up with a little, blonde dictator was almost worse.'

She got the feeling he was trying to lighten the subject so decided to help by steering it to something else. 'Why architecture?'

'Look out there, Ciara.' He pointed out to Little Havana and she noticed what he meant.

There were buildings of all shapes and sizes, each one with its own unique stamp. So very different from Miami. Though he'd shown her just how diverse Miami was tonight.

'You want to make something that's unique?' she asked, turning back to him.

He didn't look away from the window. 'Yes. But I don't know where to start. Everything I do for the business is modern, to my granddad's tastes. I'm given a project but I can't put my own stamp on it. I'd love to be able to start up on my own somehow.'

'But you don't have the money?' she asked, then bit her lip. Asking a guy how much he had in the bank surely broke some kind of rule.

He laughed. 'That's not the main problem. My granddad wants what's best for me and Elle to the point he thinks he knows what's best for us. I love him, don't get me wrong, and for the most part he lets us do what we want which is how I got my degree, but he wants us happy, settled and to have something for ourselves.'

'The business?' she asked.

He nodded, but from the way he avoided her eyes and started picking at a shrimp she got the feeling he wasn't telling her the full story. She didn't push, just finished up her meal. After all, they were only having a fling and maybe they'd already passed the point of sharing too much.

Chapter Seven

After splitting the most amazing key lime pie ever, Ciara disappeared to the bathroom and sent Elle a quick text to see if they were okay. Elle replied in seconds, saying she was missing out on the best night ever by ditching them for her cousin, but the sickly, green faced smiley and kisses assured her Elle wasn't pissed off.

When she got back, Zack was waiting by the door and held out his hand. She took it. 'You've paid the bill, haven't you?'

'Guilty as charged.' He lifted her hand and kissed the back. 'Where to now?'

'Zack, I wanted to halve it,' she said, but she wasn't miffed enough to snatch her hand back.

'Ever heard the saying, you can't always get what you want?' He winked at her and opened the door.

'Yes. But I don't feel comfortable letting you pay,' she admitted.

The sun had set by the time they got out, but the air wasn't chilly like it would be back home. Zack pulled her to a bench not far from where he'd parked the moped and sat her on his lap, despite the fact the thing was big enough to fit her bum five times over.

'I wanted to take you out, so I pay this time. If you want to cook me breakfast as a thank you, then I won't stop you.' He grinned.

Luckily she could manage breakfast. If there was anything decent in the fridge. 'I might have to treat you, since Elle doesn't believe she needs to eat when there are bikinis to wear.'

'A healthy appetite boosts stamina, don't you think?'

Without giving her a chance to voice her agreement, he pulled her face to his and kissed her. It was much, much better than the assault from earlier. Zack's lips were soft, but demanding. She answered, opening to him and when he slid his fingers into the hair at her nape, the whole combination became electrifying.

Molten blood rushed through her veins and her breath came in gasps as she twisted in his lap until she was straddling him. He grabbed her bum with one hand and pulled her so close that his erection was lined up perfectly between her legs. With her whole body aching with need, she thrust her hips to find some kind of friction and was rewarded with little currents of pleasure.

He let her lips go and trailed kisses down her neck while his hands slid under her dress. She wished her knickers weren't from the bargain bin, but it was too late to worry about that now. Unable to wait, she shoved his tee-shirt up and her fingers tingled with bliss when they connected to his warm, smooth skin.

'Ciara, we need to stop,' he said against her throat, still not slowing down with his kisses.

'I don't want to,' she said in a voice she didn't recognise.

Instead she went for his belt and managed to unbuckle it before he caught her wrists. She pouted at him, but then the breath was kicked out of her lungs at his expression. It was carnal, erotic and full of the need she felt.

He lifted her off the bench and she grabbed his shoulders in case she fell. 'What are you doing?'

After a too brief kiss, he untangled her legs and let her slide down to the pavement. 'We're going to get arrested if we keep this up and I think Elle will be too busy tonight to bail us out.'

She looked around and bit her lip. The locals and shop workers across the street were staring at them and no doubt would have seen a lot more than was appropriate if Zack hadn't kept his head. 'Oops.'

He laughed, but it sounded strained.

'We need to get back to the beach house. Now.' He took her hand and led her to the moped.

***

Her stomach was in bits by the time they arrived at the house. It didn't help that he'd made her stop off at a twenty-four hour mart and buy a bucket of ice cream either. Her mind was full of all the possibilities and the second he parked up, the nerves hit her in the form of speechlessness.

Zack led her through the house, flicking the hall light on but he left the kitchen and lounge area in darkness. 'Take a seat on the sofa, I need to grab something.'

Condoms? Her nerves fizzled under a flare of lust. Doing as he asked, she made her way to the huge white leather sofa.

He returned with a spoon and the open tub of ice cream. It was no Ben & Jerry's, but it looked good. Mint and chocolate, her favourite. She hoped he liked it too.

'Good taste, but it might be missing something,' he murmured, using the spoon to scrape up a roll of it and then slip it into his mouth. 'I know what will make it better.'

Putting the tub and spoon down on the table, he pulled her off the sofa. Ciara's heart was hammering so hard she found it hard to breathe, and when he pulled the dress over her head it seemed to double its speed.

First he just looked at her in the shadows for so long she wanted to cover herself from his scrutiny. But then she noticed

73

how dark his eyes were in the dim light, and his jaw seemed strained like he was fighting to stop himself from jumping her right there.

It gave her the confidence to unhook her bra and let it fall to the floor.

'Lie down on your back. I don't think I can touch you right now without things going too fast.'

She did as he asked, never taking her eyes off him. Zack pulled a pillow off one of the wicker chairs and put it under her head. She watched as he picked up the tub and spoon again, then knelt on the floor next to her.

Anticipation had her strung so tight she might shatter at any second. He scooped a little ice cream onto the spoon, then put it in his mouth briefly. It had melted a little when he took it out and hovered it above her breasts.

'Have you ever tried this? Using cold as a stimulant?' he asked.

Seemingly past speech again, she just shook her head and kept her attention on the spoon.

'Close your eyes, Ireland. This is about feeling,' he whispered.

She did and tried to relax back into the pillow but she was still too tense, waiting for some sensation she'd never experienced. The cold, smooth ice cream hit her nipple and she gasped with the shock of it.

'Give it a second,' he said.

She did, and suddenly the cold did something she never thought possible. It burned her nerve endings, sending a trail of fire right between her thighs. He added more to her other breast and everything doubled.

'Zack, it's... uh...' She couldn't describe how she felt, only that she was more aware of her breasts than she'd ever been. Who'd have known?

'I know.' His mouth closed over her nipple and the shift from cold to warm intensified everything.

By the time he'd lapped up the ice cream on her other side,

74

she was well on the way to coming right there and he'd only touched her breasts. She didn't have time to recover before he trailed the melted desert down the centre of her stomach, lapping it up as he went. Her breathing was coming fast now, like it did just before she went over the edge and she wondered if she should be embarrassed about coming so easily but was too lost to care.

He slid her knickers down her legs next and when they were off, parted her thighs. *Oh god, yes.*

'This is going to be more intense,' he warned with a grin, then before she could mutter out a response he parted her gently with his fingers and poured what felt like a lump of ice cream over her clit.

She muttered a string of curses as pleasure built so fast and hard at her core, but it wasn't enough to send her into a full scale orgasm. She thought ice down there would have a numbing affect. How wrong could she be?

'Look at me,' he said, his voice thick.

Ciara opened her eyes in time to see him put her leg over his shoulder and dip down. He started from below, licking the melted ice cream before it hit the sofa and his tongue dipped deep inside. She clenched around him, hoping to hold him and was surprised the sight of him using his tongue increased the pleasure instead of embarrassing her.

When he moved up and sucked her clit into his mouth, she grabbed onto the cushion and fought back a scream, opting for gasping instead. Zack never took his eyes off her, and they glittered with challenge when she bit her lip instead of giving into the moans and groans.

And accept it he did. He was merciless, bringing her to the edge of sanity again and again, then pulling her back over and over. She gave up watching, couldn't even open her eyes as her head shook from side to side on the pillow. Every time he built her back up she was sure that this was going to blow her mind and now, as he pushed her back to the brink of the biggest orgasm ever, she gave in and screamed for him not to stop.

Zack didn't and used his tongue without mercy, pushing her so high she was sure the fall would break her but she didn't care as long as he never stopped. This time the icy cold came back to her nipples as he tweaked them with sticky fingers. It was all it took for the pressure to release. The waves of ecstasy rippled through her, hard and relentless and he didn't give up, not until he'd wrung the last aftershock from her limp body.

She kept her eyes closed for a second, trying to catch her breath.

'Ciara, don't fall asleep on me. There's more where that came from,' he promised, and sucked on her nipple again, relighting the flame.

'Never,' she replied, grabbing his hair and pulling him in for a wild, desperate kiss that promised more than she knew how to give.

***

'Look what the cat dragged in,' Zack said, pulling her closer to him.

Ciara squirmed out of his hold and jumped up from the sun lounger when she saw Elle's nose wrinkle. He laughed quietly, then shifted his knee up to hide the evidence of their fumble in the sun.

'Five minutes later and we might have got a decent show,' Gem said with a grin.

Despite the fact both Gem and Elle looked like they hadn't had an hour of sleep, they both still managed to look immaculate for their walk of shame. Ciara took a seat on one of the chairs, a safe distance away from Zack. It was crazy that no matter how many times she had him last night and again this morning, she couldn't get enough.

Ignoring Gem, she asked, 'Good night?'

'You wouldn't believe it!' Gem said, collapsing on one of the loungers. 'Rye had the biggest dick ever and he used it like a porn star. I swear they must get some kind of course on the female anatomy at school here. English men don't know about half the stuff he did to me.'

Zack cleared his throat. 'I think that's my cue to leave you all to it.'

Ciara pressed her lips together to keep from giggling. He kissed her before he left, lingering a little too long and she almost forgot her friends were there when he broke away.

He whispered, 'Hopefully this Englishman didn't disappoint.'

She smiled. 'Not once.'

Ciara watched him go, gripping the side of the chair so she didn't follow. When she turned her attention back to her friends, Elle was looking at her with a weird expression – almost like pity...

Ciara wondered if she was really that in lust with Zack, or was it about something else?

'Did you get Brandon's number?' she asked, wondering if that was the problem.

Elle seemed to snap out of it. 'I gave him a bad one since he talked about hooking up for more than just sex.'

'Oh.' She didn't know what else to say. That's what she'd liked about Brandon.

Gem then went on with a more explicit breakdown of her night from the private shower in Rye's ensuite to the athletic morning fuck that left her sore but satisfied. All the while Elle was frowning at the glass wall of the house and she couldn't shake a horrible nagging feeling that Elle wasn't happy about something.

'I guess we better go spend your vouchers, Ciara. You up for a day at the shops?' Gem said.

'Sounds good,' she said, trying to hide her disappointment at having to leave the house. Or, more accurately, Zack.

'Then we'll go out for dinner. I haven't eaten anything other than lettuce in days,' Elle said distractedly. 'Excuse me.' She got up, went into the house and closed the door.

'Is she okay?' Ciara asked, hoping Elle wasn't annoyed at her. 'She doesn't mind, does she?'

'What, that you're doing her cousin? I doubt it. She's been quiet all morning,' Gem said.

She wondered what was wrong, but Elle wouldn't open up until she was ready. Her friend was quick to talk about herself until it came down to touchy subjects, then she kept her lips sealed.

'What are you getting at the mall? You should plan for Paris since we're leaving soon!' Gem said, reminding her that the clock was ticking.

And soon her fling would be over for good. The high she'd been riding all morning crashed like a surfer hitting the sand face down.

***

They didn't get home till late and the house was in darkness. After a day at the mall buying as much as we could carry, they hit a beach bar, ordered tasteless food and stayed there chatting and drinking for hours. But Ciara wasn't even tipsy when they stumbled up the path in the dark, or worried about falling in the pool. It might cool her off, since Zack didn't appear to be up.

Elle walked ahead and turned the patio lights on. She was staring a hole through Ciara's head.

'Spit it out, Elle. I'm too tired to figure out what's wrong with you.' All the guessing was making her paranoid.

'What's going on between you and Zack? Is it serious?' she asked.

Oh god, how did she answer without putting her foot in it? Elle might pretend to hate Zack but she grew up living in the

78

same house as him, and this interrogation felt a bit like Elle was worried she was going to hurt him. After all, she had the attention span of a gold fish and it wasn't like they didn't know. When they headed out to parties she was always the first to get drunk and hit the dance floor because standing around waiting to catch a guy's attention drove her bonkers.

But honesty always went down better with Elle. 'We agreed to have some fun while we were here, like a fling. He said that's all he wants too.'

Her nose wrinkled again, but then she laughed. 'Good, but make sure you don't share any of the gory details.'

'But the details are the best parts,' Gem protested.

Elle shuddered. 'It's bad enough listening to your sexcapades, never mind my cousin's!'

Gem laughed as she followed Elle into the house, but Ciara's mind was working overtime. Why had Elle relaxed when she said it was just a fling? But she knew the answer. Elle didn't want her to hurt her family, quite rightly too. She'd hurt some at uni, those who she thought she could maybe have more than the occasional hook up with and would always get bored of them a little too late to spare their feelings. Ciara definitely didn't want to do that to Zack.

Zack didn't appear as they packed away their shopping so she resigned to going to bed alone and hanging up her purchases. After a shower and a quick brush of her teeth, she climbed into bed, wondering if he was even there. They hadn't exactly been quiet when they got back.

But then her door opened and he snuck in, wearing nothing but his boxers.

'You tired?' he asked, then kissed her lightly on the nose.

'Not anymore,' she said, winding her arms around his neck. 'How was your day?'

'Good. I worked on some drawings and I'm actually happy with them.'

'Really?' She pulled back to try and see his face in the darkness. 'Can I see?'

'Tomorrow,' he promised and sealed it with a kiss.

He pulled at the hem of her new, silky nightgown she'd gotten from Bloomingdales. 'I like this, by the way. I take it you had fun shopping?'

'I bet I'd have had more with you,' she said, running her hands down his back.

He managed to get her out of the silk without her having to let him go. 'I'd put money on it.'

'Wait,' she said, pulling the sheet over her breasts. 'Isn't this a bit weird with Elle and Gem in the house.'

'Maybe.' He laughed a little. 'You'll just have to bite your lip tonight.'

By the time they'd finished with each other, she'd almost chewed it right off.

***

The sound of scratching woke her up the next day, and the first thing she noticed was Zack sitting at the dressing table in her room with a sketch pad and pencil. She stretched, feeling the burn in her muscles where she'd bent into some positions she never thought she'd been capable of.

'Good morning sleepy head,' he said.

Ciara rolled her eyes. 'I wonder what could possibly have gotten me so exhausted.'

'The hazards of bedding a stud?' he suggested.

She tossed a pillow at him, but he batted it away with a smile and put the sketch pad down. 'You're crabby this morning.'

Maybe, but it hadn't hit her until now that this would be the last morning she'd get to spend with him.

'Can I see now?' she asked, needing a distraction from the depressing thought.

He closed over the pad he'd been working on. 'This isn't finished yet, but you can look at these.' He brought a bigger notepad over to the bed and sat on the pillows next to her.

She noticed he'd been showered and dressed and realised she was probably smelling like a sweaty, sex filled night. Zack didn't seem to mind. He tugged her up so she was cradled against his shoulder, then opened the book.

'Wow.' The first design was a block of flats with a twist. Maisonette in style, but with a more modern, new build feel. He'd sketched a river next to it and the gardens looked like something out of a new age fairy tale.

'I was thinking of doing a development like this at some point. Do you really like it?' he asked.

'I love it. You're so good at this.' She flipped through the pages, all of them getting better and better until she came to one she had to stop at.

This house was huge, as big as an old Victorian mansion but wasn't flashy with it. The sides were completely glass with floating staircases inside at either end. It was very chic, a little space agey but definitely stunning. 'This is like something you see on those dream home shows.'

'It's my dream home. I'm going to build it someday, hopefully,' he said, sounding more wistful than excited.

'You should!' She grinned at him. 'It's brilliant, really. Stunning.'

'So a bit like you, then?'

She laughed at his cheesiness, but then her mood plummeted again.

Zack seemed to feel the same. 'I wish you were staying longer.'

'Me too.' She sighed and snuggled closer against him.

'We'll just have to make the most of today,' he said, finger combing her hair back from her face.

'You know, the buildings in Paris would be good inspiration.' The words were out before she could think about it. 'I… er… sorry. I didn't mean to say that out loud.'

81

His eyes were abruptly sad. 'I have to go to London tomorrow, Ciara.'

'Of course, you have responsibilities. I'm sorry,' she mumbled again.

'Don't be,' he said, shifting over so he was facing her. 'No regrets, okay?' She nodded, since she didn't want to lie and he pulled her into his arms. She hugged him close, knowing she was going to have lots of regrets when she left Miami – the biggest being that she didn't take after her loving, dependable father instead. Then maybe she'd get to keep hold of Zack a little bit longer.

Paris

Chapter Eight

Paris really was the city of romance and Ciara was reminded of it every stinking second.

'You're messing with our karma, Cia,' Elle said, but despite the words her friend didn't look annoyed with her. Her eyes were almost as sad as Ciara felt.

'I'm sorry. No more moping, I promise.' She sipped at the red wine they'd ordered in a small bar not far from the designer shops both Gem and Elle had dragged her around.

Beneath the table were all her friends' bags with so many new clothes that they were going to have to pay another excess weight fee at the airport when they left for their next stop.

'You know the best way to get over a guy is to get under another,' Gem pointed out. 'We're going to the club tonight. Maybe we'll meet a trio of gorgeous Frenchmen.'

Ciara forced a smile, feigning excitement. Elle's sharp look told her it was a wasted effort. After a few tears had appeared when they got to Miami International, her friends hadn't taken her gaze off her since. Pretending to sleep for the whole flight just to get the attention off her hadn't worked. It just made them more determined to cheer her up.

'I don't think that's what she needs, Gem.' Elle reached into her purse and pulled out a couple of notes, then left them on the table. 'But I have an idea.'

'Oh hell, what now?' Her mind was too busy churning through the possibilities that she didn't even moan at Elle for paying the bill.

'Where are we going?' Gem asked when Elle picked up her bags.

'You'll see. I didn't waste all that effort getting us into Le Baron for Ciara to wear a face like that all night.'

'Thanks Elle,' she murmured dryly. Then something clicked. 'Wait, isn't that the private club the Russian mafia lords drink in?'

She'd googled the night life in Paris before her shopping trip in Miami to try and figure out what to buy with her vouchers, and La Baron was one of the clubs she remembered, just not for the right reasons.

Elle laughed. 'It used to be, but it's under new management now. Relax.'

'So why did it take so much effort to get in?' she asked as they started off down the street.

'Because it's private. And exclusive. I want to go. Obviously.'

There really was no stopping her friend when the chin tilt appeared so she sighed and gave in for the moment. It didn't take Elle long until they got to their destination and Ciara couldn't stop her chin from dropping. Two windows showcasing sleek, black dresses would have been enough to stop her in her tracks, but above that and the door a black metal balcony with gold letters stunned her.

Elle was taking them to *Givenchy*, knowing how much Ciara loved the black dress she borrowed from Elle for a spring dance a few years before. But this was just cruel. Taking her to a shop that she couldn't even afford a scarf in.

'Come on,' Elle said, pulling her toward the door.

'I can't go in there.' Ciara tried to wrestle her arm back.

'You're going alright. Gem, get her other arm!'

They had such a tight hold on her that struggling wasn't just humiliating in front of all the passers by, but totally pointless. Strong-arming her into the shop can't have been easy with her wriggling and the bags they were already carrying, but they did a better job than she could have.

'I hate you for this! Both of you!' she hissed, closing her eyes to make it hurt less. If she saw any of the dresses, the accessories, she'd be saying 'bye, bye' to the rest of her money.

'You're going to love me soon,' Elle said, not even out of bloody breath!

'What, when I'm penniless and on the next flight to Dublin? I doubt it.'

A woman's voice asked in French if they needed assistance, but her lessons from high school failed her as she couldn't remember how to say 'yes, call the feckin' guards.'

Elle answered in fluent French, making Ciara hate her even more. Then she was being dragged again and in a bid to end this madness, she planted her feet and refused to budge.

She should have known that wouldn't stop Elle.

'Drop the bags. We'll pick this cry baby up and carry her to the changing rooms,' Elle said to Gem.

As her feet left the ground she did the most stupid thing ever and opened her eyes.

They were in a rectangular room, all grays and white but that wasn't what drew her attention. It was the minimalistic clothes hung on rails in the indentation from the walls. Dark, plain, simple and oh so pretty.

Little black jackets hung next to the matching white blouses and leather skinny jeans. The next alcove had sleek, knee length skirts and a blouse with a daring strip of red below the bust. But the loveliest, most elegant black dress draped over a mannequin with so much effortless grace stole all her attention. Her anger evaporated and she sagged against Elle, needing the support.

'Think we've found a winner,' Gem said, lowering her friend back to the floor.

Such a bittersweet feeling, seeing something she wanted so much and knowing she could never ever have it for real. She'd been having that feeling a lot lately.

Elle started up again with the French, so fast she didn't understand and then they both dragged her away from the dress. The swell of disappointment made her too weak to fight back, and she stared at the prettiest thing in the world until it was out of sight, just to make sure it was ingrained in her memory.

Gem shoved her into the dressing room and she sagged onto the sofa, feeling even more miserable than she had an hour ago.

'You're going to make me strip you too, aren't you?' Gem said, then without much of a pause got to work on doing just that. 'Just so you know, this isn't gay in the slightest.'

Ciara didn't care what it was as she let her so called friend strip her top off then her jeans.

'This has to go too, sorry.' Gem unclipped her bra and pulled it off her arms. 'You do have a nice pair, but not nice enough to turn me off the dicks for good.'

She knew Gem was trying to make her laugh, but her eyes watered instead. God, it was like she was grieving. For Zack first and now for the prettiest dress in the world.

The curtain parted to show Elle with a hand full of hangers. 'Shit, Gem. I didn't tell you to molest her.'

'I didn't, I just got her ready. Do you have it?' Gem asked.

Ciara couldn't care less what they were talking about. She knew it would only mean more torture. At least there weren't mirrors here. She could look at the panel without seeing her despair or catching a glimpse of them.

'This is ridiculous, Ciara. You should be excited, not acting like someone died,' Elle said. She thrust something at Gem, then pulled Ciara onto her feet. 'Don't make me slap you. I will.'

Like she cared either way.

'This is totally unnecessary,' Elle huffed, but then turned her around. 'Hold up your arms.'

They weren't going to leave her alone until they'd had her way, then she could go back to the massive house and lock herself in her room until they were ready to leave this horrible city.

Ciara lifted her arms and closed her eyes. Satin fabric fell down over her body effortlessly, with nothing but a thick strap over one of her shoulders. She wouldn't open her eyes and look, this was bad enough. The soft dress skimmed her curves, all the way down to her knees making her tingle and yearn.

She was turned around again and pushed forward a few steps. 'This is the one,' Elle said.

'I'll say. Wow, Ciara. You look like a model,' Gem gushed.

Ciara didn't dare look. She couldn't trust herself to hold it together if she got a flash of reflection. Her imagination was already running riot.

'You know, I'm trying to do something nice for you and here you are, being an ungrateful bitch.'

Ciara did lose it then, but not in the way she'd feared. As soon as Elle had spoken, anger flared through her, burning away all the hurt and she did open her eyes, but the image of her in the prettiest dress in the world didn't soothe her.

She whirled on Elle. 'How is this *nice*? You know I can't afford *Givenchy* but you dragged me in here anyway, torturing me with more things I can't have! As if leaving Miami wasn't bad enough, now you want to show me how fucking amazing I look in this dress, knowing I'm going to have to walk out of here without it? You're the bitch, Elle.'

Elle's eyes widened and got a little watery. 'I'd never do that to you, Ciara. The dress *is* yours and you *can* walk out of here with it. It's already paid for.'

Her anger only cranked higher as she returned to the dressing room, pulled the satin off without missing a beat then got dressed in record time. When she got back, Elle and Gem's worried expressions made her bite her tongue against the angry torrent she wanted to scream at them.

Instead she headed for the exit.

'Where are you going?' Gem asked. 'Cia, don't do this.'

'If either of you knew me at all, you'd know how much I hate being a charity case and would never have done this. Some friends you are.'

Gem called out again but Ciara kept walking until she hit the streets, then broke into a light jog as tears welled in her eyes. Her gut wrenched until she had to slow down, the sick feeling lying heavy in her stomach. It was guilt, she knew she'd overreacted but not enough to go back and accept their charity.

Instead she walked aimlessly through the city, not noticing much at all about the beauty of the place she was in. Her mind went back to her eighth birthday, when the headmaster called a meeting with her father and she'd tagged along. He'd thrown out words like genius, and good university and ever since that day her da had worked double shifts, weekends too, just to make sure she could have the best education money could buy. Money they didn't really have, but that her college friends had in spades.

She knew it was different, but the principal was still the same. She'd barely earned enough in her life to begin paying anyone back. Maybe if she had a plan for the future, she wouldn't have half of the stupid pride she did. But this was real life and she was who she was.

***

Hours might have passed, Ciara wasn't really tracking. She'd walked through most of the city and was now at a park with the clichéd couples on benches, tourists with their cameras enjoying the afternoon sun and kids running around with Viva La France footballs.

She wasn't tracking the world cup either, but most of the

tourists seemed to be and had dressed for the occasion with footie shirts galore. Finding an empty spot shaded by a massive oak tree she sat down and decided it was time to snap out of this funk.

After all, Elle and Gem had only been trying to cheer her up and the guilt had shifted to shame, so much so that each time her phone vibrated she couldn't bring herself to fish it out of her pocket.

But that was wrong, they'd be worried about her and Elle had been right, she was an ungrateful bitch. One who didn't deserve her friends. Pulling her phone out, she noticed all the missed calls, texts and voicemails and was about to dial Gem when a text from a number she didn't recognise flashed on her screen.

1pm. Le Petit Café.

The address followed. Had Elle and Gem bought a new phone to tempt her out of hiding, or worse, gotten a private investigator involved? She squeezed out a giggle, trying to convince herself the latter was ridiculous but she couldn't say for sure that they hadn't. Elle was just as prone to overreaction as her, albeit in a different way.

Jumping up, she stuffed her phone back in her pocket and then peeled out of the park, keeping a look out for the nearest taxi. She had an hour, but wanted to get there as early as possible in case her mental friends really had paid someone to find her.

Finding what she was after, she rhymed the address off to the driver as best she could, then spent the journey going over every single way she could apologise. When they hit the side streets, Ciara knew this wasn't going to be good. Elle was all about the restaurants and cafes on the main strip. A back street one away from all the designer boutiques was a foreign concept to her friends.

But then he pulled out to a main street and stopped in front of the building. It wasn't too out of the way, which gave her hope that they'd just got a new phone. After paying the driver, she climbed out and scanned the tables outside. Her friends were nowhere to be seen, but she was a little early.

She scanned the inside with no luck. Ordering a coffee, she went back outside and sat at the only empty table. The smell coming from the place was all ground beans and sweet pastries. Maybe she should have added a desert to her request, but it was too late now. She took her phone out of her pocket again and scrolled to Elle's number. It was way past time she grew girlie parts and made amends.

A shadow cast over the table and she looked up. Her mouth dropped open.

'I hear you stood up to Elle at last. Good for you, Ireland.'

Zack was here, or this was the best dream ever. He looked different though, wearing a suit instead of the shorts and tee-shirt combo she was used to. And his suit looked expensive too. Dark blue with a crisp white shirt beneath. At least he didn't have a tie on, and had open buttons. It made him seem more human and less corporate businessman.

'Ciara, are you okay?' he asked and took the chair next to her.

She closed her mouth, tried to clear the shock of seeing him from her mind. 'Why are you here?'

His brows were furrowed, like he was worried about her. 'Elle called this morning and told me what happened. I jumped on one of the company jets to see if I could help her find you.'

Oh God. She covered her face as embarrassment wrestled with guilt inside. 'You didn't have to do that, I'm so sorry. I was just being an eejit.'

He pulled her hands away then tilted her chin up. She couldn't understand why he was grinning like that, or why his eyes sparkled. Shouldn't he be mad? Being dragged away from his work just to find a stroppy bitch.

'Don't be. It gave me an excuse to see you again.' His eyes narrowed. 'And I have a thing or two I'd like to say to Elle in person.'

'Please don't, it's not her fault. I overreacted when she was trying to do something nice for me.'

His eyebrows shot up. 'By carrying you into a shop, stripping you half naked and forcing you into a dress? That's nice?'

Ciara looked down at her phone, seeing the new screen saver of the three of them huddled together with huge smiles in LA. 'They knew I'd never accept their charity, and it was the only way to get me to agree.'

Zack took her phone, put it on the table then linked his fingers with hers. The contact was so much more than electric – it thrummed away the sadness until all that was left was him.

'What's wrong with gifts? It's only a dress,' he said.

Spoken like a true Muir. The extent of their fortune was becoming frighteningly clear. He thought nothing of having a flight scheduled then hopping on to cross the channel at a moment's notice, just like Elle thought nothing of buying her an expensive dress remembering how much she'd loved the designer.

Looking into his eyes, she forgot all of that. He looked like the easy going Zack she'd met in LA with gorgeous dark eyes and lips to die for. She didn't care that what passed between them could never last or go further than this meeting. She wanted him to know as much about her as she knew about him. 'It's hard to explain.'

'I can keep up,' he said with the lopsided smile she adored.

Ciara told him about that time in the headmaster's office, letting him know everything her da went through to get her to Oxford and told him how much she loathed feeling indebted to anyone.

He listened, all the way through, letting the coffee he'd ordered go cold, and squeezing her hand when she needed him to. She left out the parts about her mother, since she hadn't been around back then and left out the parts about how much she'd missed her dad when he'd worked so much, because she knew how selfish that was when he was doing it all for her.

'So that's about it,' she said.

Zack was quiet for a long time, just looking at her with his eyes wide and maybe a little sad. When he smiled, it was kind and wiped away the hint of sadness. Or maybe she'd imagined it.

'Ciara, your dad wanted the best for you and always will. That's not charity, it's love.'

Probably more along the lines of pity, since she'd had to grow up without her ma, but she didn't tell him that.

'And never, ever tell Elle I said this.' He waited until she nodded. 'I think she loves you too, and she just wants to do nice things for you the only way she knows how.'

Her vision got blurry. 'I really am an ungrateful bitch.'

'Never say that,' he scorned, wiping a stray tear from her cheek.

She forced out a smile, but it was weak. She was back to hurting again, knowing the grieving was coming as soon as she left him. And that time had to be soon. Surely he needed to get back to work and she had serious apologising to do.

'I missed you,' she whispered.

The lopsided grin was back, making her heart take off. 'I missed you too, Ciara.'

Ciara bit her lip before the most unfair words came out. She wanted to ask him to stay, so badly it was making her tremble. His eyes darkened in that way they did when he was thinking dirty things and the breath whooshed out of her lungs.

But then he stood up. 'You should take Elle up on her offer and go enjoy yourself tonight.'

Just like that, air was kicked out of her lungs until she felt winded. She nodded, lowering her gaze to the table.

'And Ciara?' he said, tilting her chin up with her finger until she could see his face. He looked concerned again. 'Don't run off on your own in a city like this, okay?'

'I won't,' she mumbled.

His lips brushed her forehead for a second, then he seemed

to jerk away like she smelled funky. Watching him walk down the street, all she could think was she deserved this feeling of being walked out on. It's what she got for being a cow.

Chapter Nine

Ciara's heart was hammering as she stepped into the foyer and knocked on the huge black door rimmed with gold. Another of the Muir's fancy properties, and she'd wondered if Zack had had a hand in designing it as the building only looked a few years old.

But she wasn't going to think about him until she'd apologised properly and they'd been on the fun night out Elle had had planned for ages.

Gem opened the door with Elle right behind her, and though they breathed out identical sighs of relief, they watched her carefully, like she was going to erupt at any second.

She was a miserable, selfish, horrible person who had the best friends in the world. Her eyes welled and spilled over like water bursting from a damn. 'I'm so sorry.'

'You're a pig headed idiot,' Gem said, pulling her into a hug that knocked the breath out of her. 'But so are we.'

Elle joined in, wrapping her arms around them both. 'I'm unstoppable sometimes and it's not fair to you. I should be the one that's sorry.'

This all felt too easy. She didn't deserve that. 'Aren't you mad?'

Gem shook her head. 'We were worried. I'm glad Zack found you.'

'I'd have come back. Just, when I calmed down I felt so bad about storming off that I couldn't face phoning you.' She bit her tongue against asking what Zack said when they called him, and for every little detail of that convo. This was about her making up for being a cow.

'Come on, we're making dinner,' Elle said, pulling them into the house and closing the door. 'You can grovel more in the kitchen if it makes you feel better.'

She smiled a little and wiped away the tears. 'It will.'

'We should too, for dragging you into Givenchy,' Gem said.

Ciara shook her head and took a seat on one of the bar stools on the breakfast bar/wine rack. Gem went straight for the wine underneath and pulled out a bottle. 'While in France…'

While Elle chopped away at the veg and threw together a massive salad with the best olive oils and dressings money could buy, she sipped at the red wine, listening to Gem natter on about the tee-shirts she was getting printed for the Greek part of the tour.

She couldn't wait until they got to Santorini, and she could relax for a week without worrying about unpacking and packing up again within a few days of each other. Already, she'd decided Paris was her least favourite city in the world. But then if she'd come with Zack for a couple of days as a romantic break, she'd probably change her mind.

Sighing, she pulled her phone out of her bag. No more texts. He was probably back on his private jet, soaring across to London.

Elle put Ciara's plate down in front of her and noticed straight away that something wasn't right. Her chicken wasn't grilled like Elle's and Gem's. Instead it was done in the frying pan covered in spices she loved. Next, her salad had a dollop of mayo whereas she knew Elle would never, ever buy mayo, never mind serve it! And was that cubes of feta through the lettuce leaves?

'What have you done, Elle?' she asked. Her friend wouldn't ply

97

her with this kind of meal if it wasn't bad. Well, it wasn't fried chips and steak bad, but close.

Elle held up her hands. 'Don't get crazy again, but I didn't *just* buy you the dress.'

Ciara gritted her teeth, trying to call back the consequences of the last time she'd lost her temper, about eight hours ago. 'What else?'

A sheen of sweat broke out over Elle's forehead. 'Shoes – to go with the dress. But that's it, I promise!'

She took a deep breath, remembering what Zack had said about Elle loving her and only wanting to do something nice for her, so she swallowed her pride. 'Thanks, really. I love that dress and I'm sure the shoes will be stunning.'

Elle's eyes widened and Gem said, 'Do you want to repeat that? I think I was hearing things.'

'Ha. Ha.' She shoved her shoulder against Gem's. 'Really, I appreciate it and I'm sorry for being such a baby earlier. The food looks fab too.'

Ciara dug in, ignoring the look that passed between her friends. The whole day had put so much in perspective for her, and even though she still didn't feel comfortable wearing expensive clothes her friends bought, she was going to try and think of it as a nice gesture by someone who cared about her.

***

Even though the club was exclusive, there was still a line to get in. Most people weren't on the guest list and were turned away one by one. She was so glad she had something chic and sophisticated to wear, since all the women in front of her were dripping with designer and style.

'Elle, I really do love the dress and I'm sorry for—'

'I swear, Ciara. If you don't stop worrying you're going to look fifty by the time you're thirty.' Elle treated her to a dazzling smile.

Her cheeks heated. She deserved more wrath than this, had fully expected it. Especially since she'd driven her friends to call Zack. But she hadn't mentioned him since she got back. Her plan had been to apologise and the feeling of him walking away hadn't left, but she was determined to put that aside so she could enjoy the night with her friends.

'I wouldn't want to get on his shit list. He's huge,' Gem said, nodding to the tank of a bouncer who'd just come out the club. 'Definitely steroid abuse and god knows what else. You can't get a body like that naturally, even if you spend all your life in a gym.'

'Trust the biological science graduate to ruin the view,' Elle said.

The words she'd found on the Google search popped into her head again. *Russian mafia lords.* But she wasn't stupid enough to say the words out loud. Her palms got damp as the group before her were escorted in by the tank, then they were asked their names.

Elle rhymed them off, and the man with the list nodded. They had to wait for the bouncer to come back and she had a vision of a trio of lambs, waiting to be led to the slaughter. Of course, Elle and Gem looked nothing like lambs. One donned in burgundy *Prada* and the other in teal *Gucci*, for once she didn't feel out of place next to them in the prettiest dress *Givenchy* had ever made. All thanks to Elle.

When the human tank appeared, Ciara was ready to bolt but Gem took her arm and led her in behind Elle and the freak of nature. She didn't dare speak as they made their way through a dimly lit blood red hall, and didn't say a word as the bouncer led them to a table to the right of a giant room. There was a dance floor that was too shiny and expensive to dare stepping on with stilettos.

But one thing she did notice was that all around, whether the tables filled with men or mixed with women, there were classy and refined people everywhere. Sipping champagne and chatting over low French music that made her feel more relaxed. Even if it may or may not be where the gangsters came for a drink – and possibly the occasional slaughtering.

A waitress in a silver gown brought over a champagne bucket and glasses. Elle had clearly ordered ahead. Ciara wondered if they'd make it to the end of the night, then shook the thought away. It didn't *look* like the kind of place mafia lords came to party, though she only had *The Godfather* to go on and even then she had to turn off the first midway because all those guns gave her the chills.

After the waitress filled the glasses with pink champagne, they thanked the woman and she left them to it.

'When you said club, I had dancing and bathroom sex in mind,' Gem grumbled.

'It won't be long until the party starts, just wait,' Elle said, scanning the crowds, probably for a hunky bachelor to sink her claws into for the night.

Ciara took to alcohol instead of checking out the eye candy, hoping the bubbly drink would relax her enough to actually enjoy herself. She hoped Elle had ordered a crate of the stuff.

***

A few bottles of the pink champagne later and Ciara was starting to have fun people watching. The music picked up and the daring took to the dance floor. A woman dripping from head to toe in gold and rubies had to be the head of the mafia's wife, in all her finery. And the woman was hot even though she could have been old enough to be her mother.

A man approached the queen of the gangsters, but he looked too thin and wiry to be a crime lord. Maybe he didn't know who she was. Maybe he'd eat a few bullets later for his trouble.

She shivered, despite the fact the club was warm.

'He's here!' Elle said. 'I knew he'd come.'

Ciara's heart launched into her throat as she looked around desperately, hoping to see Zack among the sea of men in finery. The crash was almost devastating. Of course Elle would never be excited about her cousin being anywhere. Her reaction in LA and Miami had proved that.

'Where?' Gem asked, and Ciara followed their gazes.

The man looked powerful in a black suit that no doubt cost a fortune. His hair was greying at the temples, reminding her of a younger, sexier George Clooney and she had to admit she was digging the silver fox thing he had going.

'Pier,' Elle sighed. 'He doesn't go by a second name, like Madonna.'

Ciara frowned. 'What makes him so special?'

Both her friends looked at her like she was from a different planet.

Elle filled her in. 'He's the third richest bachelor in the world, Ciara. Keep up.'

'And you care about that, why?' It's not like they weren't rolling in it themselves.

'The money is what makes him so unattainable. A challenge.' Elle grinned. 'And you know how much I love those.'

'You want to, what, marry him or something?' Ciara had never heard either of her friends talk about a relationship where it ended in wedding bells.

'God, no. I was hoping for an invite to one of his parties. He has a loft apartment down by the river and I heard he takes a select few back with him. Imagine a man like that picking you to take home and give you his full attention.'

She knew she had a lot to learn about all this girl and boy stuff still, but didn't understand why Elle would want to be with someone who was, by what she'd said, a bit of a slut.

'Don't you dare ditch us, Elle,' Gem warned.

'Come on,' Elle said, topping up her glass. 'He's not about to pick me, is he?'

But Ciara didn't trust the glint in Elle's eyes, she doubted Gem did either.

A while later, her friends had drawn the attention of two Frenchmen who didn't seem to speak a word of English. They were gorgeous, dark haired and totally her type. Except she found she didn't even want to speak with them, even if she'd known how to. Excusing herself, she made for the bathroom again, feeling dizzier than the last time she'd tried this. God, it was awful. She was well on her way to being drunk and Elle was so polished she could still speak fluent French and flirt.

A look in the mirror showed her make-up, at least, was still intact. The golden ringlets Gem had given her seemed fine too. Still, she rummaged around the *Dolce* clutch Elle loaned her for lippy. She found her mobile instead.

Carrying it over to the sofa, she opened up her texts until she found the one from earlier.

She still had his number.

She still wanted him.

Not any of the suits in the club, not any of the posers in Miami. She wanted Zack like she'd never wanted anything else, and as she thought more about their last night together in Miami, she couldn't stop the burn of heat flooding through her veins.

Her thumbs started typing and before she knew it, she'd hit send. Re-reading the text was harder, the screen was getting blurry which was probably her cue to order a glass of water. The words she'd sent to him flared up a spike of lust.

I want you in my mouth. I want to taste you and lick you until you come for me.

She did. It was something she'd never had the pleasure of doing yet – something she'd hated doing with guys she'd dated in college. But imagining Zack in their place? Her stomach got all gooey and her mouth watered.

Gem opened the bathroom door. 'There you are! Come on, we're leaving.'

'Huh?' Ciara asked, shoving her phone in her bag and hoping her cheeks weren't as bright as they felt.

'Those two know Pier and invited us all to a private party at his place!' Gem took her hand and pulled her up.

The plush marble sinks seemed to spin with the room around her until she took a deep breath to clear her head.

'I think you should lay off the bubbly,' Gem said.

She giggled, and a rush of emotion heated her cheeks. 'I love you, Gem. And Elle too.'

She'd no idea why she thought now was the perfect time to tell them, but it felt right.

'We love you too, now come on or we'll miss the limo.' Gem put her arm around her waist and she strutted out of the bathroom, feeling very sexy in her new killer heels.

When Elle said loft, Ciara had immediately thought of a dusty old attic with a little paint and some art to make it homey. This was so not what she expected. The house *was* old, but it had been renovated so the living quarters were down stairs and the outside staircase led to a balcony, looking out over The Seine. Through the glass patio, she could see inside. Dim light, lots of corner sofas and a fully staffed bar. Plus, what was that in the middle? It looked like a massive, blood read cushion except it was bigger than a bed.

Eight of them had come, another two women, Pier and the Frenchmen who'd sat at their table in the club.

Pier went straight for Elle, leading her into his loft like a true gent, but all Ciara could think was all the women he'd had and couldn't get past it. She was handed a glass of champagne by a waiter, but decided to take this one easy since her equilibrium was on the dodgy side.

She followed Gem to one of the sofas, with the other women and one of the guys. The other Frenchman went to a wall that looked like it was made up of electronics and after a moment of touching buttons, more music she didn't recognise filled the room.

The soft voice of the singer was almost sensual, but something about it made Ciara think it was a soundtrack to a classy porn film.

'How are you now?' Gem whispered in her ear. 'You look antsy.'

She was a bit. She wanted them to put upbeat music on so she could cut some moves on Pier's plush carpet – it didn't look as easy to ruin as the dance floor at the club.

'I'm fine. Actually, I've got loads of energy,' she said, not bothering to whisper.

Hands massaged her shoulders gently and she looked behind her to see the music changer hovering over her. God, he did have gorgeous eyes with little green circles round his pupils.

He bent down so he was close to her ear. 'I'm glad to hear you're full of energy. You will need it later.'

His accent rolled around the words, making her tingle. Well, her hand tingle anyway. Wait. She snapped her attention to her bag and realised that was the cause of the buzz. 'Sorry, I have to take this call.'

'I'll be waiting,' he said, then his thumb trailed down the side of her neck.

Blood rushed to her face, but it wasn't because she was turned on by his touch. He hadn't even talked to her once before now and what, he was flirting? Hoping she'd go back to his place and fuck him?

She got off the sofa and headed outside. She knew who had called, or at least hoped she did. When she pulled her phone out her bag she realised she'd missed him three times.

Hitting call, she put the phone to her ear.

Zack answered on the first ring. 'Ciara, are you okay?'

Smiling at hearing his voice again, she turned to lean against the balcony and look out over the river. 'Why wouldn't I be?'

'You sound sloshed.'

'Tipsy.' She giggled again. She'd been doing a lot of that tonight. 'Zack you won't believe where we are. Elle got us an invite to a party and I'm on a loft balcony right now looking at the Seine. It's beautiful.'

It truly was. With the light of the moon and city shimmering over the black waves.

He laughed. 'So that last text was all talk?'

'The what…?' And then she remembered. She'd sexted him. Elle's bloody cousin. Her face burned. 'No, it wasn't all talk. It's true.'

'As in, still true or true before you got an invite back to the party?'

Did he sound jealous? She grinned and then looked over her shoulder to make sure no one had come out to hear what she was going to say next. Lowering her voice, she said, 'Oh it's still true. If you were here, I'd be on my knees right now, undoing your trousers and then licking you until you got hard.'

Zack groaned deep in his throat. 'I'm already hard, Ireland. You're killing me.'

She could imagine him (naked, of course), all aroused and waiting for her to make her next move. And she would, taking her time, exploring every line of muscle, every part of him she'd never had the chance to before.

'It's a shame you had to go back to London.' She sighed. 'I have so much energy, I could go all night.'

He cursed, obviously as frustrated as her now. At least he could relieve himself easier than she could. She had the feeling Gem and Elle were here for the duration.

'Ciara, what if I told you I wasn't in London?' he asked.

Chapter Ten

'I'd say, I hope you're not kidding,' she said, almost breathless.

'I'm not.'

He didn't elaborate and her heart started to hammer. The fact that Zack was close when she thought he'd gone home made her giddier than all the champagne.

'Why did you stay?' she asked.

He spoke slowly, like he was trying to phrase something carefully. 'You were right. Paris is good inspiration for me and I can work from the hotel just as easily as I could back home.'

'Oh.' So it wasn't because he felt the same way she did.

Though she shouldn't be so depressed by that. It was her that wanted the time limit in Miami before they got serious and she got bored. Elle might act like she hated Zack, but if Ciara screwed him over and broke his heart like her mum had broken her dad's, her best friend would never forgive her.

Ever.

'Ciara?' he asked.

'Mmm?' It was the best she could do without showing how upset she was. Surely this fixation she had with him would pass soon. After all, there was a gorgeous guy in the house flirting with her and she bet he was just like her, keeping 'relationships' short, fun and satisfying. Zack didn't seem like that at all. Or maybe it was just the fact that she liked him more than she'd liked the other guys she'd dated. Of course that would make her wary.

'We could extend the time limits. Technically, you're still on holiday for another few weeks.'

His suggestion was perfect, exactly what she wanted. Definitely more than she wanted to go back into that party and pretend she was into someone she wasn't. But she had to make sure he was clear about things. 'I don't want a relationship, Zack. Just a bit of fun. Nothing too deep or emotional.'

He sighed. 'I know. I wish you'd tell me why.'

Turning to lean against the balcony, she sighed too. 'It's complicated.'

Zack chuckled. 'You say that a lot you know.'

'I do,' she said with a grin, but then noticed something wasn't right with the scene inside the house, or maybe it was a sixth sense kind of thing but the mood had shifted somehow. 'Wait a sec.'

Ducking her head inside, she met Gem's eyes. Her friend looked freaked out, stuck in the middle of one of the woman and a guy. They were both feeling up Gem's legs and leaning over her to snog the face off each other.

'Oh god, I think we've walked into a crazy, French orgy,' she told Zack.

'*What?* Ciara, where are you? Is Elle okay?'

She tried to spot Elle and when she did, realised her friend wasn't that comfortable stuck between Pier and the other man. A woman knelt on the floor in front of Pier, unzipping his trousers as Elle was pawed by the bastard himself.

'I don't think they are.' The pleading look Elle shot her way snapped her out of the 'oh shit's.

'Can you pick us up?' she asked, hurrying back into the loft. The sensual music sounded creepier now that she knew what mood it was setting.

Lots of rustling on the other end of the phone. 'I'm coming now. Tell me exactly where you are.'

Ciara tried to give him directions, but she had no idea where she was and hadn't paid much attention when she was in the limo. As Zack started to sound more and more frustrated, she made her way to Gem and said, 'Something's come up, we need to go. Now.'

The French man grabbed her around the knee, then slid his hand a little too high. 'Stay, beautiful Ciara. I will make sure you enjoy it.'

'Put that bastard on the phone, now!' Zack shouted in her ear. Oh god she couldn't do that could she? What if they were mafia lords? They wouldn't take Zack cursing them lightly. She had to play this cool and as calm as she could.

'Sorry, but we have to go,' she said, grabbing Gem's hand.

'Don't apologise to the creep!' The sound of an engine revving almost drowned out Zack's angry shout.

Gem untangled herself, then bolted for Elle. They apologised to Pier, even though he was in the middle of having a blow job that a porn star could never pull off.

And, despite having half his dick in another woman's mouth, when Elle rose he grabbed her arm. 'Stay. I will take you first and make sure you are well seen to.'

Zack's response to that was a string of curses, but they were cut off by a beep. She looked at her phone, her eyes blurring as she realised the battery had died. Shit, shit, shit.

'I'll pass, Pier. This isn't my scene,' Elle said, but Ciara could tell that wasn't an apology in her eyes, it was cold fear. Which is probably why she hadn't dumped her glass of champagne over the guys before now.

If Elle was scared, this had to be bad.

Thinking on her feet, she lied. 'My mother's been in an accident, we have to go.'

She took Elle's arm and pulled, then they were clattering out of the loft and down the outside stairs. When Ciara got to the bottom, she felt a little slice of guilt for saying that about her ma, but it was all she could think of and it wasn't like she even knew if the woman was alive anyway.

Gem grabbed her arm and they scampered down the street, far away from Pier's.

'Elle, you need to call Zack. He's on his way but I didn't know where we were and my battery died.' She looked behind her, just to make sure they weren't being followed. The road was clear, thank god. But that didn't mean they were out of trouble yet.

Elle pulled her phone out with shaking hands, then dialled her cousin.

***

About ten minutes after their escape, a fancy black town car pulled over at the side of the road. The driver lowered the window and when she saw Zack's scowl, she could have cried with relief.

Elle was struggling to stand straight and she and Gem had to hold her up. It was scary, watching her strongest friend go into some kind of shock. At least Gem seemed okay.

'Elle, get in the front. You two in the back,' he demanded.

As she shuffled to the back of the car and climbed in, she wanted to weep for a different reason. He was mad, she could tell by the way his shoulders and jaw were rigid. But he still turned around and asked if they were okay. Both she and Gem nodded, then a black security screen rose up, separating them from Elle and Zack.

She turned to Gem and saw she was shaking. 'Are you really okay?'

'I've done stupid things before, Ciara. Gone home with men I didn't know and risked so much, but up there was different. Those men were really charming in the club and even when we got back, then all of a sudden it was sex den time and I didn't think they'd take no for an answer.'

Shuffling over, she wrapped her arms around Gem and let her friend cry against her shoulder. 'You're grand now. Zack's taking us home and you didn't get hurt.'

'It's because of you. If you hadn't come back and got us out, we'd have been used. Totally used.' Gem sobbed.

'Shh, it's okay.' She repeated that over and over again, hoping Elle wasn't in the same state and Zack was giving her hell. After all, even Ciara didn't think those men were into that stuff. Maybe they came across a little forward, but into orgys? She'd never have guessed.

When they stopped again it was outside the Muir's building. The front doors opened, but Gem was still shuddering and she didn't want to push her away just yet. Zack opened the back door at Gem's side and the anger melted from his expression.

'Hey, Gem bear. You're okay now. Come on, we'll get you inside.' Zack didn't meet Ciara's eyes as he lifted Gem out of the car and put her down on the pavement.

'Thanks, Zack,' Gem mumbled, then headed for the house.

She climbed out and was greeted with his back. She shut the car door and stood there with her stomach in bits, waiting for him to acknowledge her.

'Elle said she feels dizzy, but doesn't remember drinking much,' he said in a hard tone.

'She didn't.' It was Ciara who'd devoured most of the champagne at the club. 'Oh god, you think they drugged her?' she asked, then hurried for the house.

He caught her arm and turned her around so fast her head spun. 'She only had a sip in the party, but that's when she started to feel it come on so yes, I'd say they tried to drug her.'

Her eyes watered as she turned back to the house. She tried to remember if Gem had finished her glass, but then remembered seeing it on the table with hers, pretty much untouched. 'I don't think Gem had any there.'

'Good. Ciara, you said things to me you haven't before. How much did you drink when you got there?'

She turned back to him and saw he'd clenched his jaw. His free hand was fisted at his side. 'Nothing, honestly. I stopped drinking at the club.'

He seemed to relax, then pulled her into a hug, burying his face in her hair. 'Thank fuck for that. Honestly, if Elle wasn't so shook up I'd give her hell for dragging you all somewhere like that.'

'She didn't know,' Ciara mumbled against his shoulder. 'None of us did.'

'Well, you're all okay now. I guess that's the main thing,' he said, but sounded like Elle when she was trying not to be mad about something and failing horribly. He pulled away, then headed for the car.

'Can't you stay?' she blurted, not wanting him to leave.

'Make sure they're okay and phone a doctor if Elle gets sick. She said she didn't want one just now, but all bets are off if she even breathes wrong.'

She nodded, but her brows pulled together wondering why he had to leave.

Zack must have been down with the mind reading. 'I can't be near her right now, Ciara. I'll come over tomorrow.'

Before she could agree, or drop to her knees and beg him to stay, he was in the car with the dark windows and she couldn't see his face. She watched him drive away until she couldn't see the tail lights anymore, then turned back to the house. Coffee seemed like a good idea since she wasn't going to sleep until she knew for sure Elle was fine.

***

It was a long, long night and even the espresso she'd had at five this morning didn't help much with the exhaustion. By nine, Elle and Gem were stirring in the bed they'd shared and she breathed a sigh of relief from the not-so-comfortable tub chair she'd perched on for the last eight hours.

Elle frowned at her. 'What are you doing?'

'Making sure you don't die a horrible death by drowning in your own vomit,' she answered, trying to make light of a situation that was so not funny. But she'd decided she wasn't going to make Elle feel bad. She'd looked terrified at Pier's.

Elle turned to see Gem next to her, then sat up and rubbed her head. 'Was I that smashed last night? I can't remember drinking much.'

Ciara went cold all over. 'Don't you remember anything? The club, Pier's?'

'Pier's? What do you...' Elle's eyes got wide and terrified again, like it was all crashing back to her.

At least that was a good sign. She'd spent the night with her phone on charge, googling date rape drugs and others, and most of them wiped memories of the night before. Since Elle just had a sip, she hoped the drug hadn't taken root.

'I'm so, so sorry Ciara. Did Gem drink it?' Elle asked.

She shook her head. 'She was more freaked out about what could have happened, but its fine. We're fine.'

Physically, anyway. One good thing might come out of this, at least. Elle and Gem might be more careful before they come up with the next crazy scheme.

'Do you mind if I go to bed? I'm shattered.' Now Elle seemed fine, she could keep an eye on Gem.

Tears welled in Elle's eyes and she climbed out of the bed, careful not to disturb Gem, then pulled Ciara into a choking hug. 'You're the best friend to us. We're such fuck ups, getting you arrested – twice – and then dragging you into an orgy! Next time I have a bright idea that looks like it's going to end in disaster, you need to pull me back. Remind me of last night.'

'I will,' she promised, hugging her friend tighter. 'Just work on that stubborn streak so I have a chance.'

'It's a deal,' Elle said, and Ciara yawned. 'Go get some sleep. I'll make sure lazy bones doesn't drown in her vomit.'

'Thanks Elle.' She untangled herself from her friend's hold, and yawned again.

Doing a zombie shuffle across the room, she forced her eyes to stay open long enough to make it to her bedroom, and face plant onto the mattress. Her last thought was that she was glad she'd put her pyjamas on before she settled in to watch her friends, since she would never have been able to hang up the prettiest dress in the world right now.

***

A high pitched shriek woke Ciara from her coma. She fumbled around on top of the sheets for her phone and saw it was just past two in the afternoon. Her head hurt so much she wanted to close her eyes and never open them again.

But then came the shouting.

'I don't think you realise how serious this is, Elle.'

Zack. Oh god, he was here and she was a mess. And he was laying into Elle.

She jumped off the bed, running to the ensuite to make sure she didn't look as awful as she felt, but Elle's defence stopped her half way there.

'I don't think you realise it's none of your business. If you hadn't noticed, we're fine. We could have gotten a taxi back last night, but since you were stalking Ciara's every move, I called you because I knew if I didn't, you'd lose your shit.'

No, no, no, no, no. That wasn't how she felt about the conversation. It was her who reached out to Zack first!

'When are you ever going to grow up and act even a little bit responsibly? You could have all been raped!'

She'd never heard Zack shout before. His anger was just as impressive – and terrifying – as Elle's. And she couldn't argue with his logic. They *could* have been raped.

'Will you two keep it down, Ciara's trying to sleep!' Gem butted in, but she sounded nervous and Ciara remembered when she stopped her from getting in the middle of them in LA.

'No point, he's leaving anyway,' Elle said. 'You talk about me being responsible? Why don't you go back to London and do the right thing. This stalking stuff is getting creepy and pathetic.'

Bugger how she looked, she wasn't having Elle make Zack feel bad for their fling, not when she was the one who'd asked for it. She bolted through to the living room, just in time to hear the front door slam shut.

'Elle, why did you say that?' she asked, horrified that he'd left thinking god knew what.

Elle's cheeks were red and she had fire back in her eyes. 'Because it's true. He has shit he needs to deal with back home, and you're better off without him Ciara.'

'Isn't that for me to decide?' she asked, her own temper paying a visit. 'All he's done is get us out of trouble. He doesn't deserve to be abused for it.'

Her friend's anger seemed to melt and there was no mistaking the pity in her eyes. 'This has gone past just a fling for you, hasn't it?'

Speechless, she looked to Gem for help but there was pity in her expression too. What the hell were they keeping from her? But then, if it wasn't bad, like really, really bad, they'd have told her. Wouldn't they?

Ciara slumped down on one of the sofas, not caring at this second that she might put a dent in the precious looking silk cushions. She was exhausted again, both physically and emotionally.

'I really like him, but I know what it is and so does he.' It was all she had without worrying them that she was going to hurt him, or vice versa, since they seemed to feel sorry for *her*, not Zack.

'And what is *it*?' Elle asked in a softer voice.

Feck, she was going to make her spell it out. 'It's just a bit of fun with the first man in ages that doesn't make me feel like a slut for only wanting something short. He understands a lot that most people don't, like why I have a hard time accepting gifts that cost an arm and a leg. Honestly, Elle. It's not like I'm going to fall in love. I'd get bored by then, you know that.'

Elle didn't look convinced, neither did Gem. 'And what if he does, Ciara? I might hate him right now, but you don't. Could you hurt someone you cared about like that?'

She could, it was in her genes. But she didn't want to, and Elle knew that too.

'I wouldn't if I could help it, but if you both thought for one minute that Zack could fall in love with me, you both wouldn't be looking like *I'm* the one who's going to end up heartbroken, would you?' She stared at them both and each of them lowered their eyes. 'So if it's me you're worried about, don't be. I'd rather spend time with him while I can and deal with the rest later.'

'I wish you wouldn't.'

It was all Elle said and made her think twice about darting into her room and grabbing her phone. Anger and a flat out refusal were what Elle was famous for. This dejection with a request? She wondered again what they were hiding from her, but it was obviously something Zack didn't want her to know, or he'd have told her already.

She rubbed her eyes, thinking this was a topic she was never going to win and with Zack's sudden departure without even seeing if she was okay, she guessed it was her who was into him more.

'I need food, and more coffee,' she grumbled.

'I know a little café that does the best croissants ever. We can get showered and go there if you like?' Gem suggested.

She smiled, thankful for the break in the topic of impending broken hearts. 'Sounds good to me. Elle?'

Elle's smile was genuine and not forced at all. 'I should have known croissants would cheer you up.'

But as they all headed to get showered and dressed, Elle stopped her just outside her room. 'I really don't want whatever's happening with Zack and you to drive a wedge between us. I love you Ciara, and don't want to see you get hurt. Or him, believe it or not.'

'I don't want that either. The idea of giving him up and never seeing him again is like being told I can never have mint ice cream again.' Bad example. Her cheeks flushed remembering the way Zack had shown her how it could be enjoyed in Miami.

Elle sighed. 'I get that, I really do. And for what it's worth, I think he feels the same.'

'What are you saying?' she asked, not daring to hope.

Her friend's smile was sad. 'I'm saying… be careful. And be happy. Both of you.'

Ciara's throat got so thick she didn't have words. Instead she pulled Elle into a massive hug.

'You *really* need a shower, Ciara,' she said and laughed.

Pulling away, she wrinkled her nose. 'I really do. I'll see you in a bit.'

Or a few hours, if they were waiting for Elle to get ready…

Skipping back into the room, she was about to go for the shower but her phone caught her eye. Changing direction, she went for the bed and picked up the mobile. No missed calls, no texts, and the hurt was instant. But then Elle had called him a stalker and thrown him out saying they didn't need him.

As she scrolled to his number, she wondered if she was being selfish, or if whatever they weren't telling her was a deal breaker to the way she felt for him. Either way, she couldn't leave things the way they were. She'd dragged him out of his bed twice now to come and help them and, if nothing else, she had to thank him for that and let him know she was sorry.

Taking a deep breath, she hit call and brought the phone to her ear. It rang and rang and rang until an automated voice asked her to leave a message. After the beep, she did.

116

'Hi, it's me. I wanted to thank you for last night. For everything, really. And I'm sorry for coming between you and Elle. I'll understand if you don't want anything else to do with me.' She had to stop and clear her throat since her voice got too thick. 'I just want you to know that I meant what I said last night. I want to see you again, to extend our fling, but I know I've gone and fecked that up.'

The beep cut her off before she could ramble on. Her mood was as gloomy as it had been when she left Miami. She had a feeling this really was the end. In his shoes, she didn't think she'd have the patience to put up with all their drama and couldn't blame him for bailing while he still could.

But she wasn't about to ruin the next destination for her friends, since she'd made a right mess of Paris. Nope. She was going to grow lady balls and save the moping for when she got home. After all, this was their last summer together and she was determined to make it their best ever.

Santorini

Chapter Eleven

'That had to be the most embarrassing journey ever,' Elle complained, tugging at the tee-shirt Gem designed.

Ciara grinned at her friend's mortified expression. 'I think they're cute.'

'See? Someone appreciates my talents,' Gem said.

The printed tee-shirts were white, tight fitting, had deep 'v' necks with 'Geeks go Greek' printed across their busts in a groovy, neon pink font.

'Thank god we're here. Now I can get into my bikini,' Elle said, pointing along the dirt road they were being driven down by the Muir's driver.

After seeing the Land Rover waiting for them at the airport, Ciara had worried that the next of the Muir's properties was going to be some shack in the middle of nowhere or something, but she hadn't been prepared for this.

The house – again, if she could call it that – which Elle pointed to, was massive. It seemed to have six levels, each one backing up on the mountain like a staircase and ending with a huge raised patio over the beach. There was a hot tub, swimming pool and a stone area centred by the biggest dining table she'd ever seen.

Looked like Santorini was going to be another luxury trip.

'Wow, is that your granddad's yacht?' Gem asked as they got closer.

To the side there was a pier stretching into the clear blue sea, a boat with more multi-levels, a group of jet skis hooked to a buoy further out, and a shed that could fit ten dorm rooms, easily.

'That's a yacht?' Ciara asked. It looked more like a ship to her.

'Yes, but don't get any ideas. I haven't a clue how to sail it even if I'd go near the sea.' Elle shuddered. 'The water's disgusting.'

It looked gorgeous to Ciara – all blue, clear and shimmering in the sun. She couldn't wait to go for a dip.

'Anyway, I have so many treatments and massages booked that we won't even need to leave the house,' Elle said.

The thing was huge, no doubt about it. But, still. Ciara didn't want to be cooped up in the thing for over a week. 'Why don't we hire a car and see more of the island?'

'I'm not doing anything until I get this tee-shirt off and catch some sun,' Elle protested.

Gem scowled at her. 'I'll come with you, Ciara. Just as soon as I've unpacked.'

The driver pulled into a triple garage where she saw that the Land Rover wasn't the only thing they had here. Quad bikes and a Porsche filled the other spots and she wondered if they were Zack's, since the way Elle spoke of her granddad made her think he was a bit old to be zooming about on them. No way were they Elle's – she wouldn't want to risk messing up her hair.

More staff appeared from the house, all speaking Greek with one another and Ciara didn't even try to guess what they were saying. Unsurprisingly, Elle knew and dished out some orders fluently, then their cases were taken into the house.

'Why don't we leave exploring until tomorrow?' Elle asked, instead of demanding like she usually did. She was getting good at the tactful stuff. 'There's a restaurant not far from here and they put on really good shows at night.'

Ciara barely heard. She'd switched her phone on the second

they got off the plane and ever since had checked it every two seconds. It had been almost two days since she left Zack the voicemail and she hadn't heard from him since.

Still nothing. She tried to tell herself that didn't matter. She was in a beautiful place with lots of exotic flowers, strong sunlight, a pretty beach and the potential for some serious fun.

She wasn't going to *let* it matter. This was about enjoying time with her friends, not pining over someone who obviously didn't want her.

'Sounds fun to me. You in, Ciara?' Gem asked.

'Yes. Fun.' When they both looked at her funny, she tried to remember what they were asking her. Right, restaurant with a show. 'Really, it sounds good. I'm starving.'

They laughed and headed for the house.

'I'll ask them to make us a light lunch and we can go later. I had massages and pedicures booked for after the flight.'

By the time she'd unpacked, there was no missed call flashing on her phone and even during lunch when Gem told Elle they were going for a bike ride round the town with their Geeks Gone Greek tee-shirts and there had been loud refusals, there was still no missed calls or messages on her phone.

She'd tried to be discreet, but during a languorous foot and temple massage with them, Elle caught Ciara's mobile screen lighting up and sighed.

Elle said, 'He's not going to come, not after what I said to him in Paris. Believe it or not, he's even more stubborn than me.'

Ciara nodded, trying to keep her expression blank and obviously failing because Elle took her hand and squeezed.

'You're miserable, aren't you?' Elle asked.

'Don't be daft,' she protested but it sounded weak.

Gem peeled the cucumber slices from her eyes and pinned her with a 'mmhmm' look.

'Really,' Ciara said, glaring at them both. She handed Elle her phone. 'You keep hold of that and I'll stop obsessing. Promise.'

Elle gaped at her like she'd just handed her a kidney. 'You're giving me your phone?'

'If my da calls I'll speak to him but no one else ever does and it will stop me checking it every two seconds.'

Thankfully, she'd been wise enough to delete the sexting. And sensible enough to delete Zack's number, just in case.

Gem frowned. 'Ciara, it's your *phone.*'

She rolled her eyes. 'Exactly. It's not my arm or my leg, just a piece of plastic that wasn't affordable till I was sixteen. People did used to live without them, you know.'

'Cavemen,' Elle grumbled. 'Jesus maybe. But this is the 21st century!'

For all their smarts, when it came to history they were clueless. 'Believe it or not, even last century people got by without mobiles. And TV.'

Her friends shuddered. Drama queens.

Elle shook off the horror first then dived straight into Ciara's phone, nosing like a pro.

'There's nothing incriminating there, you know,' Ciara said.

'Good, I don't want to have to bleach my eyes before dinner. God your 4G is *slow.*' Elle had zero patience with technology and soon switched it to standby.

Ciara didn't want the gaping horror back on their faces, so didn't mention her phone barely had 3G. Instead she lay back and enjoyed the temple massage. The women Elle hired to give them the works over the next ten days definitely knew what they were doing. But she'd get bored of this soon. Lying around and being pampered was nice, just not for her.

And the down side of all this relaxing was she had too much time to think about things she shouldn't. Zack, the fact there was nothing waiting for her back home work wise – unlike her friends she lacked ambition and had spent her summers in England instead of hunting for internships, and on top of all that, she'd put on so much weight munching down on croissants in Paris that most of her trousers were tighter than her skin.

She groaned, but it had nothing to do with the fingers at her temples moving in relaxing circles – she wasn't relaxed at all.

'Enough with the sex noises, Ciara. It's disturbing,' Elle said and Gem laughed.

'Ha. Ha. Actually, I was thinking about how fat my arse has gotten since Paris.' At least in LA and Miami she'd had Zack to help her work out.

'You can always order a salad you know,' Gem said.

'And miss the chance to try proper Greek food? I don't think so.' Ciara sighed. 'But maybe I should do a few laps in the pool before we go.'

She sat up and thanked the masseuse, determined to go for a swim. After all, her friends still had pedicures to go and if she knew Elle, manicures too.

'You're insane. I'd rather starve than work myself into a sweat,' Elle griped, then reset the cucumber back over her eyes.

'To each her own,' Ciara said, then got off the massage table. Elle really hadn't been kidding when she said Greece would be about pampering and relaxation before they hit the next crazy stop on their destination.

***

The bedroom door swung open just as Ciara was wriggling into her favourite pair of white linen trousers.

Elle barged in, looking more like a glamour puss than she ever could. 'You're never allowed to moan about the length of time I take to get ready again.'

'I'm having a wardrobe disaster,' Ciara said, then had an idea. She lay on the bed, sucked in her stomach and gave her trousers a heave. Finally, they buttoned.

Elle bit her lip. 'Um, Ciara. I don't think you'll want to wear those.'

She sat up, feeling the squeeze around her hips and bum, and had to agree. But she loved these trousers and hadn't had a chance to wear them yet. She saw this as motivation, if nothing else.

'It's too late for that now, we have reservations. My top hides how much they choke me anyway.' She pulled on a loose fitting flowery smock that came down to her hips, grabbed her bag and slipped on her gold flip flops.

Elle pressed her lips together and her eyes watered like she was trying to stop herself from laughing.

Ciara gritted her teeth. 'Don't you dare, Elle. I mean it. I feel crap enough as it is!'

Having gorgeous, skinny friends was a curse. She stormed past Elle, through the massive corridor and down two flights of stairs until they were at the 'ground' level. Or at least the level with the cars.

'Just don't reach up and you'll be fine,' Elle said from behind her.

'What took you so long?' Gem asked. She was tapping her pink flip flops against the gravel. 'It's usually Elle we have to drag out kicking and screaming.'

'My trousers shrunk and my arse got bigger. Can we go now?' Her cheeks flared with irritation and a lot of mortification. So much for all the exercise she'd done.

'I really think you should get changed,' Elle said, tugging on her arm. 'You have dresses—'

'No way,' Gem butted in, grabbing her other arm. 'I'm starving. We're leaving now.'

Elle might be bossy but Gem was fierce when she wanted to be. Winning the tug of war, her friend probably gave her a bangle of bruises round her wrists but she didn't argue much. She was starved too.

On the way, Elle kept looking at her stomach and irritation flared again. 'Stop looking at me like an alien is going to burst out of there. It's fat, nothing else.'

'It's not that I'm looking at. Your trousers. They're... Um... very tight.' Elle's cheeks scored pink and she was back to pressing her lips together.

'I know that!' Feck, if she'd laughed at Elle for this she'd be one friend down. Permanently. She stared out of the window, ignoring the ache in her jaw from more teeth clenching. She was even struggling to appreciate the pretty scenery with the mood she was in.

'Elle that's bitchy, even for you,' Gem said.

'I'm being a friend, not bitchy. But it's okay, her top covers it.'

The fat. The new fat she'd acquired from comfort eating everything she could stuff into her face their last day in Paris. Served her right, really. But she was paying for it now.

'What are you talking about?' Gem asked as they pulled up in front of the restaurant.

Ciara let herself out of the Land Rover, not wanting to hear what she knew was the truth but Elle didn't make an effort to whisper.

'She's got camel-toe.'

Freezing mid-step, she tugged her top right down until the cups of her bra were on full display. Speechless didn't cover it, and it wasn't the first time a Muir had done that to her was it?

'Oh shit. Ciara turn around and let me see!' Gem said.

There were people all around on the street and she swore every set of eyes zoned in on the spot between her thighs. Her face burned hotter, adding to the humiliation.

'Ciara!' Gem said, louder this time.

She climbed back into the car, ignoring her friends. 'I'm going back. Right now.'

'Don't be a little girl. I told you, your top hides it,' Elle said.

She scowled at her prettiest friend. 'You could have told me!'

Elle scowled back. 'You told me not to, remember? Now get your arse out of here before we drag you out. We'll enjoy dinner and the show and no one will know what's going on under the table.'

Gem snorted out a laugh, then quickly covered her mouth with both hands. Ciara turned her scowl on her until she mumbled out an apology.

'Fine but I'm not staying all night and I'm *not* getting up for anything.' Ciara said.

Elle told them that after the meals had been served the performers encouraged the customers to get up and dance. No matter how drunk she got, she'd never risk putting herself on display that way.

'Deal. Now come on, you'll *love* the food,' Elle said, taking her arm and tugging.

She stumbled out of the car, pulling at her top as she went. 'Food's the bloody problem! I should be doing more laps in the pool and munching on lettuce instead.'

***

Elle was right, she did love the food. After her chicken with aubergines and feta, she swore she could never go back to plain old chicken and broccoli. And with every course and act put on, her mood lightened to the point she could almost laugh at herself.

The restaurant was pretty and rustic, with huge arched walls filled with lights aimed at the stage in the centre of the room. The food was traditional Greek too, and the dancers, who wore different coloured outfits, put on a fabulous show. Right after everyone's desserts had been cleared, the performers started pulling people up for a round or two on the dance floor.

This was the part she'd been dreading. Thank god there was lots of wine left.

'We should dance,' Gem said. 'It looks fun!'

'I'm sure it will be hilarious if I get up,' Ciara grumbled. 'I'll be the entertainment for the rest of the evening.'

'You're a crabby shit when you want to be aren't you?' Elle said.

She shook her head then sighed. 'I'm sorry, it's not your fault I ate all those croissants and now I'm bursting out of these trousers.'

Gem, obviously well on her way to sloshed, said, 'Can you really put on weight on your vag? I mean, I get hips and arse and even stomach but down there?'

Ciara didn't know if it was the honest to god curiosity in Gem's tone that pushed her toward the edge of madness or whether she'd just hit the point of cracking up, but she laughed so hard her eyes watered and her ribs hurt.

Elle joined in, and soon Gem too but she still had that burning need for knowledge glittering in her eyes.

After pulling herself together, Ciara said, 'I don't think so. I just had to tug them up too high to get them fastened.'

It wouldn't be a problem for long. First thing tomorrow she was starting her new get fit and skinny routine which meant lots and lots of exercise. Maybe even enough so she could come back here every night and enjoy a three courser. It would be her treat after being forced to lie around all day getting massages and facials and whatever else Elle had planned.

'Ladies, can I persuade you to join in?'

Elle and Gem turned to the gorgeous Mediterranean man who'd asked. By the gaga look on Gem's face and the little sheen of drool on Elle's lips, they *really* wanted to accept the offer.

'You two go have fun. I'll watch our stuff.' And the wine, though she was planning on doing more than look at it.

'You sure?' Elle asked, but Gem was already out of the chair and fawning over the male performer.

She laughed. 'Really sure. It's a pity I don't have a camera. Snapping you two would keep me busy.'

'Here!' Elle dug out her own phone and handed it to Ciara. 'Snap a few and Instagram them. The good ones I mean.'

Her eyes widened. Elle didn't hand over her 'baby' to anyone.

'It's the least I can do. I should have told you earlier whether you wanted to hear it or not,' Elle said.

Ah, so it was an offering to ease the guilt. Ciara didn't care, she'd take it. Even though she really shouldn't. Having Zack's number within a few taps on the screen was a bad idea.

'Go have fun. There's still lots of wine here to keep me company,' she assured her friend. Gem had already taken off. From what she could see, she was getting the hot dancer to show her some moves.

Elle followed her gaze and laughed. 'She wasn't down for long.'

The reminder of the night in Paris when they got a little too close to real trouble made her shiver. 'We stay together okay? And go home at the end of the night.'

Elle got serious. 'Definitely. I'll peel Gem off him, even if it ruins my new manicure.'

She relaxed a little more. Having Elle on side would mean they'd get out unscathed. 'Go learn how to dance, I know you're dying to.'

'Learn?' she bitched, but got up. 'You just make sure you snap all my sexy moves.'

Ciara tapped her way to the camera, switched the flash on then snapped a picture of Elle who posed like a pro in record time. 'You're not Kate Moss you know.'

Elle wrinkled her nose. 'Thank God for that. The whole junkie rocker look is so not my type.'

'Johnny Depp?' she asked.

'Maybe him. If he'd scrub up a bit. Keep the bad pictures on the phone, we can have a laugh at them later,' Elle said.

Her friend *must* feel bad. Elle refused to be teased ever.

She waited until Elle found a female dancer and started swinging her hips as instructed. Of course, she picked up the new dance fast and Ciara did as promised, zooming in and snapping the sexy moves.

When she spotted Gem, she laughed. No way did their other friend have two left feet, but Ciara wouldn't guess by the mess she was making of the dance. The instructor pulled her really close and danced with her then voila, Gem got it right! Rolling her eyes, she snapped a couple of pics, making sure to really capture the gorgeous guy and get one of his behind. Gem would love that.

But after a while she got bored and the wine bottle got empty. She scrolled through the pictures she'd taken, then onto the ones from the club in Paris. It was before she'd drank her weight in bubbly stuff and the way the *Givenchy* dress hugged her made her giddy and gooey eyed, but that whole night was one she'd sooner forget, so she flipped to the pictures from Miami.

Cringing, she saw exactly what Zack meant about her looking sloshed in the bar. A massive jug of cocktails downed in record time would do that to a girl. But the red stain on her chin from the drink made her remember that night all too well. And the night after, riding with Zack along Ocean Drive and into Little Havana.

Then later, with the ice cream and his way too talented tongue...

Ciara slammed the phone face down on the table and necked the last of her wine. The temperature seemed to shoot up about a hundred degrees and she was sweating all over. She tried to convince herself it was the body heat from all the customers dancing that made the place too warm, but it was such a lie.

No matter what she did, she couldn't get Elle's cousin out of her mind.

Eyeing the phone, Ciara tried to convince herself that trawling through a friend's messages was wrong. Then again, it was the first thing Elle had done when she handed over her phone earlier that day.

Her hand made up her mind for her, reaching out and grabbing the thing. She tapped out of the camera and into the messages. Her heart launched into her throat when she saw there was a conversation with Zack and today's date was the latest message. How could she not open it?

For Christ sake, Zack. Answer your phone!

That was from Elle. Today. Other than one above apologising for being a bitch which she must have sent in Paris, there were no other messages. She tapped out and hit the call log, almost biting her lip off.

He was the last person she'd called and from what her phone said, the conversation had lasted over twenty minutes. No way was that just to his voicemail. She'd been cut off much sooner.

What had Elle said to him? She couldn't exactly ask. Elle would know she'd been snooping. But the wondering was going to drive her insane, she could almost feel it coming. Still, it was none of her business. In fact, it was probably about exactly that, the Muirs' family business. Made sense. Elle was going back to work there and Zack said their granddad wanted them to work together. Elle would know she'd have to make things right with him first.

She tried not to let that depress her, and failed.

Get a grip. Tapping out of the call log, she did just that and concentrated on Instagraming the best pictures of the night she could find. It didn't stop her thinking about that which shouldn't be thought about, but she took what distraction she could.

Chapter Twelve

'Glad to see camel-toe isn't joining us today,' Gem said.

Ciara ignored her, walking right past the sun loungers where her friends were enjoying their early morning coffee with the gorgeous view of the ocean.

'I don't know, I kinda miss it,' Elle said.

'You two should do stand-up. You're hilarious,' Ciara said dryly, but didn't stop for more. She was on her way to the pool to work off last night's dinner. Not to mention the extra flab she was carrying around her hips.

'Come on, Ciara. It was pretty funny,' Gem said. 'And you did snap a few beauties of Elle last night, so you're even.'

'There weren't any bad pictures of Elle,' she said, sure she wasn't that drunk.

'There's a couple taken at dodgy angles that make my arse look square,' Elle disagreed.

Ciara rolled her eyes. 'Only you could see imperfection where it doesn't exist.'

'Stop being a crab, Ciara. I let you have my phone last night and everything. What else do I have to do to make it up to you?' Elle asked.

Yes Elle had given Ciara the phone but it had haunted her all night, wondering about the call with Zack. She almost asked but then that would be like confessing to murder as far as Elle was concerned.

'You can take me back to that restaurant tonight. I've not had a chance to wear any of the dresses I got in Miami yet.' If they still fit, that was.

'Deal,' Elle grinned.

'We were going anyway. Milo's expecting me,' Gem said, with a giddy look in her eyes.

'*Milo?*' she asked, then bit her lip before she laughed. Elle wasn't so gracious.

'What? I think it's sexy,' Gem protested.

'I think it's gay,' Elle countered. 'And by the way he dances you might be in for more heartache, Gem.'

'Come on, he's too gorgeous to be gay.' Gem really was clueless at times.

'Sorry, but I agree with Elle. He's polished, he can move and I bet you two got on like a house on fire.' Nothing like any first date she'd had, with a straight guy anyway.

Gem picked up her magazine and made like she was miffed and ending the topic. 'Jealousy gets you nowhere. You two should concentrate on pulling your own Mediterranean Gods instead of dissing mine.'

Elle rolled her eyes and then got down to catching the early morning sun. Ciara took that as her cue to leave and got busy with her new workout regime.

***

The day was filled with more pampering and just as she was about to go brain dead from boredom, they finally moved on to the restaurant. From what she could see on her journeys to and from town, there really wasn't much to Santorini at all. But then in two days it wasn't like she'd had a chance to go anywhere. At

134

least she managed to enjoy herself at the party, despite being the most uncoordinated one there.

And even after witnessing Milo teaching another man how to bump and grind on the dance floor, poor Gem was still in denial.

The next morning all she did was talk and talk about her sexy fling to-be, ignoring any jibes Elle threw in about him being more interested in Aiden Price than Gem was. But come lunch time, Ciara had way too much energy to just sit there and have her feet and calves massaged like Gem and Elle. All this exercise was starting to perk her up, and not just because it was easier to button her trousers.

'Why don't we head out on the jet skis?' she asked Elle.

'Because I want to live to my twenty-fifth birthday,' Elle replied.

Gem threw her a look that questioned her sanity. 'Lie back and enjoy this while you can. Trust me, you'll be glad you took it easy this week when we hit Ibiza.'

'If I haven't died of boredom by then,' she said, completely serious.

'I can't believe you're bored of this after two days. I could do it forever,' Elle said, relaxing back into the padded chair while the masseuse worked on her arches. 'Sun, relaxation and don't forget facials are next.'

As much as she loved all the foot rubbing and the temple grinding and even a good facial, each one came right after the other. There was only a pause to eat and that was a small, not so tasty event of plain salad without the dressing. The only thing Ciara had to look forward to was four in the afternoon when the staff left and they could get ready for dinner.

But the schedule for tomorrow was more of the same.

She really was going to go insane here. She couldn't help but wonder if this was how her ma had felt spending every day with her?

Shaking off the thought, she thanked the masseuse and stood

up. Elle wasn't the only one with the tricks to get what she wanted. 'Fine, I'll go by myself. But I didn't take you for a wimp, Elle.'

Just as planned, her friend's eyes lit up like blue fire. 'I'm no wimp, Ciara.'

'Really? Then you must not think you can win a race. I know how much you hate losing. Better to avoid it than admit defeat, isn't that right?'

Elle got out of the chair, murmuring something in Greek, then glaring at Ciara. 'I can beat you two, any day! Gem, come on. We can finish this later.'

Gem muttered something unladylike, then said louder, 'Why me? I don't care about losing. I'm fine just here.'

Elle pulled her up. 'If I'm risking my life out there then so are you. It's what friends do for each other.'

'It's the sea, Elle. Not molten lava.' Ciara tried to hold back a smile, but failed.

'You won't be saying that when you're legs are covered in shark bites!' Despite the protest, Elle marched across the deck to the small pier, shouting in Greek to a man scrubbing the deck.

He was on the jet ski next to the yacht in record time, then speeding out across the waves to the buoy where the others were. It looked so fun, but having Elle all revved up might not go well. Still, it beat lying down and being rubbed, buffed and plucked (or whatever else was planned), by a stranger.

As soon as all the jet skis were brought over, the man handed them life jackets. Then he helped them onto the machines and showed them how to turn the handle and control the speed.

'You see those white buoys out from the coast?' Elle asked, pointing to six points that highlighted a huge semi-circle area. 'We don't go past them because the current is too strong. We'll do three laps round the inside of the markers, only going as far as those in front of the beach, and the winner gets to pick what we do for the rest of the day.'

Ciara was glad to see the old Elle was back, taking charge as usual. But she was determined she wasn't going to lose and have another day full of mindless boredom. 'Got it.'

'Gem?' Elle asked.

Gem was gripping onto the handlebars like she'd fall into the water if she didn't. 'I heard you.'

Elle nodded and grabbed her handlebars just as tightly. 'Then on the count of three, we go.'

Ciara got ready, she knew what was coming and would be prepared for it.

'One... Two...'

Before three was called Elle shot off, right when Ciara twisted the handle a little too far, but it meant she was neck and neck with Elle. Leaning forward, she ignored the waves crashing against the jet ski and soaking her face with salty water and concentrated on not toppling the thing over.

Her heart roared and adrenaline kicked in as they hit the first turn. Though she'd never done it before, the physics part of her course came back to her and she calculated the perfect speed to take the curve faster than Elle did, then she was zooming back to the pier where Gem was still shaking on her immobile jet ski.

The second lap brought Elle way too close. Her friend's fear of sharks was nothing compared to her competitive drive and Ciara had relied on it to get them off their bums and out having fun.

'You're getting lapped, Cia. Don't get comfortable up there,' Elle shouted.

Ciara just laughed and risked the next bend a little faster than she should have. Shifting her weight to the side made up for the death turn and she put some much needed distance between them again.

Elle was good on the straight run though. She zipped right past Ciara full speed, standing up on the machine to balance the front out. Ciara did the same and caught up a little, but after her take-off she had visions of flipping the thing right over if she went any faster.

The bends weren't Elle's strong point and Ciara threw everything into it until her knee skimmed the surface of the ocean. On the straight she took a deep breath and stood. Ignoring the jitters in her stomach she leaned her body forward and twisted the handle until the bottom of the jet ski barely skimmed the waves.

'Bitch!' Elle screeched.

But Elle didn't have to worry. Despite twisting the handle right back she was going too fast to slow down enough for the next bend. Instead she shot through the boundary and took a wide arc toward the beach.

When she was back on the straight she saw Elle shooting across to the pier and knew she was fecked. Another day of boredom it was then.

The trip back was slower. All the excitement and thrill had been sucked out of her.

When she got to the pier, Elle was already standing with her hands on her hips and a smug smile on her face. 'You should know better than to challenge a Muir, Cia. We'll always accept and we'll always finish first.'

'Those things are terrifying. Sorry Ciara, but I'm glad Elle won. I wouldn't get on that thing again even if Aiden Price bribed me with marriage.' Gem was on the pier too, looking paler than she had after the horrible night in Paris.

'And you two accuse me of not knowing how to have fun?' she grumbled, getting off the jet ski and hoping she'd get the chance to have another go soon. But she had lost to Elle once, and she knew she'd never get the chance to again.

'That's not fun, it's horrifying and I'm soaked with salt water.' Elle pulled at her vest top. 'Shower time and then a much needed facial to get that dirt out of my pores.'

A shower sounded good since she was drenched too, but she could do without the facial. Still, Elle had won.

'Yay. Facials,' she said with as much false enthusiasm as she could muster.

'It's not like I asked you to have your nails peeled off,' Elle said.

She climbed off the jet ski and onto the pier, 'Too bad,' she grumbled, 'That sounds more fun.'

***

Ciara didn't know what was worse – having thick, sticky, green paste covering her face or the whale music Elle thought would help them relax. Her friends had fallen asleep in the upstairs spa, waiting the allotted time before more strangers were back removing the gunk and purifying their pores.

She still had a good half hour and sleep wasn't happening for her. Peeling the sliced veg off her eyes, she slid off the table and snuck out of the room. The walls facing the ocean were made completely of glass which, with the white walls *everywhere*, made this officially the brightest place she'd ever been.

It was a lovey house though, and totally modern. She had wondered if Zack had a hand in designing the place with all the twisty staircases to the different levels but the house looked older. More likely he'd been so inspired by their holiday home that he had decided architecture was what he wanted to do.

And there she was again, thinking thoughts she shouldn't.

Though she knew it wasn't going to help a thing, Ciara made her way to the kitchen. Comfort food hadn't done her favours so far, but she'd spied aubergines in the fridge earlier and after the restaurant's amazing traditional Greek food, she'd decided they were her new favourite vegetable.

A little steamed aubergine and some feta would definitely pass the time before she was preened some more.

Rounding another maze-like corridor, she found herself in one of the sitting rooms looking out over the beach and swore. She wasn't even on the right level!

'Still swearing like a sailor? Tut, tut, Ciara.'

She whirled around at the sound of his voice. Zack was here, looking just like he had in LA and Miami wearing an easy grin and a pair of shorts. His laptop was propped on his knees but she only noticed because it blocked the most important part – his bare chest.

He laughed. 'Is that you, Ireland? I recognise the voice but can't be sure with all that gunk.'

She turned away from him, mortified that she'd forgotten about the facial. 'Give me a minute.'

Or a year to live the shame down. She bolted out of the room, on the hunt for the first bathroom she could find. As soon as she got in, she shut the door, ignored the mirror and got busy washing her face in the pearly sink. Green sludge fell onto the porcelain, making her cringe even more. After furiously splashing her face, she towelled off, took a deep breath and faced the mirror.

Her skin looked smooth, but flushed from all the panicking and her hair was awful – pulled back from her face with a towelled headband covered in more gunk. She tugged it off, trying to ruffle up some waves but got limp instead. Served her right for not drying her hair after the shower.

Then it hit her again. Zack was really here, and she'd run away and left him.

A knock sounded at the bathroom door.

'You okay in there?'

His voice was muffled through the wood, but still sent little prickles of awareness dancing over her skin.

'I'm sure I'll survive,' she said shakily. Bugger.

Her voice wasn't all that shook. Her hands and knees did too. Why was he there? And why hadn't he called her?

But instead of stressing herself out in the bathroom, she could open the door and get answers. Zack beat her to it and marched straight in. His brow was low and those dark eyes sparkled with concern.

'Ciara, it was only a face mask. Trust me, growing up with Elle and her mum I saw enough to give me nightmares,' he said, then grinned. 'And to think, most kids got freaked out by Freddy Krueger or Chucky. Not me. They didn't hold a torch to the multi-coloured gunk faces and cucumber eyed monsters.'

'It was Elle's idea,' she said, still shocked senseless that he was even here. And he'd totally just walked in on her in the bathroom. He was Elle's cousin alright.

'I guessed that much,' he said, then chuckled again.

Like he'd not ignored her for days. Like he'd not just left her hanging without a bloody word. Like him showing up here without explanation was the most natural thing in the world.

'What are you doing *here?*' she asked without thinking.

The chuckling stopped and he got all serious in a way that Elle did when she was hiding something and trying to make Ciara believe that she wasn't.

'The truth, not whatever story you were going to come up with.' Looked like crabby Ciara had returned, but she didn't apologise for it. Instead she folded her arms and waited.

He inhaled slowly, studying her expression and she made sure to show him she meant business. After all, she'd done nothing wrong in Paris. She'd got his cousin home, watched her all night and even left a message apologising when really, it was Elle who'd dragged her out. And now he was here, without so much as a text or call to warn her – as far as she knew anyway. Elle still had her phone.

Still, she couldn't hold back how pissed off she was feeling.

'Let's talk back in the front room. It's not a conversation for here.' Zack turned and walked down the hall.

She followed, even though she probably shouldn't. Did Elle know he was coming? Was that what the twenty minute phone call the other day was about? At this point she was sick to death of the secrets and the half truths. If Zack brushed her off, she'd go straight to her friends and make them tell her.

He returned to the chair he'd been in and she noticed the

laptop was still open on the coffee table with accounts on the screen. So he was working, that was obvious. But why in Santorini and why now?

When he realised she wasn't going to sit, he mimicked her pose and folded his arms across her chest, pissing her off more. 'Out with it, Zack. I haven't got all day.'

Actually, she did and would much rather be here arguing with him than up there having some rough skin treatments.

'Elle called me and asked me to come,' he said.

She frowned. 'Elle?'

She couldn't imagine a universe where her friend would ask him to come on their holiday, especially after the arguments she'd witnessed between the two.

Zack nodded. 'And I did because I wanted to. I was a dick in Paris and thought what better way to apologise than in person?'

Her anger melted a little since he seemed sincere. But she was still confused. 'Why would Elle do that?'

He shrugged. 'You'd have a better chance of finding that out than I would.'

Her cheeks flamed as she realised Elle probably asked him because of what Ciara had said in Paris, that she really liked him. And when they first got here, she couldn't stop checking her phone. Another pity gesture? Ciara better watch or she was going to win the saddest case of the year award.

'So you came all this way to apologise? Then what?' Ciara asked. This wasn't going to be Paris where she had let him walk away and still held a shred of hope. If they were over for good, she needed to hear it even if she didn't want to.

'That's right.' He rose and she couldn't help notice the way his biceps bulged when he pushed himself out of the chair. Or how his abs became more defined with the effort. 'Then I was hoping you'd let me make it up to you, but I had a few work things to catch up on first. Lying around all day covered in gunk can't be much fun.'

The half-smile was back. Speechless and possibly drooling, she nodded.

'Thought so. Have you had a chance to explore the town yet?' he asked.

A head shake was all she managed.

'Great. Go grab a pair of shoes and we'll head out. I'll let Elle know.'

He turned around, treating her to a lovely view of his tanned back. Oh God, she'd gone soft in the head. 'Wait!'

He looked over his shoulder.

'I'm a mess. Let me get a shower first?' Not to mention she was in nothing but clingy shorts and the tee-shirt Gem made for her, which could have been painted on. With all the extra flab she was carrying, a smock top was a must.

'You look gorgeous, Ciara.' He turned around and stepped so close she could feel his body heat radiating in the air. 'And this is cute.'

His fingers traced the neon letters across her breasts until she was at risk of hyperventilating.

When he flicked over her nipple his expression changed. The humour was gone and replaced with a hunger she recognised. Then she remembered what she'd sexted him in the bathroom of the club in Paris, and every word from their telephone call came back at her until her heart beat so hard she wondered if he could hear it.

But after everything that happened, she had to make sure she wasn't reading this wrong. 'Do you still want me?'

Chapter Thirteen

Zack slid his hands down until they rested on her hips. His thumbs did something to her sides until she shivered in his hold, but she didn't take her eyes off his.

'I didn't stop, Ciara. Do you still want me?' he asked, his gaze flicking down to her lips.

When all she managed in reply was a breathy sigh, she decided in this instance show might be better than tell. Rising on her tip toes she took his face between her palms and pulled him down the rest of the way.

She meant for the kiss to be passionate, just enough to show exactly how she felt, but it went a bit beyond that when he pulled her hard against him. She opened her mouth and let him in, again and again all the while he melded her closer.

The next thing she knew her legs were wrapped around his waist and his hands cupped her bum, showing her exactly how creative he could be when he slid his fingers round to her clit. The thin material was barely a dampening barrier and he expertly stroked her into a frenzy. The orgasm built at break neck speed, fast and furiously.

Zack swallowed her cries, reminding her that they were not alone in this big house and stripping him naked right now and

144

having him inside her was not going to be possible.

'Take me back to the bathroom,' she said, and Zack obliged.

Her centre rubbed against his erection as they went and the friction on her oversensitive clit pushed her closer and closer to the edge again.

When they made it to the bathroom he shut the door, locked it, then pressed her up against it so she was wedged between the wood and him. Zack peeled off her tee-shirt and made quick work of her bra clasp before he put her back on her feet and tugged it off all the way.

His hands cupped her breasts and then he pinched her nipples, making her moan. Then he started working all the sensitive spots on her neck with his lips, teeth and tongue until she was putty in his hands.

'I've dreamt about this every night,' he said.

Thoughtlessly, she admitted, 'me too.'

'Then let's extend the deadline until the summer's over. What do you think?' He pulled away, studying her expression.

She didn't care that she was probably wild eyed and so flushed she'd make a tomato jealous of her skin. The way he looked at her made her feel like the sexiest woman alive. 'I say you have a deal.'

Another smile was followed by a knee melting kiss that stole her breath, but then he pulled away and cursed.

'What's wrong?' she asked.

'I didn't bring any protection. Honestly, I thought I'd have a lot more grovelling to do before you gave me the time of day again.' The half-smile was back, making him look a little rueful.

'You don't have to grovel, not after effortlessly giving me two mind-blowing orgasms.' She grabbed the top of his shorts and used it to twist him round so they swapped positions. 'And protection's not a problem. We don't need it for what I want to do.'

She unbuttoned his shorts then dove a hand in. She didn't

have far to reach, he was already close to the point of bursting out of them. She squeezed his erection until his eyes closed on a hiss.

Ciara didn't waste any time tugging the material down his hips and even less dropping to her knees. She barely felt it when they cracked against the tile but no doubt she would later. Zack opened his eyes then, meeting hers just as she flicked her tongue out to tease him.

He threaded his fingers through her hair, massaging her scalp just right so that it tingled. Who needed a masseuse when she had him?

She used her lips next, sucking on the tip of him until his eyes rolled back and his chest heaved. It made her feel powerful. And even more aroused than he was. So she took him in until she almost choked and worked her tongue around him again and again, keeping up a cheek hollowing suction.

Zack murmured encouragement between gasping for air and with every word, her confidence grew to the point she used her hands to increase the tempo and cup the silky skin beneath. All the while he used his finger tips to caress her head, but he let her set the pace and rhythm.

When his thighs tensed and his jaw clenched hard, Ciara picked up speed until he pulled his hands away and fisted them at his sides.

His gaze was crazed as he held hers. 'I'm there, Ciara.'

It was a warning to pull away, but she didn't take it. Instead she welcomed the little warm jets and swallowed every one, soothing him with her tongue as he trembled. When the bitter-sweet taste of him was gone, she pulled away, impressed that he was still erect.

With surprising strength, he pulled her off the floor and held her so close his damp skin wedged against her stomach. The kisses he gave her weren't as purposeful as before, more lethargic and simple, like he had all the time in the world to enjoy her.

Since they had much more time left than she could ever hope for, she let herself get lost in his drugging kisses.

***

When Zack finally let her go and suggested after a quick change they take the quad bikes out for a spin, Ciara happily agreed. They walked hand in hand up to her bedroom but stopped short when they saw Elle and Gem waiting for them at the top of the stairs.

Elle wrinkled her gunk free nose. 'I don't want to know.'

'Like it isn't obvious,' Gem said with a grin.

Ciara's face got so hot she reckoned she could fry an egg on her cheek.

Zack laughed and shook his head. 'Do you mind if I borrow Ciara for the rest of the day?'

'Ew. Just keep the doors and windows shut so we don't hear anything,' Elle said, faking a shudder.

'We're going out,' Ciara protested.

Gem shook her head. 'You are the only woman I know who can't just *relax*. Elle, we must have done something wrong during training.'

Ciara laughed. 'There's only so much I can deal with before I go insane. We're in a beautiful country and just stuck inside these walls.'

Zack tugged her closer and she turned her head. 'Don't worry. I'll show you the sights.'

She smiled at him.

'We have reservations at seven.' Elle glared at Zack. 'Remember to wear a shirt, it's a classy place.'

Ciara wouldn't mind if he turned up naked, but then she'd probably be arrested for not being able to keep her hands to herself.

'He can go shirtless if he wants. I don't mind the view,' Gem said.

Though she knew her friend was teasing, she still wanted to strip off her tee-shirt and force him into it so Gem would stop staring. After all, it was rude to ogle someone else's man. Even if he was only hers for the duration.

'I'll be covered up Elly, don't worry.' He led Ciara up the stairs while Elle gaped as if she couldn't believe he gave in without arguing. 'You should shut your mouth before flies get in there.'

At Elle's stumped expression, Ciara had to press her lips together to keep from giggling.

'Who are you and what have you done with Zack?' Elle asked.

He shrugged. 'You're letting me take Ireland out without an argument so I'm not going to sweat the small stuff.'

They walked past her friends and he led her down to her room. At the door, she turned to him expecting more kisses or maybe a little shower soirée, but all he did was circle his thumb around her lips.

Right, Elle and Gem were probably watching. But somehow the touch and the way his eyes melted when he looked at her felt more intimate than the most passionate of kisses.

'Garage in twenty minutes?' he asked.

Well, that left her absolutely no time to get anywhere near glam but she was too impatient to see him again to sweat the small stuff. She nodded, then hit the shower, towelled off, found a pair of tiny denim shorts that hugged her arse instead of choking it and then remembered her hair was a state.

Thankfully she was good with braids and French pleated away until she had an intricate style that used every inch of her locks. Handy for the heat and it looked pretty. Make-up was out in the midday sun but she had a nice golden sheen and decided sun cream would be enough.

When she got to the garage, Zack had already got the quads on the road leading away from the house. She wasn't too disappointed that she wouldn't get to sit behind him – she'd never been on a quad before and got giddy thinking about racing around on it.

'You're stunning,' he said, ditching the bikes and moving closer.

She was sad to see he'd put on a white tee-shirt, but she'd get it off him eventually.

Ciara tugged at the pink vest when his eyes took a trip down her body. It wasn't quite a smock but it was the loosest fit she had with her.

He took her hands and pulled her close. 'I like the curves, stop trying to hide them.'

Good, because it would take a lot more than a baggy top to hide them.

'What's in the basket?' she asked to distract him.

'Lunch. I thought we could go into town for a few things then head down to a little cove not far from here. It's pretty. And... secluded.'

The way his voice got all deep and husky made her shiver. 'Can't wait.'

***

After an embarrassing trip to a local pharmacist to pick up 'supplies', Ciara was happy to be speeding away from Caldera on the dirt roads into the more rural part of the island. She'd learned to drive the quad fairly quickly, but was nowhere near as good as Zack who could easily keep pace with her.

'It's not far now, but we'll have some climbing to do,' he said, leading her down a windy path surrounded by rocks.

'Climbing and flip flops don't really go together,' she grumbled.

Zack laughed. 'It's just a few stones. I'll carry you if I have to.'

When they reached the end of the road she saw what he meant – although she'd describe the 'rocks' as 'boulders'. Still, they did look smooth. She'd do it in her bare feet if she had to. The secluded part of the plan was that appealing.

They parked the quads and she went to the edge of the rocks, taking in the gorgeous blue of the ocean. The salty breeze meant the heat of the sun wasn't overpowering and she had to admit, she'd never been anywhere this beautiful in her life.

'You ready, Ciara?' Zack asked.

She turned to see he'd left his tee-shirt on the quad and had the basket in hand.

'Let's go.'

He'd been right about the climb being easy, it was the descent to the little cove of beach that worried her. But with Zack's help she managed to get there unscathed and soon he'd laid out a blanket in the sand and was tugging out boxes filled with goodies. She dug into a moussaka and chicken souvlaki salad while he started with some bread dipped in oil.

'I love the food here,' she said, switching the first for another olive packed salad and a hunk of the crusty bread.

Zack picked up the salad she'd abandoned and used her fork to dig in instead of his own. She wondered if this was the kind of thing people in real relationships did, the kind she figured would bore her to tears eventually. Still, it was hard to imagine that now.

'The food's just a bonus. Santorini's amazing. I'll show you the volcano with the thermal springs and we can even take a trip over to Thirassia one day if you want to.'

It was *really* hard to imagine ever wanting to leave him, but it was still new and exciting. Promising more, even to herself, would only end up hurting them both.

But then she remembered the way Elle and Gem had felt sorry for her for liking Zack and curiosity got the best of her. 'Elle didn't want us to get together, but I don't think it had anything to do with me.'

Then again, maybe it did. If she had someone who was pretty much like a brother to her, would she want him dating her friends?

He shrugged, but the movement was too jerky to be blasé. 'You know Elle.'

150

Ciara sighed. 'And you're just like her. You evade anything you don't want to talk about.'

'Some things aren't worth wasting breath on. We have a little time left together, why not make the most of it?'

She felt so stupid she couldn't meet his eyes. After all it was her who insisted on time limits. Even if she kept breaking them.

'Come here,' he said, patting the space between his legs. 'The view's great.'

'I'm sure it's exactly the same here.' But she got up anyway and lay back against his chest.

Zack packed away their lunch then held her close. 'Remember I'm not the only one being evasive. You still won't tell me why you're so anti-relationship.'

She nodded, not knowing what else to do. He'd probably think she was mad too, just like Elle and Gem did. And she wasn't sure she could open herself up like that if he wasn't willing to do the same. Some things were probably best kept out of this so they could enjoy their time together.

His arms tightened around her. 'Just tell me one thing. It's not because someone... hurt you, is it?'

She'd been devastated when her ma left, but she had a feeling that wasn't the kind of hurt Zack meant.

'No, never.' She turned in his arms and straddled him, hoping to take his mind off the conversation.

It worked. His hands started roaming around her body, pulling her closer.

She kissed him lightly, then sucked his lower lip between her teeth. His growl was feral and his eyes blazed, so she knew this was the end of the conversation. Zack crushed her against him and kissed her like he'd never kissed her before. She explored his glorious back with her fingers and may have dug her nails in too, but she was way beyond remembering to be gentle.

As he dragged her onto her feet, all but ripping her clothes off, she was glad they'd made the embarrassing trip to the pharmacist because she had a feeling they were going to need them all by the end of the afternoon.

***

The drive back wasn't a comfortable one. Despite the blanket, they both had sand in places it should never be and she was sure half the beach had made its way into her hair. But that didn't keep the smile off her face.

Since they were running late separate showers were a must or they'd never have made Elle's reservations. And even though Elle grumbled a little about cutting it fine, dinner went down without an argument and for the first time since she'd met Zack, she saw just how well he and Elle could get along.

Gem was distracted during the meal, even though Elle kept trying to drag her back into the conversation. When desert was done and Ciara's sundress was a little tighter than it should be, Gem caught the eye of her crush.

'I'm going to dance with Milo,' Gem said.

Elle rolled her eyes. 'We didn't see that coming.'

After sticking her tongue out at Elle, Gem was off across the dance floor and jumped right into Milo's arms. He lifted her up like in the end dance scene from Dirty Dancing and if that wasn't clue enough that he swung for the other side, Ciara didn't know what was.

'She knows that guy's gay, doesn't she?' Zack asked.

Elle shook her head. 'She's blissfully unaware, even though we tell her every chance we get.'

Zack laughed. 'She hasn't changed a bit.'

While they shared childhood stories about Gem and her passion for everything male, Ciara watched the topic of conversation and her new crush. Milo didn't seem completely uninterested. He ground his hips with hers, even raunchier than Baby and Johnny ever did and she wondered if he maybe didn't swing both ways.

Just then the music came to a stop and Milo bent Gem over backwards, one leg between hers, and kissed the shit out of her.

'I don't think he's gay,' Ciara said to them.

They both followed her gaze and laughed.

'Well, if anyone could turn him back to the vag it's Gem,' Elle said.

When the next song started, Gem looked like she had a hard time staying on her feet. Milo wasn't his usual gracious self too which made her more convinced they had him wrong.

'Wanna dance?' Zack asked her.

'Yes please.' But then she remembered Elle. 'Um, you two can go first though.'

'I'm not dancing with him! Go have fun. I'll do the Instagraming tonight. Time for the world to find out about Gem's talents.' Elle smirked.

Ciara took Zack's outstretched hand and followed him around the table. 'We'll be back soon.'

'Just make sure you don't put on a show like Gem and her boy toy. I don't think I'll be able to keep my dinner down if you do,' Elle jibed.

'We won't,' Ciara said.

'I'm not making promises I can't keep,' Zack said, pulling her onto the dance floor.

He could move much better than her, despite having watched the dances for the last two nights. Saying he held her indecently close would be an understatement. If they were naked there wouldn't be a part of her that wasn't flush against his skin.

The temperature flared again but she didn't bother to lie to herself this time. Zack could make her flush from just a look, but now that they were grinding to the music and she could feel exactly how much he was into it, she was beyond turned on.

'This is getting ridiculous,' she whispered in his ear. 'I've lost count of the amount of times I've come today and I still want more.'

He nibbled on her earlobe and slid his hands down to palm her bum. 'I'm not done yet.'

He squeezed her against his growing erection so she had no doubts about what he meant.

'I think we need to hurry up and get back to the house,' she said, not sure if she could wait that long.

'Later. Right now I want you on the edge.'

His smirk was so unfair.

'I'm about to topple over it if you keep rubbing me there.' With every sway his erection was rubbing her clit into a frenzy.

'That suits me too. Do you know how hot you are when you come for me?' he asked, his eyes darkening.

Her already flushed face felt molten. 'You wouldn't dare do that to me here.'

Zack cocked a brow. 'Is that a challenge?'

Shit. She remembered too late what Elle said the day before when she won the race. 'Don't, Zack. Please don't.'

He laughed. 'Don't worry, I'm not into public displays. When you come later it will be in my bed and on my tongue.'

The flood of moisture in her panties from the possession in his voice was startling. Who'd have known she'd be into cavemen lines?

'Sounds like a plan,' she said and let him swing her around the dance floor.

Chapter Fourteen

Ciara was so hot and sticky she couldn't sleep another second. Peeling her face off Zack's chest, she took stock of her surroundings.

His room was a mess, totally destroyed from their too-hot-for-each-other-to-make-the-bed antics. Her dress was next to a smashed lamp on the floor near the dresser where he'd taken her first. She didn't mind that he'd broken his promise to use his tongue since she'd come twice in a row as he'd taken her furiously.

The paintings had fallen from the walls and she was sure even three levels up, Gem and Elle would have heard her but then again Ciara wasn't the only one having fun last night. Gem hadn't come back alone and she and Milo had been just as keen to get privacy.

'Good morning, Ireland.' Zack's voice, thick with sleep, made a shiver run down her spine.

'Morning,' she said, snuggling back into his chest to hide her face. Who knew what her hair looked like and morning breath wasn't sexy.

He didn't seem to agree, because he pulled her up to share his pillow and cupped her cheek. She did her best to breathe through her nose.

'Guess we were wrong about Milo,' he said.

Ciara grinned and tried for a non-breathy answer. 'I hope Elle had headphones to drown out the noise.'

He smiled and twirled a strand of hair around his finger. 'What do you want to do today?'

Brush her teeth, shower, brush some more…

'Whatever you want, but I'm going to go for a swim first,' she said, remembering the camel-toe incident, although she was sure the day before must have burnt off at least a thousand calories. 'I should probably get some work done.'

He sighed and she was about to ask why he bothered if he hated it but he pulled her into a kiss that made her very aware of how naked they both were. Questions forgotten, she made use of the fact the sheets were also on the floor somewhere and pressed herself against him.

But then she pulled away, just in case her breath knocked him out or worse, made him run for the hills. Not that he was minty fresh either, but she loved the taste of him to the point she worried about her sanity.

'I'll let you get on,' she said, slipping out of his hold.

'I wish you meant that literally.' Zack grinned.

'You're insatiable,' she said, stunned. 'I thought after yesterday you'd need at least 24 hours to recover.'

But he didn't seem to. He was already growing hard and would more than likely be up for another marathon session.

'You do this to me,' he said, sliding his hand down his stomach. 'You sure you don't want to get your workout here?'

Grabbing his dick, he stroked lazily and she recognised the look that came into his eyes. He really was insatiable. She bit her lip, torn between wanting to help him and being unable to stop watching him pleasure himself.

'This doesn't feel as good as being inside you,' he said, fisting his hand tighter and sliding it all the way up so the tip disappeared behind his fingers.

Ciara's core clenched, remembering all too well how it felt to have him inside.

'I don't think you've had enough yet, either,' he said, but the strain in his voice was more evident now.

She picked the condoms off the bedside table – the only thing still left on it – and ripped the packet open with her teeth. Pushing his hand away, she covered him down to the base, making sure to squeeze as she did.

Zack groaned and took hold of her nipples, teasing them into sensitive peaks. Lust crashed through her, holding her hostage and she straddled his hips, unable to wait a second longer.

He grabbed her hips before she could take him in, but she knew him well enough not to be disappointed. Sliding his fingers inside was easy since she was more than ready for him and the action made it worse. She gasped as his thumb found her clit and swirled.

'You're always ready for me,' he groaned.

His patience must have expired because after pulling his fingers out he thrust up and filled her completely.

Ciara clenched him tight, savouring the feel of him inside even though there were inches to spare. She lowered further until he was on the bed and her bum was almost touching his thighs.

Rising, she took his offered hands, linked her fingers with his and studied every detail of his face. He really was gorgeous, laid out in the early morning sun waiting for her to take him. She'd never appreciated him properly all those times when he was filling her over and over, driving her closer to another toe curling orgasm. Not until now.

She'd never noticed the way his chest heaved or the way his jaw and eyes clenched tight when the pleasure of what she was doing got too much to bear. And, most mesmerising of all, she'd never noticed how he watched her when she went into a slow burning orgasm that stole her breath.

Still, she swung her hips, intent on driving him towards his goal but something had shifted between them as she kept eye contact throughout. He looked a little awed and she couldn't help feeling the same as she watched his eyes close as he trembled with his own orgasm.

Totally magnificent.

Absolutely terrifying.

Because there was no doubt now that she was being dragged into dangerous water and she didn't think she had the strength to swim back to shore.

***

A week in and Ciara couldn't believe she'd thought Santorini was dull. Her time had been filled by Zack to the point she was amazed she had any energy left at all. They'd gone scuba diving, seeing the volcanic stones and bottomless depth of the Caldera. Just yesterday he'd taken her to Thirassia with a picnic and they'd spent the whole day exploring the Potamos and Manolas settlements.

Even though she'd ditched her early morning exercise regime for a more fun start to the day, they'd still gone swimming in Korfos twice and had lunch in the tavernas.

And everything seemed to work out with Gem and Elle too. Metrosexual Milo loved being pampered as much as her friends so he'd spent every day playing the replacement BFF and after his shift he'd switched to the Milo who knew how to treat a woman.

Since it was their last day in Greece and Milo was off work, Zack agreed to take the yacht out for the day. Elle grumbled about risking her life but Gem was happy since she could catch up with her sunbathing and, unlike the jet ski, there was almost no risk she'd fall off.

Soon they were bikini clad (Zack's shorts and Milo's speedo withstanding) and sailing out across the ocean. While Gem and

Elle stayed back from the front of the boat, Ciara stood by the railing with Milo, enjoying the wind rushing by.

'Is this your first time sailing?' Milo asked, noticing her excitement.

She shook her head. 'When I was little we went on a boat trip in Tenerife. I didn't get to see any dolphins or wales though.'

She'd been gutted about that.

'There are a few dolphins out this way.' He pointed to the right. 'They hunt for food there.'

Elle must have heard them talking because she shouted at Zack. 'Take us left! I'm not being tipped to my death by shark wannabes.'

'Learn to sail and you can take it wherever you want, Elly,' he shouted back.

Milo chuckled. 'They're always like this?'

She nodded, rolling her eyes.

'This is mild,' Gem said. 'You should see them when they really go for it.'

Elle gave them an insight to the real problem – Zack – and threw in a good few examples to make her case stronger. So she wasn't dragged into the debate, Ciara went down to the galley to make up a pitcher of mojitos with all the ingredients they'd brought. She'd never have guessed a boat could have such a pretty kitchen with appliances for absolutely everything. And it wasn't small either. She reckoned the Muirs could fit a good few chefs in here and have a party on deck in the middle of the ocean.

Maybe that was the point in having it, though god knew why when they had a house the size of theirs.

She took the pitcher and a load of plastic glasses up to the deck and realised they'd stopped moving. The ocean really was beautiful and she could see the whole curve of the island with the white houses scattered around greenery and more rural, rustic areas.

'There's something you don't see every day,' Zack said, appearing beside her.

'I can make things myself you know, I don't need to ask the staff to do it for me.' She held up the jug to prove her point.

'What's got you all fired up? I was talking about the view.' He jerked his head to indicate the island across the water.

'Nothing,' she lied.

The truth was, she'd been too scared to ask if he was joining them in Ibiza, but had been losing sleep wondering if he'd come. No one had mentioned it, not even Zack and she'd tried to bring it up but they were always busy and she didn't want to spoil the time they had left.

'You're a crap liar,' he said with a grin. 'But I'm not going to push. Let's get this party started.'

He took the pitcher to the front where the others were sprawled on sun loungers.

'You better be careful. Elle will freak if the captain of the ship gets sloshed,' she teased, pushing aside the fact this might be their last full day together.

'You're absolutely right,' Elle said, sitting up on her sun lounger. 'No cocktails for you!'

Zack shook his head and handed his cousin the jug and cups. When Elle handed Ciara a glass, she took a long drink and silently thanked Gem's super fast internet for the recipe.

'I'll just have to enjoy it this way,' Zack said and then pulled her into a not-so-friendly kiss.

His tongue left no inch of her mouth untouched and she was gasping for air in seconds.

'*Ew*, do you two *mind*? Anymore of that and I'll need to bleach my eyeballs. And the sockets,' Elle complained.

Ciara reluctantly pulled away and saw the mischievous glint in his eyes, giving her an idea. 'I think we should go swimming.'

'*I* think the two of you need your baby making bits removed,' Elle countered. 'It's really not normal.'

'She must have a resilient fufu,' Gem said, making Ciara's cheeks burn and her chin drop.

Milo tried to smother a giggle and failed.

Bitches, all of them.

'Elle go worry about your own sex life, or lack thereof,' Zack said.

Even though she knew he was sticking up for her, she gave him a light dig on the shoulder. 'That's mean.'

He raised an eyebrow, then lowered his voice. 'When you get off this boat I'll show you how not-mean I can be.'

She barely heard the retching sound – probably from Elle, not when he looked at her like he wanted to eat every inch of her.

'Last one in…' she said, taking off to the railing.

Zack was over faster, then did a perfect dive into the water sending some spray back onto the deck. Gem cursed and Ciara giggled, thinking it served her right for the vag joke.

He surfaced all wet and sexy, so she decided to show off a little and somersaulted off the boat. It backfired when she landed dodgy and lost her bikini top along the way.

'Bugger,' she said, kicking her feet out and spinning to see if she could find it.

'What's wrong?' Zack asked, swimming closer.

'I've lost my top!' She tried searching with her hands next and got a mouthful of bitter, salty water.

'Is that an Irish expression or are you being serious?' he asked.

'I'm serious! Can you help me look for it please?' She spun around again, hoping to see a scrap of pink glinting on the surface. No such luck. It was only water all around and if it slipped under the boat she was in trouble.

Zack pulled her to the back end of the yacht and she kept a look-out, hoping he'd seen something she hadn't.

'Here will do,' he said, then pulled her against his chest.

He was strong enough to keep them both above water, and that distracted her a little as she wrapped her legs around his torso to stay afloat. Then she noticed the sexy grin he sported and realised he'd dragged her back here for another reason.

'Zack! I need to find it,' she whispered.

'You're looking at this all wrong, Ireland,' he said with a grin. 'It's just one less thing I'll need to take off.'

'We can't do that here!' But when his hands cupped her bare breasts she lost her train of thought.

'Can't isn't a word I have in my vocabulary,' he said, then kissed her slowly, smoulderingly.

Feck it! She held onto his neck, upping the intensity of the salty kiss and before she knew it Zack had shoved her bikini bottoms to the side and was rubbing her in a way that should be illegal.

Moaning 'more' seemed all she could manage and his groan sounded like sweet surrender. He freed himself from his shorts and pulled her down until she was filled by him. The stab of heat was instant and she knew it wouldn't be long until she was coming hard. Using her hold on him, she tilted her hips and rode him until she was biting her lip to hold in the cries of relief.

Someone screamed and both she and Zack froze. She could see the lust haze faze from his eyes until they became sharp and more aware.

'Get out of there!' Elle shrieked.

They looked up to see her at the ladder. For the second time in forever, Elle looked scared but now it was closer to terror.

Ciara was glad the water wasn't as clear out here because Elle would have seen a lot more than she bargained for beneath the waves.

'What's up, Elle?' he asked, discreetly unjoining them.

That was until her red hot cheeks gave them away.

'Sharks! You're going to be dinner if you don't move now!' Elle shouted, pointing across to the front of the boat.

Ciara knew she should be swimming for that drop down ladder as fast as she could, feck the bikini top she'd lost. But she couldn't move. Even her legs were frozen in a vice grip around Zack's waist.

Four or five dark grey fins protruded from the water up ahead, but they were closing in fast and then they disappeared below the surface.

She started to tremble.

'It's okay,' Zack said, cupping her cheek. 'There aren't sharks out here. It's probably dolphins.'

'*Have you lost it? Zack get my best friend out of there now!*'

But he didn't and all Ciara could do was imagine a sharp, incomprehensible pain in her thighs as the sharks took chunks out of her and dragged her under.

'Don't panic, they won't hurt us. They're probably just curious.' He didn't look scared at all, in fact the excited glint in his eyes made him look younger.

Just then one of the creatures broke the surface and the sound of dolphins singing stunned her. She'd heard it before on Elle's silly relaxing nature tapes and from the beak on the animals that popped out around them she knew they weren't sharks.

'Elle, they're dolphins.' She reached out to one but it backed away, opening its mouth to yatter something.

'Look at those *teeth*! That's no dolphin,' Elle shouted from the deck.

Gem and Milo laughed so hard they had to hold their stomach's for support.

'I'm positive it is. Now stop freaking out or they're going to swim away,' Zack said.

Elle fisted her hands and glared, but since they were relaxed now the potential danger was over, she aimed her anger at Gem and Milo then stormed away out of sight.

'I suppose I should give you this back now,' Zack said, pulling something out of his back pocket.

Not *something*. The missing part of her bikini! She snatched it out of his hand. 'That was mean.'

His grin was wicked. 'I'd say I more than made up for it.'

Her cheeks flared again, but the heat spread to other parts too.

She tied the bikini on then went in for a quick kiss. 'You did. But I don't think we both finished.'

He laughed a little. 'I think the dolphins are a bit young to see that.' More seriously, he added, 'And we don't have any protection. Later, I promise.'

What a thing to forget! Still, he hadn't finished. And she was on the mini pill to regulate her periods so the risk was minimal. 'I'll hold you to that.'

**

After swimming with the dolphins they'd gone back to the boat in time for lunch. Drying off in the sun next to Zack was the perfect way to spend a lazy afternoon as far as she was concerned. As they all listened to Elle and her cousin try to top each other with the most embarrassing stories, Ciara felt at peace, like that antsy need to get up and do something had completely deserted her.

She couldn't hold out hope that it would last. The restlessness was buried too deep inside. She'd even debated with Gem that it could be hereditary and her friend, though not quite an expert in the gene field, had been swayed a little by that argument.

But now she could pretend for a while that she was different and being held by Zack certainly helped. This close to him she almost felt normal. Like a woman experiencing what it was like to be happy, carefree and without a tenth of the worries she had.

Until Elle went and ruined it.

'Zack, did you manage to book a seat on our flight?' Elle asked.

Since Ciara was leaning on his chest, she could feel every muscle go rigid. Oh God, he wasn't coming and now Elle was going to make him say it and ruin her perfect day.

'I've got a meeting in Munich first,' he said.

She didn't understand why the vein at the side of Elle's head became pronounced like it did when she was mad, or why her friend's eyes became icy cold chips that looked sharp enough to cut through leather.

'You're. Going. To. Munich?'

Okay, mad was an understatement. Elle was using her livid-disbelief tone.

She looked to Gem for some kind of hint at why that was a bad thing, but Gem just shrugged.

'Careful, Elle. I'm not in the mood. We have a meeting there with one of the buyers.' Zack didn't sound so pleased either, but when she tried to pull away so she could turn round and see him, he held her so close she struggled to breathe.

'We?' Elle asked through clenched teeth.

'I'm going with Granddad. After that I'll be straight on a plane to Ibiza,' he said.

She relaxed back into him, closing her eyes with relief. Elle was probably pissed that she was missing out on some deal, even though for a second she'd been worried it might have more to do with the things Zack refused to tell her. Again, not her problem and definitely not worth worrying about after a day like today.

'I'll miss you,' she said, linking her fingers through his.

He turned her around and his easy smile knocked the breath out of her. 'You too. Make sure my cousin doesn't get you into any more trouble.'

'I thought you were only going to be gone for a day?' Elle bitched.

His eyes tightened a little. 'I will.'

She couldn't be sure whether it was the sibling rivalry these two seemed to have acquired over the years or something else, but she wasn't going to dwell on it since now she knew for sure she'd see him again.

Instead she kissed him like they were alone and thanked her lucky stars that this part of her holiday didn't have to end just yet.

Ibiza

Chapter Fifteen

Since they only had four full days in what Gem called the clubbing capital of the world, they didn't waste time unpacking and
hit the shops the second their bags were dumped on the hotel
room floor.

As they sauntered along the little market stalls looking at tack
and skimpy swimwear, Elle was unusually chatty, probably because
Gem had been glum since Milo bent her over in the airport and
kissed her with movie-esque finesse.

'Is it just me or do you feel like we're slumming it in that
hotel?' Elle asked.

Gem shrugged.

'It's five star, Elle. What more do you need?' Ciara asked.

It wasn't quite the Muir style of living the girls were used to
on this trip, but it was hardly the pokey rooms Ciara had to share
with her family when they'd travelled abroad. They were in the
penthouse apartment of the fanciest hotel in Ibiza.

As well as having separate ensuite rooms, there was a living
room, dining room and even a spa room.

'It's no Santorini beach house,' Gem said on a sigh.

'Gem, snap out of it. Remember we're going to Amnesia
tonight! Dave Call will be there,' Elle said.

Ciara didn't even know who the DJ was until Elle got to reception and asked who was playing in the clubs that night. Apparently he was famous – despite the ridiculous name. And according to Gem, he was gorgeous. Still, that didn't seem to snap her out of the Milo withdrawals.

Since Ciara missed Zack just as much, she could sympathise completely.

'It's not like we'd get within a hundred feet of him, he'll have security,' Gem said, and Ciara had to bite her lip before she asked if her friend knew that through her stalker experience. This so wasn't time for teasing.

Elle frowned. 'Where did my friend go? I want the girl back who strutted into a celebrity party and chatted up a movie star without blinking an eye.'

'She's heartbroken.' Gem even stopped to cup her hands over the organ in question.

Elle *pffd*. 'You'd think someone who studied the human body would know how impossible that is.'

'Actually, it's quite possible for a heart to break. It's what keeps heart surgeons in a job,' Gem retorted, but Ciara had hope it was a good thing since her friend had some of her spunk back.

'Honey, if anyone is going to be heartbroken it will be the man you left behind. You're resilient and officially on the rebound. Over here.' Elle grabbed Gem's arm and dragged her over to a stall.

'He's probably over me already,' Gem grumbled.

'Unlikely,' Ciara said, trailing behind. 'You teased me for having a resilient vag but yours must have held up its own.'

Elle wrinkled her nose, but recovered quick. 'Not to mention all the spa treatments and facials he had with us. I'll bet he misses us more than you miss him.'

That made Gem smile. 'You're right.'

True to form, the idea that she was pined over snapped Gem right out of her funk.

'I'm always right,' Elle said, then pulled a dark blue sundress off the rail of the stall. 'And I'm going to be right once more saying this is the dress that's going to get you laid tonight.'

She held out the material to Gem, whose eyes got all wide and excited. 'It's perfect!'

It really was, and would look great with her new sunglow and fire red hair.

A golden scrap of a bikini hanging above the owner of the stall caught Ciara's eye. It was daring, but all the wild sex and walking for miles in the last week meant even her white linen trousers were hanging off her. The croissants were a distant memory. For the first time in a long time she was toned and her stomach was completely flat. If there was ever a time to pull something like that off it was now.

'Can I see that?' she asked the woman behind the counter, pointing to the bikini.

'And you were wondering where I went? I think it's Ciara we should be worried about,' Gem said.

She turned to stick her tongue out at them while the woman brought the bikini over.

Elle's eyes were shiny and her smile was proud as punch. 'Our baby's all grown up.'

'Eejits,' Ciara mumbled and took the offered bikini from the woman. It would never cover all her lady bits fully, but thankfully the bikini wax was one of the treatments she'd subjected herself to in Santorini.

And when she saw it was a measly thirty Euros, she decided there and then that it was going to be hers.

'I'll take it,' she told the woman, digging into her bag for her purse.

'And I'll take this!' Gem said, slapping the dress down on the counter and pulling out her Amex.

The woman shook her head at the card and Gem pouted. '*Everywhere* takes Amex.'

'I don't think that applies to stuff you buy at markets, Gem,' Ciara said, pulling some notes out to cover both purchases. 'It's okay, I've got it.'

'I love you, Ciara!' Gem said, hugging her so hard her boobs got squished against Gem's. 'Maybe even in a gay way.'

'Ew,' Ciara said, pushing her away with a laugh. 'I like the dicks too much to turn, even for you.'

'Yeah me too,' Gem said, then sighed. 'I think I need to concentrate on finding a replacement for Milo.'

'Well I'm not playing the fifth wheel again so I guess I'm on the lookout too,' Elle said from the other side of the rack. 'What do you think about this?'

She held up a deep purple bikini that would rival Ciara's on the skimpy scale, and suit Elle with her dark tan and sun-kissed hair.

'If we hit the beach with you wearing that I'll never get noticed,' Gem said, darting over to the rail to dig out her own skimpy scrap.

'Relax, I only brought out a couple of hundred euros…' When Elle and Gem were on a mission to outdo each other it could cost thousands, even in a market.

'No problem, Cia. Wait here and watch the purchases. We're going to find a cash machine.' Elle passed her the bikini and then linked arms with Gem, dragging her away into the crowd.

She didn't see a point in mentioning that they'd be charged for using their cards to withdraw money, especially abroad. The interest on the funds they had in accounts probably covered it anyway.

Sighing, she smiled at the woman and used a twirling finger at her temple to explain in any language how crazy her friends could be.

***

172

When the sun set it seemed like the population doubled. Even though they'd gotten ready early to hit a bar before they went out for some serious clubbing, the streets were mobbed with people their age and younger, all seemingly with the same idea.

Ciara instantly regretted going for comfort than insta-glam when she saw the way other girls had dressed, but feck it. She was on a mission to dance the night away and anything other than the tiny shorts would flash her knickers.

Leaflets were shoved into their hands by jittery street reps who either had an insomnia or drug problem – probably both by the way they jerked around.

'No thanks,' Elle said, handing the thing back.

'What's Destiny?' Ciara asked.

A picture of all the people dancing and a hot looking DJ on the decks was the advertisement for the 'best of the best in Ibiza'.

'It's a *free* club, need I say more?' Elle asked.

Free sounded good to her, especially when she'd heard what the cover fee for Amnesia cost.

'And if those junkies are any indication of the clientele I'm out,' Gem added. 'There are better chemical reactions than drugs, thank you very much.'

'Endorphins?' Elle guessed, no doubt correctly.

'Super endorphins.' Gem grinned.

Ciara giggled. 'Let me guess, you get those from sterling orgasms?'

Her friend nodded. 'But only when you're chemically compatible. You have to be attracted to both looks and the pheromones. The super endorphins follow the spectacular orgasms. It's quite addicting.'

'How much did you drink before we left?' Elle asked. 'That sounds like voodoo, not science.'

'Just dumbing it down for you two.' Gem dodged Elle's swing of her handbag. 'But really you should try it.'

'I think I know what you mean. Zack does something to me—'

'And that's the end of this conversation,' Elle said, cutting her off.

'Stop being a prude, Elle. I want details,' Gem protested.

'You can get them when I lose my hearing. Come on, here looks okay.' Elle led the way into the quietest looking bar on the strip.

'Wrong. It looks boring,' Gem protested. 'I'm guessing a quickie in the bathroom before we hit the club is a no, no here.'

Ciara didn't think that would be an option. The cocktail bar had a different atmosphere from most pubs they'd passed. The music was just loud enough to hear but they could easily talk over it and the inside didn't have that students-gone-wild-every-night-for-a-decade look.

They made their way to the chrome bar and she noticed the thing barely had a scratch. There was a man sitting at the end with his pint perched on a coaster and she guessed that was why the bar remained unscathed.

'I feel like we should have wiped our feet first,' Ciara said, because there wasn't a sticky patch of resistance anywhere.

Elle rolled her eyes, then approached the barmaid. 'Do you have Crystal?'

'Coming right up,' she said.

The woman disappeared through the back and Gem pulled out her Amex. 'I wonder if we can open a tab.'

'We should be able to in a place like this,' Elle said.

Ciara sighed, no doubt that meant her money would be no good here.

'You're welcome to open one as long as you leave your card details,' the man said.

He was pretty cute even with the longer hair, skinny jeans and questionable fashion sense. Or was that his style? It reminded her of the American skater boys but with his own stamp.

Surprisingly, Elle was the one to approach him and when she spoke, it was with her flirting voice. 'Thank you. I'm Elle Muir and these are my friends, Ciara and Gem.'

Elle stuck out her hand for a shake. Skater boy – who was the last person in the world she'd think her friend would be interested in – stood up so he was towering over Elle. He took her hand and brought it to his lips.

'It's a pleasure to meet you. I'm Kieran and this is my place,' he said.

'Are you seeing what I'm seeing?' Gem whispered.

The way Kieran looked at Elle was so intense that she swore her friend was blushing, but that couldn't be right. Elle went for the polished, put together men who looked clean cut and scrubbed up well.

Kieran looked like he'd rolled out of bed an hour before, finger combed that shiny black hair and pulled on the first clothes that he stumbled across.

'I'm seeing it, but I'm not sure I believe it,' Ciara whispered back.

She and Gem were distracted by the waitress bringing back the Crystal, opening the bottle and filling up their glasses. Kieran signalled for Elle's to be brought the five steps down the bar to her.

'Let's leave them to it,' Gem suggested, picking up the ice bucket with the drink and her glass.

Ciara hesitated, wondering if it was what Elle wanted but they'd only be a few feet away if she needed them so Ciara followed Gem over to a table within spying distance.

'This is new,' Gem said and Ciara nodded. 'I wonder if Elle's feeling the chemistry.'

Ciara grinned. 'I'll bet it's all that talk about super endorphins. Maybe she thinks Kieran is the key.'

'Good for her.'

They watched their friend playing coy while Kieran inched closer so they were almost touching. Their voices didn't carry but by the way Elle appeared to be flirting right back Ciara was sure she was into it.

'So, now Ms Prude is out the way, I want details!' Gem said.

Ciara knew exactly what details her friend was after, but somehow sharing the ins and outs of her private time with Zack felt like a betrayal. She decided vague was the way to go.

'When he touches me everything becomes clearer, sharper and even holding his hand is electrifying. It all quadruples when it's just us and I can't seem to get enough of him.'

From Gem's disappointed pout, she clocked what Ciara was up to.

'The endorphins are definitely super, but when he leaves it's like a sugar crash. I feel a bit depressed.' All true and probably a reason to start worrying about where their fling was going.

'Sounds like more than a temporary thing to me,' Gem said, watching her closely.

Ciara shrugged. 'Temporary is all I can do.'

'Even though you had me convinced for a while that a flaky gene could be hereditary, I don't think that applies to you.'

'Let's look at the facts,' she said, using her fingers to count off her many flaws. 'I can't stay in one place for a long time without feeling like I'm going to crack if there's nothing else to do. My past relationships have ended before they've even begun. I'm worried about going home because there is nowhere I can imagine working that wouldn't have me running out after a month. And I know deep down, even if I fall for Zack and he falls for me, there are no guarantees that will stick. Just look at my ma.'

Gem shook her head. 'You like to keep busy, there's nothing wrong with that. As for the job, I think the issue there is you're scared to fail. And—'

'Excuse me?' Ciara asked. She was not that kind of a wimp.

'It's true and don't worry, I feel exactly the same. You're not the only one whose family has high expectations, you know. Mine want me to go straight to work and they're expecting insta-greatness.'

Gem played with the stem of her glass, leaving Ciara speechless. She'd thought her friends were excited to go back and tackle their futures head on but it seemed Gem was as worried as her.

'And as for Zack, I think you're wrong. It isn't just endorphins, it's like you two are halves of the whole,' Gem said.

Ciara rolled her eyes. 'I thought you didn't believe in that soul mate nonsense.'

Gem shrugged. 'I didn't until I saw you two together.'

Her palms got damp. Even the cynical Gem who was convinced attraction boiled down to nothing more than a chemical reaction was coming round to the idea that two people were meant to be together. But there was more to it than just her fear of leaving him someday. Gem and Elle had been worried for her too.

'You both seem to think it's me who'll get hurt at the end of this. Why is that?' she asked, going for broke. It was long past time she knew the truth.

Gem shot a glance Elle's way – who was now holding hands and laughing quietly with Kieran. 'Before we went to university, Zack was dating this girl Vanessa and they'd been together for years. She proposed to him on a leap year and he turned her down.'

Wow. He'd been with her for years. Saying no must have been the worst slap in the face ever.

'But I saw those two together when I stayed over at Elle's. They didn't have much of a spark. It seemed like they were put together by his granddad and her father. They're business partners.'

'So it wasn't the problem with commitment, more like an arranged match up he didn't want?' Ciara asked, hoping Gem would alleviate her fears.

Gem shrugged again. 'You'd really have to ask Zack. Even Elle doesn't know.'

'Elle doesn't know what?' the Muir in question asked.

Ciara's face burned like she'd been caught doing something she shouldn't. Elle and Kieran had decided to join them, hand in hand.

Gem recovered first and saved her. 'Where do you want me to start? I have a list longer than my arm.'

'Funny, Gem. Seriously though, I came to ask if you wanted to leave the clubbing until tomorrow? Kieran's also in a band and they're playing here later,' Elle said.

He was in a band? Maybe that explained the eyeliner.

'Is there a hot bass player?' Gem asked.

Kieran laughed. 'If you mean in a sweaty way, yeah. The drummer might be more your type.'

'Then I'm in!' Gem said with a grin.

'Me too,' Ciara agreed. For some reason she'd lost the drive to party the night away and was actually relieved by Elle's change in plans.

***

'It's official, I'm so tired I might actually sleep for the next week.' Elle rolled over on the sun lounger, wincing as she did.

Gem laughed. 'If you did more than sunbathe and starve yourself you wouldn't be so sore today.'

Elle smiled, stretching out on her stomach. 'I held my own last night.'

Ciara wrinkled her nose, trying not to remember Kieran's less than quiet performance. 'Who knew he'd be the screamer.'

'He didn't scream. He was just vocal about what he enjoyed,' Elle defended.

'Milo was a screamer. And a biter.' Gem sighed. 'I really miss him.'

'You should have given the drummer a chance,' Ciara said, though she'd been secretly glad since hearing one friend hump the night away had been enough.

Elle wasn't the only one tired today, and on this trip to the beach Ciara felt more mellow than she had in a while. She didn't even want to get up and do anything. Even with the dock waiting to be explored and the beach dying to be walked on, sleep sounded as much as she could manage.

Gem sighed. 'He was hot, but that kiss after the show barely made me warm and fuzzy. It would be like having an orgasm with a vibrator. Boring and predictable.'

'Some girls would be happy just to have an orgasm,' Ciara pointed out.

Gem gasped. 'Don't tell me Zack's shit in bed.'

'Don't tell her *anything*,' Elle chimed in. 'My stomach's queasy enough as it is.'

Ciara decided a little payback was in order since her friend had kept her up past five this morning. 'He's amazing. Gem you wouldn't believe the things he can do with his tongue and a tub of ice cream.'

'That's disgusting.' Elle got up, showing off just how amazing she looked in her new bikini. 'I'm going for a walk if you keep this up.'

'Tell me about the ice cream,' Gem said. 'Did he lick it off you?'

They waited until Elle stormed away before giggling.

'Serves her right for not remembering how thin the walls are.' Gem turned to lie on her side. 'I do want the details though.'

Ciara just shook her head.

'You're such a bore.'

Ciara's phone chimed so she dug it out of her bag and read the text. 'Zack's here.'

She didn't want to find out why that news wiped away the exhaustion and made her more excited than she'd been waiting for Santa to come on Christmas Eve.

Gem grinned. 'Looks like you'll get your payback tonight.'

Ciara smiled back, hoping the day went in quickly.

Chapter Sixteen

Ciara knew something was wrong the second Zack walked into their hotel room suite. He didn't say more than a quick hello before disappearing into her room and stripping out of his suit. She couldn't blame him. The sun was at its hottest around now and he must be boiling in all those layers.

But she'd come back to meet him, leaving Gem and Elle at the beach, hoping for more than a kiss on the cheek. He hadn't even looked twice at her new bikini!

As she waited in the main room for him to shower, the thought of what happened to make him like this was driving her insane. On the other hand, if he wanted to talk about it he would have and pushing wouldn't do her any good.

Then she remembered what Gem said about his ex and wondered if he really was a commitment phoebe. That at least would make sense. She'd been having stronger than appropriate feelings for him and maybe he noticed. Maybe coming to meet him looked like she was desperate or something.

She scrubbed her face with her hands. 'What a way to feck up a good thing, Ciara.'

The sound of the shower cutting off had her pulling herself together. He'd come here after all. If he thought she was too clingy or was planning on cutting their time short he could have easily done that over the phone. Whatever was wrong was clearly unrelated to her.

She hoped.

Next she heard the bed springs protest and frowned. It didn't sound like he was in a rush to get ready and hit the beach.

Before she could overthink things more, she got up and went to the doorway. Zack was on the edge of the bed in nothing but a towel, with his elbows on his knees and his hands fisted in his hair.

The sight of him broke her heart. Without her permission her legs carried her across to him and she reached out, placing a hand on his shoulder. Zack looked up and she saw the desolation in his eyes.

'Are you okay?' she asked stupidly. He clearly wasn't.

'It's nothing.'

He wrapped his arms around her, resting his head between her breasts but there was nothing sexual about it. She guessed he was looking for comfort, just couldn't figure out why. Still, she ran her fingers through his hair because it was all she could do.

'I've missed you,' she whispered.

The way he tensed against her was like a slap in the face.

'Me too,' he said, but it sounded wary.

Was this how it ended between him and Vanessa? Pulling away from her emotionally so as to lower the blow when it all came crashing down. But that was ridiculous. And she was different to Vanessa. She and Zack were only having a fling. It wasn't serious.

So then why did that feel like a lie?

She wriggled out of his hold. After all she refused to be the clingy woman he didn't want. Whether she was his cousin's friend or not, she'd rather be dumped now than become a pity fuck.

'What's up with you?' he asked, frowning.

'I asked you first,' she said, folding her arms across her chest.

He sighed and rubbed his face with his palm. 'Munich was

rough. My granddad wants me to stop arsing around and grow up. We had a few disagreements.'

'Oh.' She relaxed her stance. 'Do you want to talk about it?'

'Truthfully, no. I'd like to pretend it never happened if you don't mind.'

It's not that she was annoyed he wasn't opening up to her, just knew from personal experience that burying your head in the sand didn't make anything go away. She'd tried it when her ma left but the pain and heartache was still there, just waiting for her to grow up and deal with it.

'It might be none of my business – and you don't have to talk to me about it – but I think you should take the time to think about what it is you want to do.'

He looked at her seriously and nodded. 'You're right, I do. First, I'm sure in my moping I forgot to mention how sexy you are in that bikini.'

It wasn't misery in his eyes as he took in her body from head to toe and she decided to drop the serious stuff for now. If he wanted to talk things through she was sure he would when he was ready.

Instead she struck a pose, placing her hands on her hips and pointing one foot in front of the other. 'Sexy is an understatement. I look incredible, thank you very much.'

His smile melted away the last of the tension in his expression. 'You look better than that. Now come here so I can show you how much I missed you.'

***

By the time they got to the beach Ciara was exhausted in the best possible way. They hit the refreshment stand first, grabbing slushies like a couple of kids then walked hand in hand to where she'd left Elle and Gem earlier.

The amount of heads Zack turned with his beautiful torso was startling, but she reckoned some of the guys were giving her a once over too. Some maybe even twice.

'I love the bikini, but I don't love the way every boy here is drooling over you,' he said, squeezing her hand.

'They could be ogling you, ya know.'

Zack laughed and pulled her in for a kiss. 'There. Now they'll have no doubt who I'm attracted to.'

'I'm not sure. That felt more like a friendly peck than a lust fuelled snog.' She sipped at her drink.

He pulled her to a stop then dropped her hand. 'This should change their minds.'

With his free hand he grabbed her bum and pressed her so close their sun cream was all that stood between them. The kiss he treated her to was long, a little frantic and had a lot of tongue on both sides.

Lost in the moment, she let go of her slush in favour of the muscles covering his ribs and clung on until he'd worked her into a passion fuelled frenzy. It didn't matter that she'd had him less than an hour ago. She wanted him again, right there and didn't care who saw.

Luckily Zack had a bit more sense and pulled away with a grin. 'I think that's enough or we'll end up giving them a show they didn't bargain for.'

She pouted and he swooped down for another, gentler kiss.

'I can't wait to get you back to the hotel,' he said.

'I vote you take me now.' She was still clinging to him, tracing the ridges of his muscles with her fingers and thumbs. But there was so much more to touch, that was just a teaser.

'Ciara!'

Gem's shout snapped her mind out of the gutter.

She turned to see her friend waving a flyer around a few meters away.

'Later,' Zack promised and took her hand again. They started towards her friends. 'I take it you weren't a fan of the slush?'

Ciara's cheeks flamed. 'I had better things to hold.'

He laughed and the deep, happy sound made her smile. Whatever had happened in Munich was clearly forgotten about for the moment and, though she was glad he was in a better mood, she still worried about what happened.

But Gem and Elle's obvious excitement distracted her.

'*Look!*' Gem said, shoving the flyer into her hands.

It was advertising a British magazine's competition for the next Ibiza Top Model. The grand prize was a private party with other models, a few top photographers in the industry and David Call would be there too.

'We're so entering. Three chances are better than one,' Elle said.

'What? I'm not entering.' She may look sexy in her new bikini but she was not model material.

'Cia you *have* to. One of us should win and we'll get to meet Dave!' The way Gem turned his name into a sigh was impressive.

'I'm sure you and Elle will manage without me.'

Zack squeezed her hand and she looked away from Gem's disappointed pout and into his dark eyes. 'I think you should.'

'Come on! I'm not embarrassing myself when there will be gazillions of gorgeous, stick thin girls.' Despite being trimmer than normal, she didn't have the lean, petite frame to pull it off.

'You're stunning and incredibly sexy. There's no reason why you can't win it.' Since Zack sounded serious and her friends didn't immediately laugh like he was joking, she wondered if they'd all lost their grip on reality.

'He's right, you know,' Elle said.

She turned to Elle, completely speechless. If any of them could go by stunning it would be her.

'Of course I'm right, and you're not just beautiful with make-up, you're naturally gorgeous,' he added.

Her face burned so hot she swore it was on fire.

'Obviously, I'm going to win.' Elle said with a smile. 'But if for some unknown reason they don't love me, then you and Gem will be in with a chance.'

'Modesty isn't your strong suit, Elly.'

Gem giggled and Elle frowned. 'I don't see anything wrong with stating the facts. Anyway, how was Munich?'

His hand squeezed so hard on hers that her bones creaked. 'Ow, Zack!'

He loosened his hold and brought her hand up and pressed it against the cold slush. 'Sorry.'

'Guess that answers that,' Elle said and Zack's expression got hard like he was going back to the place he'd been earlier.

'Elle, enough,' Ciara said, glaring at her friend.

Though Elle's chin dropped for a second, the surprise vanished under that pity look she hated. Now she knew about Vanessa, she could relax a bit because if it was commitment that was his problem then that was fine by her. They weren't permanent or anything.

The thing was it felt like a problem, especially with the way her lungs tightened when she thought of going back to Dublin without him.

***

Becoming Ibiza's Top Model wasn't as easy as Gem had told her it would be. Later that day they found a rep who put them through their paces snapping them in different poses, checking how they strutted their stuff and there was even an inspection for flaws that he called 'skin snakes'.

Like having stretch marks weren't bad enough, he had to go and call them something uglier.

Eventually he was satisfied with their bodies and put them through to the next round. Where Elle and Gem seemed to burst with excitement, Ciara hung back and felt more objectified than anything else.

While they waited by the pool at the Ibiza Rocks hotel with a dozen other gorgeous girls, Zack pulled her onto his knee and rested his chin on her shoulder.

'You don't look happy to be here,' he said, wrapping his arms around her waist.

'I just wish it was over already.' She looked around at all the women preening in the sun, feeling alone with her wish. Even Elle and Gem were fixing their hair and applying subtle make-up.

'Every other girl is eating up the attention but you're shying away from it,' Zack said, sounding confused like he couldn't figure her out.

'I was the ultimate geek growing up. My classmates teased me all the time and the fact I dressed like a boy didn't help much either. I liked my baggy jeans and loose jumpers.' She smiled as she remembered how horrified Elle and Gem had been when they discovered she'd never owned a dress.

'What changed?' he asked, sounding more curious than put off.

'Me, I suppose. Elle and Gem helped a lot too. I was done being the brainy outsider and going to Oxford meant I was in similar company. Instead of being a geek, I was just another statistic.'

He kissed her shoulder. 'You don't have a high enough opinion of yourself.'

'I'm honest. There's no point pretending to be someone I'm not.'

'I know exactly what you mean,' he said.

She wondered if he was referring to working with the family business instead of following his dreams, or remembering how he broke up with his girlfriend.

Since he didn't know she knew about Vanessa and her friends were well out of ear shot, she decided to pry a little.

'What about you?' she asked, relaxing back into him. 'I thought a stud like you would have been snapped up years ago.'

He laughed, holding her close. 'My parents. Granddad always said how much they loved each other. Even though he had someone else lined up for my dad, he accepted my mum into the family.'

It was old fashioned to think about arranged marriages this side of the century but her upbringing had been so different. She'd thought her parents were in love till her ma did a disappearing act. Her da hadn't found anyone else. It was like his heart and trust had both been shattered beyond repair.

'Still, you didn't answer my question,' she pressed.

Zack paused for so long she was sure he wasn't going to answer, but then he said, 'There was a girl I thought I loved. When it came down to it, I knew we were all wrong for each other.'

She wished she could see his face because the calm tone of his voice sounded too forced.

'That must have been rough for both of you,' she said, linking her fingers through his over her stomach.

'Mmm,' he said, but it didn't sound like an agreement. 'What about you, since we're sharing? Has no one tried to solder a ring onto your finger?'

Shaking her head, she said, 'Geek, remember?'

He hugged her closer. 'Cutest geek I've met by a long shot.'

As they watched photographers and journalists appear from the hotel, Ciara reckoned her chance to find out more would have to be later.

'God, I hate getting my picture taken,' she grumbled.

'Maybe we should have practiced in private. You know, to help you get over your embarrassment,' he said.

'I think this is a little different than those kinds of pictures,' she said, imagining posing in inviting positions while Zack snapped her with his phone.

'Much less fun though,' he said.

She had to agree.

***

187

To no one's surprise, Elle scooped the title of Ibiza's Top Model 2014 and would be featured in not just the magazine, but in advertisements for clubs and other things over the coming year. She got a healthy cheque for her troubles too, but Elle had her eye on the biggest prize.

A section of the beach was being closed off for the private party and Elle managed to get them all invites – to Gem's delight. So they were back at the hotel for a quick bite to eat, shower and change.

When she'd finished with the room service meal, Zack said, 'How about that shower?'

Elle scowled at them. 'The walls are paper thin. If you make me bring up my dinner I'll kick you both out.'

Gem was the one who jumped to their defence. 'You only know that because of the racket you made last night. I think it's our turn for payback.'

'Too much information,' Zack protested.

Since a frisk in the shower would be weird with her friends listening in, she told him to go first. Though he looked disappointed, he did and when her friends cleared out for their showers, Ciara went to her room and lay on the bed until he'd finished.

Closing her eyes, she listened to the sound of the shower pelting down on him and though heat stirred in the pit of her stomach imagining him all naked, wet and soaped up, she couldn't get into the fantasy.

Talking about her childhood brought back things she didn't want to worry about, like what she was going to do with her life and how she'd feel saying goodbye to Zack for the last time.

Then there were her friends. Both would be returning to their corners of the UK which was further than a few doors down in their college. She'd been so used to having them close for years, the ocean separating them would make it feel like she was on the other side of the planet.

Rolling over she pulled a pillow over her head and tried to drive out the thoughts. All stuff that would happen weeks from now, not straight away. But then she sat up, checked her mobile and the date hit her hard.

It was August already. Where had the time gone? They only had one more stop left, just a few measly days spread out between here and there. It wasn't weeks at all.

Her hands started to shake and the screen blurred as tears formed in her eyes. Eight days and she'd have to say goodbye to Zack and the two best friends she'd ever had. If she thought she'd felt bad in Paris, the thick, dark cloud surrounding her now made that look like a stroll in the park.

'Ciara, what's wrong?' Zack asked.

She hadn't heard the shower stop or see him come into the room but then her gaze had been glued to the date on her phone. The bed dipped under his weight and his solid, shower fresh body brought out another wave of sadness.

As tears streamed down her face she struggled to wipe them away, dropping the evil phone onto the covers.

He pulled her into his arms and let her cry on his shoulder until she had no tears left.

How could she leave him?

'Are you sad because you have to go home soon?' he asked.

'Yes, and no. I'll miss you all like mad but it will be good to see my da and get home.' She was lying about the last bit. Of course she wanted to see her da but the home part hadn't been happy for a long time. Everywhere there was a constant reminder of who was missing from their little family and that was almost as painful as never seeing Zack again.

'I'm sure it's not the end of your friendship. My cousin is far too stubborn to give up on someone she cares about,' he said, pulling back to see her face.

What about you? she wanted to ask, but the lump in her throat stopped her.

'Instead of being upset, why not choose to make the most of what time you have left?' he asked.

'That's a change of attitude from earlier.' He'd been the miserable one just hours ago, now it was her on the bed looking like nothing could lighten her mood.

'And it was you who cheered me up. I'm returning the favour.'

She rubbed her eyes until they were dry and a little sore. 'I should get a move on before Elle comes in to drag me out.'

He looked at her in that way Elle did when she wanted to say something she knew she shouldn't, except Elle would have barrelled on anyway. He just kissed her head and told her he'd wait in the kitchen.

She rushed through her shower, feeling guilty for shunning Zack the way she did. He was right, she had to start focusing on the now or she'd ruin what little time they had left.

Keeping the towel wrapped around her, she darted through the suite until she got to the kitchen. Elle's voice stopped her dead, but only because it was more like a whisper. When she heard Zack's name she stayed behind the partition and waited like the sneaky eavesdropper she was.

'I spoke with him, Zack. He told me everything,' Elle said.

He cursed under his breath, or she assumed it was a curse. 'Why can't you stay out of my business? I don't stick my nose in yours.'

'Because what you choose to do now affects my friend and I won't let you lead her on like this, it's not fair.' Elle sounded so angry her voice rose a few octaves.

All the while Ciara's body temperature dropped. He was leading her on?

'I'm not leading anyone on. I care about Ciara.'

'So stop fucking about and make a choice!' Elle obviously wasn't as mollified as she was.

'It's not that easy. He clearly didn't tell you everything.' Zack's voice was starting to rise too, he sounded more frustrated than she'd ever heard him.

'He's pissed off but he'll calm down. You need to tell Ciara.'

She bit her lip, preparing for the refusal that would cut her deep.

'I can't put that on her, it's not fair.' He sighed.

'Fair or not, she needs a reality check whatever she decides to do. If nothing else it will make your decision easier.'

She wondered if Elle was talking in riddles because she knew Ciara was listening in and wanted to pay her back. But the reality check comment pissed her off more than the riddles. Why couldn't they just spit it out?

'Nothing about this is going to be easy, either way I have to give up something I can't imagine living without.' The sadness in his voice brought tears to her eyes.

'If that's true then you have to decide what means more to you,' Elle said, then Ciara heard the sound of footsteps on the tile floor and bolted to her room.

Chapter Seventeen

She'd been expecting more gloom from Zack when she'd finished getting ready, but instead he treated her to a tummy flipping grin and compliments about how sexy she looked in her little blue dress.

The taxi to the beach party was full of tension though. Gem was blissfully unaware, telling them about her plans to chat up Dave Call but Ciara didn't miss the pointed glances Elle kept throwing at Zack.

He was doing a good job of pretending not to notice and after a few drinks surrounded by gorgeous people, he seemed to have forgotten the conversation she'd listened in on altogether.

But Ciara hadn't. She wondered what it was he didn't want to 'put on her' and couldn't seem to relax and enjoy herself. Until Zack took her hand and led her down the beach, away from the bright lights and loud music.

'Why are we out here?' she asked.

'You didn't seem into the party,' he said, then sat down pulling her with him until she was straddling his hips. 'I really love that dress on you.'

'I got it in Miami,' she said, smoothing it down over her legs.

The breeze coming off the sea made her shiver a bit until he bent his knees and rested his forearms on her shoulders. Like this they were intimately close but the dynamic between them wasn't just sexual. It was so much more.

'We can go back if you're cold,' he said.

Ciara shook her head. Freezing or not, he had that look again that said he had something to say but was still hesitating.

She decided a little push was in order. 'I can read you as well as I can read Elle, you know. You have that look again that says you want to say something.'

His lips pulled up at one side. 'Can't get anything past you, can I?'

'We geeks can be intuitive.'

'Earlier, when I first got here, you asked what was wrong. That disagreement with my granddad was more like an ultimatum.' He played with a strand of her hair, avoiding her eyes.

'That's awful,' she said, placing her palm on his cheek. 'Why would he do that?'

'He wants me to do things I don't, I want to focus on architecture instead of the business. He said I'd be on my own if I decided to go that way.'

'*What?* He'd just give up on you?' She'd never been so mad at anyone as she was at his granddad right then.

'No, but he'd cut me off. I'd be financially on my own. I mean, I have savings but without the income I'm getting now they wouldn't last as long as they'd need to.'

'Your savings would probably last someone else a year or two.' She knew the Muirs could spend and he was clearly no different, thinking nothing of jumping on a flight to Paris a few hours after he was asked to go.

He laughed. 'You're probably right.'

'Do you want to know what I think?' she asked.

'It couldn't hurt.'

'You're so lucky to know what your dream career is. I haven't a clue what I want to do with my life and that's scarier than the thought of having no money. If it was me I'd go with my heart and try to make it work.'

'I don't think you follow your heart as much as you should,' he said. 'But I know you're right. Walking away from the business is a huge step and not something my parents would have wanted, which is what's making it harder to decide.'

She took his face in her hands and kissed him softly. 'I'll bet your parents are proud of you whatever you do.'

'Thank you. I think I needed to hear that.'

He kissed her this time, slowly and softly but with purpose. Threading her fingers through her hair, she kissed him back, switching the gears until she was panting and the fire in her veins smouldered through her like a drug.

She didn't care if it was a chemical reaction or whatever Gem called this, it felt right and exciting and she never wanted it to stop.

When his lips left her mouth in favour of her neck she shivered again.

'Do you want to get out of here?' he asked.

She shook her head. Then remembered she hadn't asked what his granddad wanted him to do other than run the business.

He didn't give her time to mull it over long. Sliding his hands under her dress, he set her skin on fire with his touch and she did the same with him, exploring his abs, chest and sides until she got so hot she forgot where they were and why, only that she was with him.

Making quick work of his buckle and zipper, she freed his erection and squeezed it until he gasped. Zack used his thumb to press against her clit until pleasure spiked through her.

'Please tell me you brought condoms,' she panted while he went to work on her.

In response, he pulled a foil package from his pocket and she snatched it off him, making short work of the task.

He grinned. 'Always impatient.'

'It feels like it's been years, not hours,' she said, then tugged her knickers to the side and slid down on him.

She rode him fast while the pressure built unbearably quickly. Just a little longer and she was having her cry swallowed by Zack's mouth. Though she was limp, he wasn't done and rolled them over so her back was on the sand and she didn't care that she'd be uncomfortable for the rest of the night. Not when she was clinging on as he fucked her like he couldn't get enough of her.

As the pressure built again Zack jerked with his own release and she couldn't keep the disappointment from showing. Gutted was an understatement.

'Sorry,' he said, between pants. 'Give me a sec and I'll make it up to you.'

But as she took all his weight as his chest heaved with hers, she didn't mind so much. They were still joined together and she felt closer to him than she'd ever been.

Zack was obviously determined to keep his word because he disposed of the condom in a tissue and then kissed his way down her stomach.

'You can't do that after we've just—'

He didn't listen, nor did the idea seem to ick him out. He pulled her knickers down to her knees, hiked her legs over his shoulders and then swirled his tongue around her clit in a way that made her writhe on the sand – hair and dress forgotten about.

'Oh, feck that's good.'

Good wasn't what he was going for though. Soon he added a few fingers to the mix, rubbing gently against both of her g-spots at the same time. The waves of pleasure crashing through her body made her unable to hold back her screams when she went into spasms. Not even when he rung the last aftershock from her trembling body.

'Better?' he asked with a grin.

Ciara just closed her eyes and tried for a nod. Her muscles

felt jelly-like. Moving anytime soon was not going to happen, that was for sure.

'Thankfully there's no one around or that could have gotten us in trouble.' He righted her dress then lay down on the sand beside her.

His face was illuminated by the moonlight and to her, he looked more gorgeous than ever.

'I got a bit carried away,' she admitted.

'It's like that for me every time I'm with you,' he said and linked his fingers through hers.

Side by side, they both looked up at the stars shining above them. Even if she got the feeling back in her legs anytime soon, she just wanted to lie there with him for as long as they could. It was just a pity that her time would be up before she was, but she was done dwelling for now.

***

The next day she hit the shops with Elle and Gem, getting her ear chewed off by one for not keeping her moans and groans to herself that morning, while the other went through her failed seduction with Dave Call trying to figure out where she'd gone wrong.

Ciara took the earful from Elle and even managed the odd apology with a promise not to be so loud again while encouraging Gem to try for someone else. By the time they'd stopped at a café to order some lattes, her mind had drifted back to Zack.

She'd left him working on a contract for the company and could tell his heart hadn't been in it. She was sad to think he hadn't made up his mind yet and wondered again what else his granddad wanted him to do that made Zack so upset.

Because despite him saying it was nothing, he did look genuinely upset when he arrived the day before.

'Are you going to keep pretending your listening to us or are you actually going to join in with the conversation,' Elle asked, sounding more and more miffed every time she spoke.

Well her friend wasn't the only one miffed. She remembered the comment about Ciara needing a reality check yesterday and she didn't care if her friend found out she'd been eavesdropping.

'Get off your high horse, Elle. Maybe you should start by telling me why you think I need a reality check?'

Elle paled to the point even her tan looked peaky. 'What do you mean?'

'I heard you and Zack in the kitchen yesterday. What is he hiding and don't say "ask him" because he told me about the ultimatum.' Just not all the things their granddad wanted him to do.

· 'You know what they say about eavesdroppers, don't you?' Elle said calmly and if it wasn't for the forced poker face Ciara might have believed she was being silly.

'Since you think it affects me, I have a right to know.' She tried to take a deep breath to calm down but it was tough since Elle didn't look like she was going to budge.

'What's this about?' Gem asked. 'Ciara why are you getting angry?'

She unclenched her fists and pulled her hands under the table. More deep breaths.

'It's not my place to say,' Elle hedged. Ever the evader.

'You're both my best friends. If I knew something that could hurt you I wouldn't hesitate to tell you both. Please, Elle.'

'Spit it out, Elle,' Gem added.

'Cia seriously, do you think I'm doing this to be a bitch?' Elle asked.

She shook her head, though she wasn't so sure.

'I know things have changed for you. I can see it in the way you look at Zack. What I meant by reality check is that I wanted him to tell you himself. That way you might get over this stupid fear of what your mum did and take a chance for once.'

Elle reached across to touch Ciara's shoulder but she shifted away. 'It's not stupid. It's who I am.'

'You're being ridiculous!' Elle folded her arms. 'Seriously, you are the most loyal person I know. You'd never walk out on anyone when the going got tough, you'd work hard, deal and get through it.'

'I think she's right,' Gem chimed in. 'And I think you need to face what's really going on between you and Zack before one or both of you end up hurt.'

That was going to happen either way, but she didn't bother telling them that. Even if she could get past the idea she might one day hurt him, there was still the distance between them. He lived in London and she suspected he was going to go back to work regardless of what she said or did.

'He told me once that your granddad took him in and that everything he does is because he wants what's best. I don't think Zack could let him down and the thought of living without the security blanket of an income is putting him off too.'

Not that she thought he was all in it for the money, that wasn't him at all. But there was no doubt he was used to the good things in life. The switchover would be tough for anyone.

'Maybe, but Granddad wants him to be happy too. Ciara, if anyone can show Zack that living on a budget doesn't mean he has to be miserable, it's you. And I don't mean that in a bitchy way.'

Elle was right. She did know how to watch her spending but there wasn't much time left and she hated wasting what little they had as it was.

'He will tell you, I'll make sure of it but you have to be honest too. Let him know why you won't commit and maybe then he'll have a fighting chance of showing you how wrong you are,' Elle said.

If only he wanted her that way, but she couldn't be sure. She supposed Elle was right though. And she couldn't expect him to be completely honest when she wasn't.

'I'll try,' she said, not able to promise more than that.

'Glad we got that sorted,' Gem said. 'Now let's talk about tonight! I think it's time we got in some serious clubbing.'

The lighter, less touchy subject got her mind off what she was going to do about Zack. At least now she better understood why he'd rather forget about it than deal. Wasn't that what she was doing when it came to going home?

***

Zack stayed in the hotel that night saying he had urgent stuff to deal with and an important call to take later. Despite being in a tee-shirt and shorts, he looked every bit the serious businessman who was no doubt as good at his job as he was at designing buildings.

But what played on Ciara's mind all night, even after they'd bumped into Kieran and hit Amnesia, was the look in his eyes when she'd left him. It was almost like he'd given up hope that he could make a go of things for himself, either that or the guilt for letting down his family had won over his happiness.

Gem and Elle tried to ply her into having a good time, buying her shot after shot and dragging her onto the dance floor when a song they recognised came on. But every time she let her guard down and started to enjoy herself, she got a dose of the guilts herself.

Then later, just as the DJs changed over, the place transformed completely. As well as strobe lights they were surrounded in bubbles that would no doubt stain her dress, and since she'd opted for the *Givenchy* number she was *not* letting it get ruined by a club still stuck in the 90s. Or so she told Elle and Gem when she left them there.

Really, she just wanted to see Zack.

The hotel was quiet when she got in but then a phone rang and Zack answered in fluent German. Amazing how many languages he and Elle knew. No wonder their business did so well internationally.

She couldn't understand the words but could see the frustration creasing his brow when she found him on the sofa. His half smile was all for her and it melted her heart. He offered his free hand and when she took it, he pulled her over so she was sitting beside him.

Zack's words were clipped and dry to whoever he was speaking to and every now and again she squeezed his hand, just to check he was okay. Each time he'd smile at her and roll his eyes but it seemed like an act.

She decided a massage might do the trick and climbed over the sofa, ignoring his puzzled look. While the brisk conversation continued, she rubbed his bare shoulders, kneading the muscle with her fingers and when he rested his head on the back of the sofa, she bent down and nibbled his earlobe.

His breath hitched and the next time he spoke he sounded much more polite to the caller. Ciara decided she liked this game and walked around to stand in front of him. His eyes were hooded and dark as he took her in from head to toe, and his grin was too seductive to resist.

She slipped the strap off her shoulder and unzipped the side of the dress until it slid down her body to the floor. Though it wasn't sexy, she picked up the prettiest dress in the world to make sure it stayed wrinkle free, but soon got back to her pose, sliding her fingertips down the front of her knickers.

His throat worked as he swallowed hard, watching her so carefully he actually sputtered out his next sentence.

Feeling brave, Ciara slid one hand up her stomach slowly until she was cupping her breast. The fact that he was watching made the space between her legs throb and she gave into the urge, sliding her other hand all the way down and rubbing herself.

The way his whole body tensed like he was struggling to hold himself back made everything that more intense. She squeezed her nipples, revelling in the sharp bursts of pleasure/pain while building up to an orgasm that would take her lip off if she had to hold the cry in.

'I need to go,' he said, switching to English. He ended the call and then turned back to watch her. 'Fucking hell, Ciara.'

'Zack,' she said on a gasp, just as the pressure burst and pulsed through her body.

He didn't give her a chance to recover, pulling her down on his lap into a kiss that was furious and desperate. It didn't take long to rip off what little clothes they had left and the second the protection was in place, he took her hard and fast on the sofa.

She cried his name over and over again as she clung onto him and took his powerful thrusts, one after another until her second orgasm blended into her third or was that her fourth?

He didn't stop once, not even after his body jerked and he panted her name like little oaths. The sofa hit the wall before they were both through and she didn't care how sore she'd be in the morning, not when she felt this incredible now.

Gem really was onto something with the super endorphins.

A little while later when they'd caught their breath, Zack broke the silence. 'Not that I mind, but why are you back so early?'

She looked into his eyes, wishing she could promise him so much but she wasn't sure it was what she wanted and there were no guarantees she'd be able to keep them. Well, accept one.

'Don't make up your mind just yet. I want to show you how good life can be, even on a budget.'

His frown and the way his eyes narrowed made her wonder if she'd gone too far into his business.

'Why would you want to do that?' he asked.

'Because I hate seeing you sad and I think you always will be if you don't follow your dreams. If I had any, I'd do everything I could to make them a reality.'

After a deep breath, he said, 'Okay, I'm in.'

She grinned, so happy he was letting her help out that she couldn't stop herself. 'As soon as we land in Florence we'll start.'

'Well, since we're still in Ibiza and technically I'm still employed, is it safe to give you something?' he asked.

Ciara bit her lip. 'What kind of something?'

'Relax, it's not a dress or a pair of designer shoes.'

He let her go and crossed to their room. A minute later he returned with a box just a bit bigger than what a watch would go in. She frowned, thinking watches were awfully expensive.

'Open it,' he said, holding it out to her.

She lifted the lid to see a bronze cuff with pearl markings and a diamante in the middle. It was so pretty and unique, she'd never seen anything like it. 'I love it.'

'A local jeweller makes one of a kind trinkets. I saw it walking by the store and thought of you.'

Her eyes got a little blurry and she had to blink so she could see him properly. 'Thank you, Zack. It's beautiful.'

Not to mention it was something she would always have to remember him by. Instead of embarrassing herself with that mush, she went for teasing instead. 'But remember in Florence, trinkets aren't allowed.'

'I'm sure I'll manage to get by without them,' he said with a grin and she laughed.

'I'm positive you will.'

Florence

Chapter Eighteen

'*This* is much, much better,' Elle said as she led them through the door of another of the Muirs' luxury properties.

Ciara realised that the Hollywood mansion in LA, the beach house in Miami, the townhouse in Paris and the spectacular multi-levelled house in Santorini were only a taster of their family's wealth.

Everything here was marble and gold with Renaissance art in the form of statues and paintings she'd have thought would be in museums, not in someone's entrance hall. Again there was a spiral staircase and she could see their granddad's style in the structure, or maybe Zack had helped with the design.

Either way, now she knew why Zack was worried about giving all this up. It must be terrifying to go from having everything to nothing. Not to mention the fact he thought he'd be letting so many people down.

'Elly, you're talking like you've spent the last few days in a Travelodge,' Zack teased.

Travelodges were perfectly fine accommodation in Ciara's opinion. The five star hotel they'd just left was stunning.

'A hotel never has the same comforts,' Elle said and on that note a woman dressed in black wearing a white apron came to greet them.

Unsurprisingly, both of the Muirs spoke perfect Italian – or at least she assumed it was perfect by the unfaltering string of words delivered with confidence. More staff appeared and Elle must have instructed them to take the luggage upstairs because that's what they did.

'Okay, I say we get showered and then hit the bars. The sun's going down and I don't want to waste a night stuck in here,' Elle said, then turned to the stairs assuming everyone would agree instantly.

'There's nothing wrong with a quiet night,' Ciara protested. After all, her funds were running low and she'd promised Elle she'd show Zack he could have a great time without spending a fortune.

Elle whirled on her. 'A night out isn't going to break the bank, Cia.'

A night out with those three could put her in debt for the rest of her life. But they had a point too. She didn't want to spend the last stop of her trip stuck in a house, even if the house was massive and incredible.

Luckily, she'd abused the wifi at the airport and had pre-planned their trip to the city thanks to travel websites. And the cheapest place for a night out was somewhere the tourists didn't go much, or so said the reviewer.

'Fine but if we're going anywhere it's the bars in Piazza di Santo Spirito. I hear it's not as touristy as the other places.'

Elle liked exclusive and Ciara took her shrug as a win.

'I think tonight I'm going for classy rather than slutty,' Gem said, following Elle up the stairs.

Hand in hand with Zack, they trailed up behind her friends.

Elle laughed. 'There's more to it than wearing a nice dress, Gem. If you get on a guy's knee two minutes after you meet him, it doesn't matter what you've got on.'

'It's not slutty if he's into it. What do you think Zack? Is it better to go with the buzz or be a tease and frustrate the guy?' Gem turned to them with genuine curiosity in her eyes.

His cheekbones darkened. 'Um, I don't think I should answer that.'

Gem stopped on the stairs and scowled. 'So you think it's slutty?'

He held his hands up. 'Didn't say that. I meant different guys see things differently. Just like you three.'

'What do *you* think?' Gem was relentless when her temper got the better of her.

'Well, that depends on the girl.'

Ciara was beginning to *hate* this conversation. 'Look, to each her own. Can we drop this?'

'You don't need to be jealous, Ciara. He's all about your fufu. I want a guy's opinion on this.' Gem folded her arms and waited while Ciara's face flushed.

'Just bloody answer her so we can get ready!' Elle demanded.

Zack took his time in answering, despite Elle's death glare. 'Some guys like it when a woman takes charge and makes the first move, and almost every man I've met wants complete honesty up front. If you're clear it's just about sex, I don't think that's slutty. It's actually kinda hot.'

Ciara had to bite her lip to stop herself from asking if that was a jibe at her. It wasn't like she lied to him in LA. It had been crazy sex – the wild, furious, all-night-long kind – and she'd been clear about her no-relationship rule the next day.

But now… her reasons for keeping things light were weak and if he asked where she thought they were she'd be lying if she said they were still in holiday fling territory. Sometime after she'd left Miami she'd realised that much pain wasn't normal – it was more like she'd been grieving.

So she tuned out of the rest of the conversation and let Zack lead her to their room, situated at the opposite side of the house from Elle's. But even if she was in the mood for a round before they went out, she doubted any sound would carry through the thick concrete walls.

She went to her case and started to unpack a few dresses while Zack disappeared to the ensuite to start the shower.

It was better to keep her mouth shut and not ask if he meant *her* when he'd been talking to Gem. After all she'd been the one to kiss him first. Feck, she'd been the one so frantic to get him naked but unwilling to let him go that he had to make the decision for her.

And putting it all down to super pheromones and chemical reactions seemed like a stretch, especially since she cared about him to the point she hurt when he hurt – which she'd been doing ever since he got to Ibiza.

God this really was a feckin mess, wasn't it?

'Wanna share to save time?' Zack asked. He'd disposed of his clothes and was gloriously naked as he leaned against the doorway to the bathroom.

Her mouth got dry and her fingers stung at the tips, like they'd been away from him for far too long and were having withdrawals.

No way was this just pheromones. Borderline addiction, but not a chemical reaction.

But that was the thing about addicts, they got bored and moved onto a bigger high eventually, didn't they?

'Ciara are you okay?' he asked.

'Yes, I'm fine. Look why don't you go first? If I get in there the water will be cold before we get out.' She didn't mean to sound so distant, but the idea that she was hooked on him was freaking her out.

'Gem's wrong. That's not why I'm here. It's about more than sex. I like spending time with you, too.'

It took her mind a minute to grasp what he meant – Gem's vag jokes. She rolled her eyes and forced a smile. 'After four years I know when not to take Gem seriously.'

He treated her to a delicious half-smile. 'Good. Now how about you let me wash your back?'

Her gaze darted to his hands. His long fingered, strong hands that happened to be hanging by his sides, framing his hips and a very impressive appendage. Heat sizzled in her lower belly until all her worries disappeared under a craving so deep, she wasn't sure it would ever disappear.

And Ciara wasn't enough of an eejit to refuse what he was offering. No woman on the planet would be. Especially since time was running out.

***

Thanks to Ciara's online hunt for cheap and cheerful nightlife, they found a little restaurant on the Piazza where the food smelled heavenly and the dishes were reasonably priced. Even Elle didn't seem to mind when she clocked a table full of delicious Italian men in suits nearby.

'Okay this wasn't a terrible idea,' Elle admitted, using the menu as a prop to spy on the men. 'You don't see local talent like that in the mainstream bars.'

'I bet they're out to relax after a hard week at the office. I'd be happy to help them de-stress,' Gem added.

Ciara wrinkled her nose but couldn't stop from grinning. She'd had a perma-smile since the not-so-relaxing shower she'd shared with Zack earlier. And now, even with Elle and Gem sharing the same table, there was definitely a romantic feel in the air. The sun was almost down for the night and the outside tables were covered by a canopy lined with lanterns giving the restaurant a magical aura.

Zack leaned close to whisper in her ear. 'You're awfully quiet this evening.'

It wasn't intentional. They'd been in Ibiza a mere eight hours ago. All that morning sex, travelling and then a bout of pre-evening sex had really done her in. Not to mention the looming deadline reminding her that she was a few days away from never seeing Zack again. It didn't help that he didn't seem bothered by the impending separation, and worse was the fact she shouldn't care either.

'I'm starving,' she said so she didn't have to bend the truth.

He laughed and linked his fingers through hers beneath the table. 'You'll need to top up your energy levels for later. I have plans.'

'Ice cream plans?' she asked, then bit her lip when she realised her friends were at the table too.

Elle made a gagging noise while Gem moaned, 'Are we ever going to get the details?'

'If you want sex advice, Gem, watch porn or better yet, google it,' Zack replied.

Gem crossed her arms and frowned at him. 'I don't *need* advice, I just love the details.'

'Well I don't,' Elle butted in. 'Let's order then talk about something else.'

'Fine by me,' Zack said, then swooped down to nibble on Ciara's earlobe.

Her reaction was instant. Blood simmered through her veins and her breath caught in her throat. Anywhere else she'd give into the sensations but here, now and with her friends as witnesses, she fought for composure and pulled away.

'*Zack!*'

His grin was wicked and his eyes were so dark she could drown in them. The heat raged on in her stomach but she refused to give into it – she couldn't.

'This is getting ridiculous. You two need to lock yourself in a room for a week and get it out of your systems so you can both act normal in public,' Elle said.

Ice spread through her veins as reality set in. That was never going to happen. They were leaving soon, far too soon. Even a week didn't seem long enough. Even if they had a month left she doubted she'd be ready to say goodbye.

The amusement disappeared from Zack's eyes too and he squeezed her hand. 'I'll behave.'

'Thank God for that!' Elle, seemingly satisfied with his promise, waved over a waiter to give their order.

Ciara's head was spinning so much she ordered the first thing that jumped out at her on the menu. Luckily it was a gorgeous, creamy pasta dish and Zack ordered something with a tomato and basil sauce which she got to try.

Still, she didn't track much of the conversation and when the place mostly cleared out and shifted gears for the night, she barely even touched the glass of wine she'd ordered as she pretended to listen to the others.

Zack didn't exactly behave, but even Elle couldn't moan at the occasional kisses he placed on Ciara's head or when he wrapped his arms around her to pull her back so she rested against his chest. She was very aware of him, just not much else and gave up pretending to listen in favour of looking around the Piazza at the church and quaint little buildings.

'Florence is gorgeous, isn't it?' he asked.

She nodded, thinking now was the time to snap out of this heavy mood. Turning to face him, she said, 'I've found a way to see all of it and for under a hundred Euros. Impressed?'

Zack's eyebrows climbed his forehead.

'Don't be dubious. It'll be fun.' She hoped.

'Count us out,' Elle said.

'We didn't come to one of the top fifty fashion capitals of the world to look at paintings,' Gem agreed. 'And the designer outlets here are full of great deals!'

The day she could afford *Prada*, even at 10% off, she might refer to the designer clothes as deals.

'What are you inflicting on me tomorrow then?' he asked.

'Can I borrow your phone?' she held her hands out. When his

brows pulled together she explained, 'There's this Arttour iPhone app I want to download.'

He handed it over silently while Elle laughed.

'Looks like she's dragging you round the museums tomorrow,' Elle said, like that was the most horrifying thing ever.

'Some of the Renaissance pieces are incredible.' He grinned at her, all of his confusion gone.

Ciara couldn't resist, she stuck her tongue out at Elle. She *knew* he'd be into art. After quickly downloading the app she handed back his phone to show she had no ulterior motives – like checking his texts, Twitter account or call log. No matter how tempting.

'You two are weird,' Gem said.

Elle grinned at Gem. 'And perfectly matched. Oh well, it means we can spend some serious time at the shops!'

The waiter set down a bottle of wine with fresh glasses in front of Elle and Gem that none of them had ordered. 'The gentlemen to your right insist that you try this.'

Ciara glanced over at the same time the others did. The table of businessmen was down to two and she had to admit, they were the finest of the bunch.

Elle told the waiter she'd be sure to let them know how the wine was, then poured a glass for her and Gem. 'Okay, before we go over there are ground rules.'

'I really don't think Zack and I were invited,' Ciara said, not really wanting to watch her friends go into full-on flirt mode. She'd much rather go back to the house and have a long, slow, lazy session with her date.

'The rules are for Gem.'

Gem pouted and she and Zack both covered their mouths to stop from laughing.

'I'm not following your five-point seduction plan. They bought us expensive wine which means they want into our knickers, why bother with small talk?'

Now that she had a better understanding of the pressure on

Gem to succeed, she could see why she'd want to go out and have as much fun as she could before real life started. Elle didn't seem impressed though.

'I don't think they're the kind of men we can just walk over and invite home, Gem. A little tact goes a long way.'

'I think this might be our cue to leave them to it,' Zack said to her and she nodded.

Gem tilted her chin, a sign she wasn't happy with Elle. 'Fine, I'll be tactful but the one at the far side's mine. He's making me tingly already.'

'Definitely time to go,' Zack said, pulling her up from the chair.

Ciara had to agree.

He pulled a few notes from his wallet and put them down on the table. A few hundred Euro notes!

She waited until they'd said goodbye and they were walking through the dimly lit streets before she turned to him. 'Why did you leave all that money there? The whole thing probably didn't cost more than a hundred and we were supposed to split it.'

He stopped walking and frowned. 'Habit, I guess. I forgot.'

He forgot to make sure he didn't have to give away more than she had left for the rest of the trip? She wanted to laugh and cry at the same time.

'Zack, do you even want to follow your dreams? I can't help if you think nothing of paying that kind of money for things on a daily basis.'

'I get it, Ciara. It was a mistake. Can we drop this?' he asked, all his usual humour gone as he got serious.

Great, now she was a nagging non-girlfriend. 'I'm sorry. I shouldn't have said anything.'

He sighed and pulled her close. Tucking a loose strand of hair behind her ear, he said, 'It's me who should be sorry. I asked for your help. Getting annoyed because you're helping isn't fair.'

'Nagging isn't fair either.'

That stunning half grin was back making her stomach flip over.

'I promise I'll try harder tomorrow.' He sighed again. 'It's crazy, I've never had to think about money like this before. It's not as easy as people make it seem.'

She rolled her eyes. 'Most people worry about money all the time, but it doesn't make their lives any less happy because of it. You'll be fine.'

The smile disappeared and he nodded, but not in a way that looked like he agreed. Maybe he really didn't want to follow his dreams. Still, the idea of him going back to the office and being miserable day in, day out made her feel just as bad.

'Tomorrow will be fun, I promise.' She'd make sure they had a blast and focus on the important things, like spending quality time with him while she still could.

'I'll hold you to that, Ireland,' he said, his mood seemingly doing a one eighty again.

'Anyway, let's get back. You said you had plans for me?' She was imagining everything he wanted to do to her.

His grin was wicked as he took her hand and led her down the street. 'When don't I?'

Chapter Nineteen

Ciara's hopes for a night of long, lazy sex had been shattered the second Zack got her naked. He'd not only stripped her of clothes, but her inhibitions too. His attention had gone on for hours, using his fingers and tongue until she didn't think it was possible to feel anymore.

That's when he'd made love to her. It hadn't been sex, the emotions coursing through her refused to let her think about it that way.

They'd made love again and again and she could see in his eyes he looked at what they did the same way. She'd never made love to anyone before – it wasn't something she'd ever wanted to do but with Zack she was coming to realise all bets were off.

The next day she threw all her energy into guiding Zack through the artisan workshops in Florence and when she discovered what type of art he preferred, she led him through the Uffizi Gallery with the help of her friend Google so they managed to make it out before tea time. She was determined not to show how affected she was by the night before.

She figured Gem and Elle would still be at the shops so made a point of packing up a basket of food and a bottle of wine quickly. Before he could suggest putting dinner off for later, she dragged him out of the house.

'Where to now?' he asked as they neared the Ponte Vecchio Bridge.

'You'll see.'

She could see all the stalls were lined up, bustling with tourists buying trinkets and gifts to take back home. That actually wasn't a bad idea. When they reached the line of stalls she wasn't impressed with the quality of the merchandise but then for her budget, affordable tat would have to do.

'Looking for something for your dad?' he asked.

Ciara nodded, still scanning the stalls in the hope something would jump out at her. A stand with wooden carved ornaments did and she took off for a closer look. Zack beat her to it, leaving the basket of food and his sketch pad on top to pick up a little carved building.

'This is incredible,' he said.

'What is it?' To her it was a little mini-masterpiece, barely bigger than his hand.

'It's a mini replica of the Duomo. Almost perfect too.'

Thank you Google, at least she'd heard of that Cathedral. 'It's really pretty.'

But the price tag caught her eye and the number on it, wasn't. So much for affordable…

She scanned the others in the stall, all little replicas of buildings and places around the city. There was even a mini carving of Michelangelo's *David*. Still, the cheapest thing there was fifty Euro.

'Let's go, I want to get along the river by sunset.' She picked up his sketch pad and the basket, straining with the thing just to get it off the ground.

'I'll take that,' he said, taking the basket off her. 'Why don't you get your dad one of the sculptures? They're amazing.'

But she was already walking over the bridge, away from the

216

pretty things she couldn't afford. Maybe one day, when she figured out what she wanted to do for a living, she could come back and pick one up. After she'd paid back her da for Oxford of course—

'Ciara, stop for a second.'

She turned around, surprised to realise they weren't just off the bridge but a good twenty feet down the riverbank.

Zack's frown was full of concern. 'It's like you've been running on auto-pilot all day. What's wrong?'

What was *right*? Ciara wasn't sure if she could keep up the pretence anymore. Wasn't this supposed to be all about fun? She tried to remember back to Miami when she'd made the decision to ask Zack to be her holiday fling. She was so sure that's all it would be, just like the others before him she'd get bored after a week or two and be able to walk away with some happy memories.

More. Fool. Her.

But he was still waiting for an answer, and she wasn't sure she had one. One thing she was certain about was that she couldn't lie to him, not when he looked like he genuinely cared.

'There's a bench about half a mile along I thought we could watch the sunset. Can we talk there?' Hopefully by then she'd know what she wanted to say.

He pressed his lips together, clearly not pleased at her evasion but he nodded and then led the way. Guilt was an awful thing she didn't care much for – it had lined her stomach like churning acid for the best part of her life. But it wasn't like she needed the time to think of a lie. She just couldn't put what she was feeling into words yet.

Before she knew it they were at the bench and her mind was blank. While Zack unpacked the food and wine in the middle of the bench, panic tightened her chest until it got hard to breathe.

He glanced over his shoulder then got to pouring the wine. 'I'd rather you said nothing than lied to me. Let's just enjoy the night, no pressure, okay?'

But the pressure didn't ease and now she had an extra well of guilt to add to the mix. 'I wasn't going to lie to you. I just don't know how to put what I'm feeling into words.'

He handed her a plastic glass full of wine, his expression the perfect poker face. Just like Elle's. 'This didn't turn out like either of us expected, did it?'

She shook her head. 'Every time I think about going home I get all miserable.'

The corner of his mouth tilted up. 'Snap.'

'Really?' It was a stupid question considering he'd just told her, but somehow the thought that she wasn't alone with this gave her comfort. But there was still terror there too.

He nodded and sat at the far side of the bench, looking out over the river Arno. 'There's only so long you can go on lying to yourself before it starts to eat you up inside.'

'I'm not sure what you mean.' She sat at the other side of the food, but didn't take her eyes off him.

'You asked if I had ever been in love. I never thought I was. I wanted to be. So I told myself I really was. It ended up hurting us both.'

She knew he meant Vanessa, the woman Gem said asked him to marry her.

'You think I'm lying to myself?' she asked.

He turned to her with a smile that looked more sad than happy. 'I think we both were when we thought it would be easy to walk away from each other with no regrets.'

If regrets were all he had at the end of this, he'd be lucky. She was sure lots of pain was in her immediate future and wasn't looking forward to it one bit. Picking up a sandwich so she had something else to focus on was the only way she could hide her feelings from him. Though she suspected he already knew.

'The question is, where do we go from here?' he asked.

There really only was two options.

'We can enjoy the rest of Italy and deal with what happens

after, or I guess we'll have to say goodbye now.' A sharp pain seemed to filter through her heart when she thought the latter could actually happen. He could get up right now and walk away from her forever.

'You're very black and white, Ireland. Where's the colour, or even the grey?'

She shrugged. 'It's the way my life is, it's either one way or the other. It's always been like that.'

'Life's pointless without colour. Look over there,' he said, pointing to the edge of the city where the sun was setting for the night. 'It's never just night or day. There isn't just bright blue skies then black. Right now there's a full spectrum of oranges, blues and even a little pink.'

She could see what he meant and the sight of the sun setting over the prettiest city she'd ever seen took her breath away. Or maybe that was what Zack was trying to do, talk her around to want more than what they could have. What he didn't know was that she *did* want it, more than anything.

But never, ever at the risk of breaking him the way her ma broke her da.

The reminder of who she could be was exactly what she needed to focus on what this was really about. Now she just had to tweak her plans a tiny bit to make sure things between them didn't fall back into dangerous waters.

***

'Elle Muir if you don't get out of bed right now I'm going to throw every pair of shoes you own out of the window!'

The half-empty threat worked like a charm. Elle sat up, rubbing her eyes and grumbling, 'When did you get so dramatic?'

Gem, who was the first target of Ciara's wake-up call, shuffled into the room behind her. 'I blame you since you're the bossy one by nature. You've created a monster.'

Ignoring the jibe, Ciara walked to the window and pulled the heavy curtains apart until sunlight streamed in through the glass. 'We've got plans today so we need to get moving.'

'We're shopping today,' Elle protested. 'Marco and Luca cut our trip short yesterday to whisk us away to lunch.'

'There's two days left for shopping. I need you with me today and if you try to wiggle out of it, I still have seven more threats to change your mind.' Part one of her new plan was to minimise alone time with Zack and today she had the perfect way to do it.

But she couldn't tell her friends until they got there, otherwise they'd climb back into bed and really, she only had one more threat and there was no way she'd follow through.

'How come Zack's getting out of it?' Elle asked.

Ciara rolled her eyes. 'He's not, we're all going. You both have half an hour before we leave so get to it!'

Zack had insisted on driving which cut the cost considerably and since she'd blown a chunk of her budget on this day trip, she had to be grateful.

He hadn't even moaned when she said she wanted her friends to come with them, which just made it all that harder to stay detached from her feelings, but she was determined to try.

It did take longer than half an hour for her friends to appear in the kitchen demanding coffee before they went anywhere. By the time they'd hit the road to Montalcino it was closer to lunchtime than she'd planned. She just hoped that having her friends there as buffers for anything too deep would work. No doubt Elle would take one look at what she had planned and phone a taxi to take her back to Florence.

So she refused to tell her friends where they were going and when they got to the vineyard, they perked up. Still, it wasn't just wine tasting on the menu and that was the news she was worried about sharing.

'If you'd told us we were going to spend the day getting sloshed at a vineyard we'd have gotten a move on sooner,' Gem said.

'We're not here to get sloshed.' Although tasting first might be a better way to loosen her friends up.

'We could book a hotel close by and make a day of it,' Zack suggested.

Even though she was the one trying to make the fling more about fun than seriousness, the fact that he seemed to be giving up on watching what he spent made her sad. Was it his way of saying he'd made his choice?

'We have dates tomorrow so would have to get back to Florence before noon,' Elle said.

'Easily done. Gem, Ciara, are you in?' he asked.

'Of course,' Gem said.

Ciara nodded, less enthusiastic about his suggestion as they pulled up in front of a massive palazzo in the middle of miles and miles of grapevines. She couldn't blame them for assuming she'd be happy with staying since she'd recommended they take a change of clothes but when she'd told them that it wasn't so they could spend the night and Zack knew it.

'Why don't you three go and meet the tour guide while I sort out a hotel?' he said, pulling his phone from his pocket.

There didn't seem to be a point to grumbling about the cost or much else anymore so she did as he suggested, leading the way into the house with Elle and Gem trailing behind.

***

Ciara suggested discretely to the tour guide that they do a tasting first. They crossed the land to where the red was stored after Zack had caught up. He didn't take her hand, but that might have been because she probably looked like she was in full-on strop mode. Or maybe he just didn't want to anymore. Not something she could blame him for since she was the one choosing to live her life without colour.

221

But nothing was safer than black and white.

After being instructed on how to drink the mouthfuls of wine to fully appreciate the flavours, they were given glasses and glasses of the stuff. Ciara couldn't discern any particular tastes and ended up just necking a few. Before she knew it her head was fuzzy and her mood had improved considerably.

It really was some top quality alcohol, whether she could describe the flavours or not.

She grabbed another with the goal of getting it down as fast as she could but Elle snatched the glass away from her.

'Slow down, Ciara. I don't want to have to clean your sick off the floor later,' Elle said.

'I'm *never* sick when I drink wine,' she protested, going for the glass again.

Gem handed her a glass of water. 'This is to clean your pallet – or sober you up a bit. We've still got the white to try, and then the rose.'

'Sober's no fun,' she said, ignoring the cup of water and going for another wine glass. They both frowned but didn't try to stop her this time and before she knew it she'd necked the sample.

'I liked that one. Is there more of that one, mister?' She pointed to the glasses and the tour host went for a fresh bottle. He was a lovely man.

'Come walk with me, Ciara,' Zack said, prying the empty glass from her hand.

'I'm waiting for wine,' she said, not even slurring her words. What was their problem?

He grinned and it stole her breath. 'It'll be here when we get back. Two minutes, I promise.'

He did look earnest with his pretty dark eyes all wide and sincere. She took his offered hand and walked with him until they were surrounded by grapevines on every side. But Zack was all she could focus on and he had that look again – the one that said he had something to say he knew she wouldn't want to hear.

'You wanted to talk?' she asked, wanting it over with so she could get back to drowning the feelings inside.

'I want a lot of things. Right now, more than anything, I want to go back there and drink every bottle there is just to stop wanting everything else.'

Why did people always speak in riddles around her? 'Why?'

He shrugged. 'Probably the same reason you do.'

Doubtful. All she wanted to do was to revel in the giddy wine glow and not worry about anything else. 'Why did you book a hotel?'

'It seemed like a good idea at the time. Could you face another two hour drive to get back to Florence? I'd rather stay here, get a good night's sleep and go back tomorrow.'

He had a point. Even with the aircon in the car the heat had been uncomfortable. And this way he got the full experience of the day trip too. 'You're right.'

And she was being selfish. She hugged her shoulders.

He tilted her chin up until she was lost in his intense gaze.

'I'd rather you didn't pretend to be okay when you're not. If you don't want to talk about it to me your friends are here. I can keep myself busy for a few hours if you need time with them.'

She didn't deserve him. Even for a fling. 'I couldn't do that to you.'

He smiled again and it was beautiful. He was beautiful. Maybe she did need to slow down on the wine…

'I've brought my sketch pads and have a few ideas I'd like to get drafted before I forget, so it's not a problem. Really.'

Emotions made her throat feel tight and she couldn't think of a way to thank him. Instead she threw her arms around his neck and kissed him with everything she was feeling until they were both gasping and his hands were wandering.

Too soon, he broke away. 'Plus I'm not looking forward to Elle's bitching when you break the news about the other activity on the agenda.'

She wasn't either. She'd hoped Zack would be there to act as a buffer. 'I'm sure after a few more glasses of wine she'll be okay.'

Thing was, she wasn't sure and by the raised brows, neither was he.

Chapter Twenty

'You have got to be kidding?' Elle said, leaving her mouth hang open.

Ciara bit her lip to hold in the giggle at Elle's expression. It was like she'd never seen a barrel full of grapes before.

'This is *amazing*, Ciara! How did you manage to pull this off?' Gem asked.

At least one of her friends looked excited to be here.

'Come on, it's supposed to be fun,' she said, removing her flip flops like they'd been instructed and scrubbing her feet with the water provided.

Gem took the wash basin next to her and scrubbed her feet with gusto. Before they knew it Gem climbed over the edge of the barrel and jumped onto the grapes. The juice being popped out under her weight made a horrible squishing sound and red stains splatted her sundress, but Gem was grinning so wide she didn't seem to care.

'No flippin' way am I getting in there,' Elle said, edging back.

'Wuss,' Ciara said, pulling herself over the barrel to join Gem.

The sensation of the grapes bursting beneath her feet and between her toes was icky, in a really, really fun way like when she was little and thought it was a great idea to go down by the river back home and paddle in the muddy bank.

Elle scowled at them. 'I. Am. Not. A. Wuss. If you were wearing *Gucci* you wouldn't be in there either.'

Gem twirled, stomping the grapes as she went. 'This baby's *Gucci* and it doesn't seem to mind. Clothes are made to be lived in, Elle.'

Ciara tried a little stomping, slipped on the juices and fell into the side of the barrel giggling all the way. 'Come on, Elle. It's *fun*.'

'You and I have very different perspectives on that word.' Elle folded her arms, clearly not willing to budge.

'Fine, don't say you didn't ask for it!' Gem crouched down, picked up a handful of squished red grapes and then lobbed them at Elle.

Their friend tried to move but wasn't quick enough and they splatted the bottom of her purple dress leaving an ugly dark stain.

Gem grinned. 'There, now you don't have the excuse of ruining Gucci.'

'That was out of order!' Elle said, her voice rising an octave or two.

'It's not like you'll ever wear it again. Come on, this *is* fun.'

And Gem was right on both parts. Elle did treat clothes like paper napkins, throwing them out after one use.

'Please, Elle. I know you'll love it!' Ciara added big, puppy dog eyes to her plea.

'Fine if it will shut you both up.' Elle got with the feet scrubbing and she shared a victory grin with Gem. 'Where's Zack anyway. Why isn't he getting forced to do this?'

'He said he was giving us girl time,' she lied. Well it wasn't quite a lie, just not the whole truth.

Elle climbed in, wrinkling her nose as her feet touched the grapes. 'More like he planned a lucky escape. Ewww.'

Gem upped the stomping until Elle shot her a death glare. Ciara couldn't hold back the giggle. 'Let's get wine making!'

It was hard not to find Elle's expression funny as she gingerly lowered foot after foot into the barrel, probably avoiding all the lumpy bits on purpose. Once the fruit was mostly gunk, they slowed down a bit and focused on the areas still needing to be squished.

That's when Gem decided to get perceptive. 'I'll bet Zack not being here has something to do with the way you guzzled that wine earlier.'

'What *was* that about?' Elle asked, shifting to sit on the edge of the barrel, then scowling at the gunk on her feet.

She really did need girl time but this talking stuff was getting harder, especially when it came to him. 'The thought of leaving soon is depressing me. I'll never get to see you both a fraction as much.'

'We'll only be an hour away on the plane,' Gem said, hugging her round her waist. 'And we'll talk all the time, I promise.'

Her eyes got all blurry as she hugged Gem back. But when she saw the annoyance on Elle's face, shock stopped them in their tracks.

'And Zack?' her friend asked.

'Has he said what he wants to do yet?' Gem threw in.

Ciara shook her head slowly. 'I'll miss him, too. And I don't know if he'll follow his dream or stay working for the company. We haven't talked about it since Ibiza.'

Elle didn't look mollified. 'That's not what I meant.'

Ciara had a feeling she knew what Elle meant and an argument about why she should try to make things work was not what she had in mind when Zack suggested she speak to them. 'Nothing's changed for either of us. Can we drop it please?'

'Sometimes you can be so stupid it's a wonder you got into Oxford at all,' Elle said, then sighed. 'But you're wrong. Everything's changed. That's the last I'm saying about it.'

Ciara nodded, but it was more of an acknowledgement than agreement. 'I think we're done with the grape squishing.'

'Thank God.' Elle jumped out of the barrel and headed straight to the washbasins. 'Remind me never to believe you when you say you have a fun day planned.'

'I thought it was fun, and we've got more wine to taste later,' Gem said.

Ciara had a feeling she was going to need more. Lots more.

***

They went back to the hotel to change for the evening and send their clothes to be laundered so they had something to wear home tomorrow. She found Zack in their room on the bed, scribbling super-fast across his sketch book. There were rulers and other weird shaped measuring devices on the bed next to him and he was so engrossed in what he was doing, he didn't notice she was there until she slid onto the mattress beside him.

'Wow, that's incredible,' she said, gaping at the sketch of a building he'd drawn.

It looked like an old block of flats that had been given a facelift and she recognised something about the shape of them, like she'd seen it somewhere before. He distracted her from delving into her memory.

'Did you all have fun?'

'All bar Elle.' She grinned remembering her friend's discomfort. 'She wasn't so keen on squishing fruit with her feet.'

'I can imagine. I'd have loved to see her face.' He closed the pad and put it on the cabinet next to the bed.

'It was a picture. What are you working on?'

He shrugged. 'Nothing much. Just a potential project.'

'For your company?'

He shook his head.

'Zack that's amazing! And it's really, really good. How can they not want your drawings?' She threw her arms around him, completely forgetting her dress was covered in grape juice.

228

'There's more to it than that. The closing date's coming up and I'm not the only one interested.'

He didn't meet her eyes when he spoke and she could sense his discomfort in his rigid pose. The where's, how's and when's would have to wait until he was ready to talk to her, but she could just burst with excitement for him.

And happiness. He was going to make his dream come true after all!

'I'll keep everything crossed for you,' she said, climbing onto his lap. 'Now how about some celebrating?'

'Don't you normally wait until you have something worth celebrating?' he asked, but it didn't stop him from sliding his hands beneath her dress to squeeze her bum.

'This is worth it! We'll celebrate the possibility.' Before he could say anything else, she threaded her fingers through his hair and kissed him.

This was always so easy, almost natural, but her reaction was overpowering each time their lips met and now was no different.

He slid his hands up to expertly unhook her bra and that's all it took for her patience to expire. She broke the kiss, ripping at his shirt buttons until they popped free and she could get her hands on all that gorgeously smooth, ripped muscle.

Zack didn't make a comment about her impatience, even though he generally did. She guessed he was just as desperate for this as she was, like it had been much, much longer than a day since she'd joined with him.

Soon they were naked and she was ready for him, bugger wasting time with foreplay – no matter how amazing it was with him.

He lay her back so her head was close to the bottom of the bed and he followed her down so it was just them, skin on skin with nothing in the way. Just how she liked it.

Tilting her hips was the only invitation he needed until he slid home. Ciara revelled in the stretch of her muscles, digging her heels into his backside to bring him in all the way. He stopped moving, pulled her arms above her head and linked fingers with her.

She looked right into his eyes and she could see the emotion burning there. The same emotion burning through her. 'This really feels like you're mine, Ciara. It makes me never want to let you go.'

She didn't have a chance to reply or even to think about what he'd said. He took her mouth and started moving in a way that wiped her mind clean of everything else except her and him, joined together and hurtling towards something incredible.

Chapter Twenty-One

After a lovely dinner and more wine tasting, Ciara was too shattered to think, never mind find a way to broach a conversation about what he meant earlier. Zack must have been too because he let her fall asleep in his arms that night without an attempt at seduction or a hint that he wanted to talk.

By the time they'd got back to Florence and Elle got all the bitching about losing precious shopping time out of her system, Ciara decided a long, long bubble bath might help her put her thoughts together.

It only served to make her even more confused and finding Zack's note saying he'd just nipped out for a bit meant she was left in the big house by herself. She tried flipping on the TV but the subtitles started to annoy her. Next she tried organising her case so she only had to pack whatever she wore from now until tomorrow night could be crammed in and she'd be ready to go.

It didn't take as long as she hoped.

Next she tried for a little sunbathing in the garden which seemed like a good idea since her tan from Greece was fading fast, but even then her mind churned and uneasiness pulsed through her muscles, making her jittery.

More proof, like she needed it, that there was no hope for her to keep Zack at all.

Or a job – if she could get one.

And that would mean no kids, no family of her own.

So much for figuring things out. More like drive herself insane.

Her phone chimed with a text from Elle saying they were staying out tonight with Marco and Luca.

Brilliant. Now she had no buffer against Zack.

Giving up sunbathing, she headed for the kitchen in search of food. Since Zack was with them the fridge was full of the good things in life with barely a lettuce leaf to be found. She fried some tomatoes and scrambled a few eggs with Worcester sauce and as she sat down at the table to eat her comfort food, his sketch pads caught her eye.

Ciara went for the smaller one since she'd never had a peek in it yet and almost choked on a mouthful of eggs when she opened it.

It was a sketch of her, asleep the night she stayed in LA. At least she assumed it was her. The cheekbones looked softer in the drawing and the shadows across her face made the woman look more beautiful than she could be. Then there was her hair, which was smooth and perfect, unlike her scary, strewn-across-the-pillow look.

Shoving the plate aside she brought the pad closer and flipped to the next page.

This one was definitely from Miami. She was lying on the sofa, completely naked – although her lady bits were tactfully shaded out. It wasn't creepy like she'd expected something like this would be. He'd focused on her face, managing to catch an expression that could only be described as wonder.

A lump formed in her throat as she remembered that feeling so well. And it hadn't anything to do with what he could do with a tub of mint choc chip and his tongue. It had been the man beneath the talent that had fascinated her.

She could see an outline of something else through the paper but her eyes were watering now and she couldn't face anymore, so shut the pad.

All that worrying in Paris that he didn't want her and after, in Santorini when she worried he wouldn't come with her for the rest of the trip. She shook her head.

She'd been so self-absorbed she hadn't noticed Zack was falling for her all along, her own angst about how she felt overshadowing everything. She'd gone and done what she swore she never would and hurt someone she cared about.

Or at least she'd have to now.

A tear slid down her cheek and landed on the paper, but she wiped the rest away determined to pull it together. She had to stop this now, bugger how miserable she'd be.

The time for being selfish was over. She just hoped it wasn't too late for him.

***

Zack returned a little while later with a box of pizza and a few bags. She ignored the delicious smell of grilled cheese and herbs – her appetite had long since vanished.

'Sorry, I didn't mean to be gone so long so I come bearing pizza. Are the girls still out?' he asked, putting the box and bags down on the kitchen table.

'They have dates.'

He kissed her before she could stop him. It was brief and sweet, but also sad considering it would be her last.

'Good, then we have the house to ourselves.' His grin almost sent her over the edge into full blown misery.

'Zack, we need to talk.'

He took the opposite chair, opened the pizza box and removed a slice. 'I'm listening.'

She could almost believe he didn't know what this was about

if it wasn't for the mechanical way he chewed and the forced air of nonchalance.

The lump in her throat got so big it was hard to breathe, never mind speak but she had to force the words out. 'It feels like we're falling into a relationship and I never meant for that to happen. *We* can't happen. Not for the long haul.'

He placed the slice of pizza back in the box and folded his arms. 'If you didn't want it to go this far, why didn't you pull back sooner?'

Her mouth opened and closed but the only sound was her breath hitching in her throat.

He nodded, like she'd proved his point. Like he was expecting this conversation at some point. 'Because like me, deep down, you didn't want to.'

He couldn't be more right, but that was the selfish bitch in her. 'I can't be with you properly. It would never work and I'll end up hurting you.'

'If you're going to throw away everything we have, I think the least you can do is explain why you think that.'

He seemed too calm and collected for a conversation that must be killing him. Either he believed she'd come round somehow or would keep trying to change her mind. Maybe if he knew the real reason she could never risk a relationship, he'd stop trying.

'Okay, I'll explain. Do we have any wine left from yesterday?' She didn't even care if it was wine or absinth, the stronger the better.

Zack shook his head. 'We do this just me and you with clear heads.'

Dammit. She took up playing with her fingers to steel her attention away from legs that wanted to bolt for the nearest exit.

'My ma left us when I was little. From what I remember, she had a different job every month, got bored so easily that she was always off on mad adventures with her friends, eating out all the time and hitting the pubs or bingo at night. I can't honestly remember a night where she made us dinner or stayed in to tuck me into bed.'

Her eyes watered again remembering and she had to wipe her eyes.

'I'm so sorry, Ciara. She sounds like a really shitty mum.' He reached across for her hand but she pulled them beneath the table.

'I didn't tell you so you'd feel sorry for me. What I'm trying to say is I'm exactly like my ma.'

His brows pulled together. 'You're not a party girl.'

'That's not what I mean. My ma had the same… itch, I suppose, to keep busy. It's like adrenaline burning through us making us so jittery we just need to go do something. I focused on school-work to keep me occupied seeing how upset my da was after she'd had enough of family life and disappeared.'

She scrubbed her eyes again, but they were dry this time. 'It's why deep down I'm worried I'll never be satisfied in a job. I've had enough short-term boyfriends and got bored of them to know I can't guarantee that five, maybe ten years from now I'll walk away from a family. I'd never want to do that.'

His poker face was back, making her shift on her chair. 'And to make sure you don't, you refuse to put yourself in a position where you risk hurting them.'

'That's it, exactly.' She sighed, relieved that he understood.

'So tell me, at what point would you say it's okay to walk away, making sure both parties stay unscathed?'

The edge to the question explained the poker face. He didn't understand, he was flat out mad and trying to hide it. 'It's not a science, Zack. I didn't mean for things to go this far with us. I got so caught up in everything I didn't realise how much time had gone by until we were leaving Santorini.'

He ran a hand down his face and unclenched his jaw. 'Yeah, I know. I'm just trying to work it all out. Have you asked your dad why she left?'

'He said she had things she needed to do and he didn't know when she'd be back. I knew she wasn't ever coming though. She didn't just go through jobs, but friends too and when I got older I heard rumours about her affairs, though I didn't really believe them. Still, it wouldn't surprise me. We weren't enough to hold her attention.'

Even her da's seemingly undying love wasn't enough. Their bedroom was still like a shrine to her. He filled up vases with different flowers every week like she'd done because every week she wanted something new and exciting. Their wedding photo still stood proud on the mantelpiece, like he was just waiting for her to come back to show he still loved her but Ciara knew better.

The only difference between her and her ma was she'd witnessed what it was like to be left by someone, she'd felt the agony of it too. She could *never* inflict that on anyone. The guilt would eat her up inside.

'You're not like her at all,' he said confidently. 'Sorry, Ireland, but your mum was self-centred and only cared about herself. You're her opposite.'

'The basics are the same. I still get bored easily, just ask Elle and Gem. I drove them mad in Miami before you got there and in Santorini I almost went crazy at having nothing to do. Now university is over I need to find something else to take that itch away so I don't hurt my da, too.'

'I've never seen you like that.'

He came round the table and took the seat next to her. His aftershave mixed with the fizzle between them acted like a black hole, effortlessly sucking her in but she had to find a way to break free from him. Either that or she'd end up giving in and hurting them both.

'You've never felt like that around me, have you?' he pressed.

'That's not the point. Who says a month or even a year down the line that won't change? It's not now I'm worried about.' She let him see her honesty, hoping he'd get it.

236

'Even if I believed you could just walk away if you got 'bored', isn't it my risk to take? Ciara, I don't want to be without you.'

She imagined giving in all too easily. They'd be happy for a while, maybe even longer than a while. If he could talk her into a relationship then why not marriage and someday, kids? Then she'd have more on her conscience when the day came that she couldn't fight the jittery burn that came with repetition.

'No, I'm sorry. I can't risk doing that to you.' She rose to go and he did too, trapping her against him and the table. 'Zack, please don't do this.'

'Funny, I was about to say the same thing to you. Tell me if this is something you'll always miss, always crave, or can imagine never wanting again.'

His mouth met hers with a fierce determination that knocked her off-kilter. All she could do was cling to him as he pushed through her resistance, kissing her like he'd never kissed her before.

Though she kissed him back, tears ran down her cheeks because she wanted this, she couldn't imagine never wanting this but she couldn't see the future. Statistics and experience was all she had to go on and the likelihood that she'd leave was favoured by her calculations.

So when he pulled away she tried to let her apology shine from her eyes, but she was too devastated by his cold expression to speak.

'You don't need to say anything else, I get the message.' He pulled away and the chilly air that replaced his heat might as well have been liquid nitrogen. 'There's something for your dad in the bags and something for you too.'

'Zack…' Her voice was just a whisper. She didn't have a clue what to say.

'Don't.' He held up a hand. 'Honestly, I wish I could say I have no regrets but that's not true.'

'I'm so, so, sorry.' But he didn't hear her. He was already on his way out of the kitchen.

Glancing over his shoulder, he said, 'I thought what my granddad was offering was the worst thing for me, but I never expected this from you. Scared or not, I never thought you'd give up love so easily, especially after what your mother did.'

Love? Was that why her heart felt like it was shattering into a thousand tiny splinters in her chest? Before she could process the thought or control the heartache the front door slammed shut, shattering the silence with his departure.

She sunk into the chair, pushed the pizza box out of the way, let the tears flow free and her chest rip through the sobs.

***

That night was the longest and most depressing of her life. Zack hadn't returned, neither had Gem or Elle and all she had for company was his drawings of her, the wooden carving of the cathedral he'd bought for her dad and a personalised phone cover he'd had made with pictures of Gem, Elle and her from LA to Santorini.

It was the sweetest thing anyone had ever done and more than once she'd had to stop herself from calling him and saying she'd made a mistake.

But reality always won out. He was hurting now and so was she but it could be much, much worse if she gave in.

The sun had long since come up when her tears ran dry and sleep claimed her, but in no time at all she was being shaken back to consciousness.

'What's wrong?' she asked, her voice still groggy from sleep.

'We could ask you the same thing!' Gem said at the same time Elle demanded, 'Where's Zack?'

She sat up, rubbed her eyes and realised it was dark outside. Shit, she'd slept through the whole day?

'I don't know where he is,' she said, wondering if he came back to talk and she'd missed it.

'Did you two have a fight?' Gem asked, sitting down next to her. Ciara nodded. 'Why didn't you call us?'

'I didn't want to ruin your dates.' She'd made a mess of her love life, why should her friends suffer more of the same?

Elle's eyes narrowed. 'So you're saying this happened last night. What else aren't you telling us? Zack can be stubborn but he'd never leave you alone for a full day without calling me.'

Her vision blurred again – and here she'd thought she was all cried out. 'We broke up.'

'Aw Ciara,' Gem said, wrapping her arms around her.

'You mean you dumped him.' Elle folded her hands across her chest, looking more pissed off than she'd ever seen her. 'How *could* you?'

'How could I not? We were going to go our separate ways tomorrow anyway. I just realised that it was getting too deep so stopped it before anyone could get really hurt.' But even she knew it was too little too late.

Elle shook her head. 'I suppose the puffy eyes you're sporting are from laughing all night? Do you honestly believe that shit you're talking?'

'Elle, stop,' Gem pleaded.

Elle threw her hands in the air. 'Why? I'm sick of hearing it. You know what I think, Ciara? That you're not trying to protect guys but instead so terrified to fall in love in case they *leave you* one day like your mum did. And so you've fucked over every single one who's been unlucky enough to like you and now Zack, who I actually believe really loves you.'

She couldn't respond, not to deny or agree because it felt more like Elle had kicked her in the ribs than shouted at her.

'Elle, stop being a bitch. She's hurting.' Now Gem was the one scowling.

'It's her choice to hurt! If she didn't dump him she'd still be

239

happy. If you're going to feel sorry for anyone it should be Zack.' Elle's face was flushed with fury as she shrieked out the words, each one feeling like a lash of a whip to her skin.

Ciara didn't back down though, because she knew she'd done the right thing. Even if it was a little too late. 'I know I deserve to be upset, I deserve much worse for letting things get this far. But what about later, when he is in love with me or if we ever got married and have kids? It would be worse then. Much worse.'

Elle got in her face. 'You're walking away from the best thing that's ever happened to you because of some lie you tell yourself. You might share a selfish bitch gene with your mum but boredom isn't an illness, Ciara.'

'Elle, Cia, *please*. We shouldn't be fighting like this!' Gem said, and Elle turned her fury to their friend.

'So what? I just ignore the fact that she broke my cousin's heart. And even if I could, do you know what this means now? Our granddad doesn't just want him to take over the business but thinks Zack marrying Vanessa would be a perfect way to secure the partnership between our company and her dad's. The only reason he managed to get out of the shot gun wedding in Munich was because he cared about Ciara.'

She was too stunned to speak. But that explained so much, especially his misery when he got to Ibiza.

Elle turned to her and poked a finger into her chest. 'And, since you heard our conversation in the kitchen you'll know he was given an ultimatum. He could leave and do what he wanted but without a salary or funds to help him set up, or stay at the company and hopefully see sense about Vanessa. He said either way he'd be giving up something he couldn't live without and *you* were one of those things.'

Gem's mouth popped open. 'What was the other thing?'

'Granddad. He was pissed off that Zack left to come with us for a girl he'd never met and didn't trust. Zack thought he'd lose him if he chose Ciara.'

'I didn't realise staying a director would mean he had to marry his ex,' Ciara said, gobsmacked that he left out that little bit of info.

'It wouldn't, not when granddad calmed down. He doesn't want Zack wasting his life and thinks at thirty he should be settled down already. From what I hear the fight was awful.' Elle seemed calmer, like she'd gotten the worst of her fury out.

Ciara rubbed her temples. 'It all sounds insane.'

Elle shook her head and crossed to the dresser, picking up Ciara's phone. 'What's insane is that you haven't called him yet. Here,' she tossed over the phone. 'Tell him you're sorry and ask if you can talk. He'll come back, Cia.'

She stared wide-eyed at the little bit of plastic. If only what Elle said changed something, changed her even, but it didn't. All she knew now was that she'd broken his heart, just like she'd feared all those weeks ago that she would.

'I can't do that, Elle. We're over.'

They stared at each other until her eyes stung. Finally, something cracked through Elle's expression that looked suspiciously like hatred.

'You're not the person I thought you were. I don't have time in my life for callous shits like you.'

Ciara covered her mouth to stop the sob as Elle turned around and left. Like Zack last night, she just slammed the front door and she had a horrible feeling Elle wouldn't be back either. After all, they could easily send for their things and get a rescheduled flight home.

'Gem, I don't think she'll ever forgive me.' Ciara couldn't hold in the sobs anymore.

'I think you might be right,' Gem said, pulling her close and letting Ciara cry against her shoulder for what felt like hours.

Dublin/Home

Chapter Twenty-Two

Week Two

Ciara flipped to the help wanted page of the third weekly news-paper she'd bought that day. She didn't have much hope that this one would be any different from the other two but she had to try.

The café she'd chosen to wait for Gem was quiet despite it being a Saturday morning but then she guessed most people would be out at the shops or maybe even at home with their families.

Not that her da was around to spend time with. Business was booming and he was out working the weekend with two of his new employees. She couldn't believe that even after he'd paid her tuition he was still working himself to the bone. Then again she could relate too. She wished she had something to keep her mind busy. Zack invaded her thoughts more and more as the days went on.

'Another latte?' the waitress asked.

'Please,' Ciara said, handing over her empty mug.

'We're looking for someone to cover maternity here if you need a job,' the woman said.

She looked around the café, seriously considering applying

since she'd still to find anything else. 'Do I just hand in a CV? I've worked at a café like this when I was at university.'

'Even better, it means you can work your way round a coffee machine. You wouldn't believe how many people manage to block it by filling the thing in the wrong compartments.'

Instead of saying she knew exactly what the woman meant by doing the same thing her first time filling a coffee machine, she smiled. 'I'll drop it in on Monday.'

It didn't take long until she had a fresh latte in hand and a glimmer of hope that her almost empty purse might see a penny or two in the near future.

'Sorry I'm late,' Gem said, when she burst through the door.

Ciara's smile got wider. It had been almost two weeks since she saw her friend, despite texting and emailing. But it hadn't been a happy fortnight. 'Let me guess, you hung back again to see if you could catch a glimpse of the pilot?'

Gem rolled her eyes. 'Any other time you'd be right, but not today.' After dumping her brolly and removing her coat, she said, 'Does it ever stop raining in Dublin?'

'Not since I got back.' It felt like the dingy sky and miserable weather was underscoring her mood.

Her friend sat down across from her and Ciara could tell by the serious expression she wasn't going to like whatever Gem had to say. 'I got a call from Elle when I landed and missed my taxi.'

Her heart started pounding fast until she blurted, 'How is she? I haven't heard from her since… well, you were there.'

She still hated remembering their argument, never mind talking about it but she had tried like mad to make things right to the point she could give a stalker a run for their money.

'I do. Cia, she asked me to tell you to stop calling. She has nothing to say. I'm so sorry.'

'Oh.' It was hardly surprising. Elle had rejected every one of her calls, ignored her text and emails and even unfriended her on social media.

'I told her to stop being a cow but you know Elle. That just made her mad.' Gem wrinkled her nose. 'This is getting ridiculous though.'

'Don't give her a hard time. It's my fault. If I'd just gone to bed alone the first night we were in LA instead of kissing him, we'd still be friends.'

That's the part she was struggling with the most. On one hand, she couldn't regret what happened with Zack – just how it ended between them. On the other, she lost a friend and possibly the best thing that had ever happened to her.

'You can't help how you felt. I totally get the forbidden lust thing.' Gem sighed.

'Don't tell me you met someone you can't have?' she asked with faux disbelief, more than happy to change the subject.

Gem nodded, then took a sip of Ciara's latte. 'This is really good.'

'You can have it if you spill. Come on, I want gossip!' For the first time in ages she actually did. She'd spent so long asking her da about the gossip in town and what happened at work at the end of each day just to keep her mind busy but this was different.

Gem studied her carefully, probably to make sure a story of boy-meets-girl didn't set off the waterworks.

'I'm fine, really.'

Gem nodded. 'One of my dad's lab assistants, Brian. I know, the name's dishwater dull but he's not. He's older though, like 34 but the pheromone levels are off the charts. I swear I'm going home every night running through my vibrators like a sex craved maniac.' Gem shivered. 'I tingle just thinking about it.'

She wished Elle was there to stop Gem before she got into the lurid fantasy bit, but she wasn't and Ciara refused to dwell on the whys. For now. 'Surely he notices your hotness?'

Gem's cheeks actually turned pink – which was a first. 'I think he feels it too, and he's definitely into me. I've seen him eyeing up my arse.'

'So why are you blushing?' She had to ask. It was the first time she'd seen Gem embarrassed about anything.

'We were working late on some research and I couldn't concentrate, I was too revved up! So I kissed him. Just as I thought he was getting into it I took things a step further and he pushed me away.'

'He didn't want anything to happen?' That baffled her. Gem was gorgeous.

'Oh he wanted it. His dick was so hard it was bursting out of his trousers.' Gem's eyes glazed over and the shiver was back. 'It's. HUGE.'

This was just getting more and more confusing. 'Why did he stop? Oh, is it because he works for your dad?'

'Not even close. I tried again, even propositioned a night or two of hot, sweaty and *kinky* sex. I was that desperate! He said he was looking for more than a bit of fun, but if I wanted to date him he'd take me out. Can you believe the nerve? I practically throw myself at him and he says 'no sex until we've dated first'!'

'Isn't that a good thing? It means he doesn't want to use you.' It was more than most guys would do.

'I explained my super orgasm theory and that I reckoned with him it would be beneficial for us to get down and dirty as soon as possible. He *laughed* at me. Then said that might be true, but if I don't agree to date him first I'll never know for sure. Can you believe him?' Gem fisted her hands, but the blush was brighter than ever.

'Gem, do you want to date him?' she asked.

More blushing. Right to the hairline. 'No. Maybe.' She threw her hands up in an Elle-like gesture. 'How would I know? I've never dated anyone.'

'Maybe it would be a nice change for you. And I think you really like him too, and not just for what his dick can do for you.' It would explain the blush and why she was getting all worked up over a guy she hadn't had sex with.

Her lips twisted in that way they did when she was thinking something through. 'I could try it. Then record the progress, like an experiment.'

Ciara shook her head, wondering why she bothered at all. 'Or you could just get to know him and he can get to know you, like normal people do when they're dating.'

'I like the experiment idea better.'

Ciara grinned, completely unsurprised. 'I've missed your inner geek.'

'Same here! Now are we going back to Blessington to hit the pubs? I can't wait to be surrounded by Irish men.' Gem's eyes glittered again.

'What about Brian?' she asked, pulling her coat on.

'We aren't dating *yet*.'

Ciara rolled her eyes and left a few coins on the table.

Week Three

'I bumped into Mrs Hodge this morning,' her da said as he came into the kitchen.

Ciara had his dinner on the table for him coming home since she'd only worked the morning shift at the café. It felt good to work, even better to come home at the end of the day and spend some quality time with him.

'Mmm,' she said, not really caring what Mrs Hodge had to say but it was going to be a long depressing night where she'd send another email to Elle which would no doubt go unanswered, go over and over the reason why she'd lost her friend and end up crying into her pillow when she realised how much she *still* missed Zack. So she asked, 'What did she say?'

'You remember her son, Tony? He's at the high school now but he's struggling with math. She asked if you'd mind helping him some nights and said she'd give you something for your trouble.'

'Like a tutor?' she asked, skewering a hunk of cod with her fork and popping it into her mouth.

'I suppose that's what they're called,' he said, joining her at the table. 'It would be nice if you could find a use for that fancy degree of yours.'

He dug into his own meal, letting her think things through. He was right of course, if she didn't do something vaguely math related then she'd wasted four years of her life and a *lot* of her family's money. And how hard could it be? She'd been working at college level by the time she hit high school.

'I'll help,' she said, feeling a zing of excitement for the first time in weeks. 'It could be really fun.'

He tried to hide his smile behind a hunk of fish but she caught it. 'That's great, because I told her you'd be round at seven.'

She rolled her eyes. It had been the same thing with Oxford. He'd applied and then, when she got accepted, planted the suggestion until she came round to the idea. At least this time there wasn't an argument about it.

'Can't wait.'

***

To: Elle Muir, Gemma Howard
From: Ciara Bree

Subject: Catching up

Hi girls,

Just checking in to see what you've been up to? Gem, any progress with Brian yet?

Elle, I really hope you're settling into the business. Gem tells me your granddad is really proud of how far you've come. I'm so happy for you and I bet you're loving bossing around those interns!

This week has been crazy busy. I started working at a café in Dublin part-time and twice a week I'm tutoring a local boy in maths. I'm really enjoying it and have just discovered an open learning university are looking for part-time distance learning tutors! It's got me really excited, but of course I might not get the job. Fingers crossed!

I miss you both so, so much. Sometimes I wish we were back at uni, chatting about this stuff over a bottle of something strong. Those days were the best. I'm so glad I met you girls.

Love you both,

Cia

xxx

***

To: Ciara Bree, Elle Muir
From: Gemma Howard

Subject: Zomifuckinggod!

Ladies, forget super hormones, even super pheromones. You need to find yourselves a Brian! After dating this fine specimen for over a week, I begged on my hands and knees for him to give me a go on his disco stick and what a go it was! I spent the weekend in his bed and we were late to work on Monday because I couldn't get enough. I will give you the details later. I'm too knackered to get it right. Oh and the dating isn't as bad as I thought it was going to be, though it does include a LOT of non-naked time which is a shame.

Cia, that's great! Did you get the job? Sorry I've been MIA.

Elle, what's new? You've been quiet.

Love Gem

(Definitely not in a gay way. I'll never turn now I've had a go of Brian's dick)

xxx

***

To: Elle Muir, Gemma Howard
From: Ciara Bree

Subject: Re Zomifuckinggod

SEE? I told you dating wouldn't be so bad! My retinas could have done without the page long description of his privates, followed by a verse on how talented his tongue is around your body – but I'm so happy that you've found someone you gel with, in and out of the bedroom.

Still, I feel like I know Brian better than I should… ;o)

I got the job! And the course I'll teach starts at the end of this month – I can't wait! Oh and I've got two more private students, one who's struggling with the math part of his uni course in Dublin and another who's in school. I really think this is my calling, I just hope it sticks.

I've been speaking with my da about the way I get sometimes. He said I should go to the doctor so I've made an appointment next week. I know it's a waste of time, I am who I am and can't change that but he's worried about me so I'll go.

Elle, I'm sorry for calling all the time. I know you don't want to talk to me, so I promise I'll stop. I'm always here if you ever want to talk, or anything. I miss you so much. You're the glue that put us all together and you taught me everything about being a woman. I fucked up really bad and can't ever put that right if you don't let me try.

Love you both, always

(Maybe even in a gay way)

Cia

xxx

***

To: Ciara Bree
From: Gemma Howard

Subject: Just remember I love you too…

Cia,

I think visiting the doctor was a great idea. How did it go? I called earlier but I guess you're working. Hope things are okay.

Sorry I didn't get back over the weekend – I went down to London to visit Elle.

I wanted to tell you but with work and Brian I never seem to have much me-time anymore.

The silly cow has a stubborn streak to rival Hitler's, I swear. She's so thick-skulled that she'd probably survive if I swung a golf club full force at her head! I know you're worried about her but don't be. Remember Marco? The guy she met in Florence? Well, they've been hooking up every other weekend and I think she wants to get close to him. Still, you know Elle. She hates giving up the upper ground and refuses to admit she likes him. He's the same so there's no moving forward as far as I can see.

She does still care about you though, I can tell with how upset she got when I mentioned you. Please don't give up on her. She needs time but she'll come around eventually, I know she will.

Elle told me something I'm not sure you'll want to know, but I can't let you go on worrying. Zack didn't stay to run the company. Elle says he's off somewhere trying to start his own business doing what he loves. She didn't give details. I actually think she told me so I could pass the info on. We both know how much you care about him.

I had to do this privately but include Elle in a reply about what the doctor said. Love never goes away completely.

Listen to me with all this love shit! It's like I've quit science in favour of witchcraft.

LOVE Gem.

Mwah!

xxx

***

To: Gemma Howard, Elle Muir
From: Ciara Bree

Subject: The verdict

Sorry I haven't replied, Gem. It's been a rough couple of weeks and I didn't feel much like talking to anyone.

The doctor told me it sounded like I had problems with anxiety. Me. Anxiety? Not that easy to believe considering all I've been through and managed to keep so calm that the slogan could be named after me.

He referred me to a feckin psychiatrist! Can you believe it? I've never heard so much shit come out of a GPs mouth before but there you go. I need help, apparently.

I'm only going to humour my da. He's been pushing me to make the appointment so I did, on the condition he told me the real reason my mam left us.

He told me he'd loved her since he first laid eyes on her. He wanted a family so badly but knew deep down it wasn't the right place for her!

He'd hoped she'd love him back but she never did and got bored with the village life so basically buggered off one day after fucking half the townsfolk. Now she lives in Belfast with another man who likes keeping on the go like her. They could be swingers for all I know!

After wondering if she was even alive for all these years and watching da suffer, I'm so furious with her that some days I wish she had just died and saved us all this shit. I know that's awful to think and maybe a psychiatrist is a good thing so I can get all this out of my head and move on with my life. Maybe it won't do a thing.

Either way, I'll know for sure next week.

Will keep you posted.

Cia

xxx

***

To: Elle Muir, Gemma Howard
From: Ciara Bree

Subject: Non-ranty email. Promise.

Thanks Gem. I've calmed down since I sent the other email. You don't need to come over, I'm fine, promise. It would be good to see you though. And Brian, I'd love to meet him! Obviously you two can't stay here. I don't think my da could take the noise ;o)

You're more than welcome too, Elle. I hope things with you and Marco are going well.

I saw the psychiatrist and I'm so glad I did. He helped me dig into things in my past that I had no idea still affected me. It took me ages to accept ma leaving and even longer to actually feel anything after. I threw myself into school work to take my mind off it and studied like mad, just to avoid letting the pain in. He thinks that's why I can't relax now, why I always have to be on the go and I agree. Whenever I felt antsy it was because I didn't want to think about anything too deeply, like exam stress, my ma.

Zack.

I wish I'd done this sooner, because maybe things could have been different. We talked about Zack a lot. Sorry, Elle. I don't know if you even read these emails anymore but if you do, then this is me finally able to put what I feel into words and I think you should hear it.

You were right. I was shit scared to love him, just not for the reason I believed. Now I see that growing up and watching my dad in pain made me subconsciously avoid anything that could cause that kind of agony to me. All that, along with my own repressed feelings is likely the cause of my anxiety.

But even though I was scared, I did do love him. I know it's too little, too late, but I wanted you to know everything so you can see I didn't do this on purpose.

More than anything, I just want my friend back. With you two in my life I can get through all the other shit.

Cia

xxx

Chapter Twenty-Three

Week Six
The sun beat down on Ciara's little 2004 Ford Fiesta as she waited in another traffic jam to get out of the city. Making a mental note to reschedule her Thursday appointment to later in the evening, she turned off the motorway opting to take the country route back home.

It was amazing what a few weeks of therapy, Rita Ora blaring from the speakers and a job she loved could do to make her happy. And even if Elle still wasn't talking to her she had Gem. She had her da and was working on forgiving her ma – everything as per her psychiatrist's suggestions.

Her phone chimed and she picked it up. Elle's name flashed on the screen and she was so stunned to receive a text from her friend that she missed the turnoff to Blessington. She kept going until she saw a good spot to park up, then opened the message.

Cia, I don't know what to say anymore, it's been so long. I wanted you to know I am here. I do care. And if you really did too, you'd visit this address.

She didn't recognise the rural address and still hadn't upgraded her phone – not that it would matter out here in the sticks. She was surprised even a text got through. Grabbing for the gear stick she pressed down on the clutch, checked her mirrors then froze. There was only one person Elle would want her to visit – Zack. Ciara pulled the handbrake on and sat there, listening to the rapid heartbeat in her ears. She tried the deep breathing technique the psychiatrist had taught her and it worked a little. But from the panic constricting her chest she knew she wasn't ready to go find him. Maybe she wouldn't be for a long time.

Maybe she wouldn't be ever.

His expression in Florence when she broke his heart flashed into her mind and wouldn't leave. Whether Elle wanted her to apologise to Zack or try to build a relationship with him, there were no guarantees he'd even want to see her.

She noticed the time on her dashboard and remembered she'd promised to bring back pizza tonight and spend some time with her da. Her heart slowed and she thanked the stars that she didn't have to make this decision now.

Pulling away again, she turned and headed back to the junction that would take her home – even though part of her wanted to speed away and find the address, just to see if it really was Zack.

Later that night she struggled to focus on a conversation with her dad or even on tutoring. She realised she needed to talk to someone, but sharing her worries with Elle was out.

Instead she called Gem, but it went to voicemail.

From: Ciara Bree
To: Gemma Howard

Subject: HELP!!!

Sorry for calling, Gem. You're probably with Brian. I'm freaking

out a bit. Elle texted, asking me to visit an address and I'm almost positive it's Zack.

I want to go but at the same time I'm terrified he'll chuck me out before I even get to say sorry. Plus I'm just starting to get my life in order and my health.

The fear I can get over, I suppose. I want to see him more than anything. But is it shitty of me to try and start something with him when I'm still a bit of a mess?

Cia xxx

She didn't hear anything until the morning, even though she'd spent the night refreshing her inbox every two seconds. Oh, and she'd found the address, even written down directions.

There was no point in lying to herself. She wanted to go. The only thing that could stop her was Gem telling her it was a bad idea. But that's not what Gem said.

To: Ciara Bree
From: Gemma Howard

Subject: Re HELP!!!

Don't apologise, that's what friends are for – to help with the stupid freak-outs :-)

Go, Cia. If you don't you'll always regret it. And Elle didn't tell you where he is because she wants to crush you. She told you because you must both be miserable. Whether you're seeing a psychiatrist or not doesn't matter.

Let me know how it goes. I expect a full break-down tonight

– if you two aren't bonking each other's brains out.

Take some cream for your fufu!

Love, Gem

xxx

***

Ciara didn't waste time after that. She jumped in her car, following the directions she'd mostly memorised. Ten minutes into her drive and her hands were all sweaty on the steering wheel, not to mention her heart was palpitating. But she wasn't going to stop in case she chickened out.

She took one of the turns, drove a little further but then had to pull over. Down the road a bit was a block of old stone flats, three stories high and almost desolate. There was scaffolding all around and renovation works had started, but a year ago none of that would have stopped her in her tracks.

It was the *design*. The gable wall with the staircase had been torn down to be replaced with glass. Old to modern, edgy and classy. The front windows were also being torn out and the upper floor had been replaced with French doors, like the architect was making each column of levels into three storey town houses.

And not just any architect – she recognised the signature instantly.

He'd done it. Elle hadn't been kidding.

She shifted the car into gear and sped down the road, her breaks screeching out a protest when she stopped in front of the building. All the workmen stopped to gape at her and she rolled down the window.

'Is he here? Zack, I mean.'

One of the workers came closer. 'Na, the boss is at a meeting.'

Her heart thrummed so hard in her chest she could hardly breathe. 'Is he coming back today?'

He shook his head. 'That's him. Said he was going home for the weekend.'

'When?' she asked.

'Tomorrow, I think. You okay, lady? You look like you're going into shock.'

Hmm, she possibly was. But adrenaline was pumping fast and furiously through her veins making her mouth work ten seconds ahead of her brain. She rhymed off the address in Elle's text, asking for confirmation if Zack still lived there, just in case she'd misunderstood her friend.

'That's the one, Miss,' the worker confirmed.

'Thanks.'

She started the car, but panic started to kick in again.

Shit, what if he'd moved on and hadn't told Elle? It had been over a month since she'd seen him. Six weeks, maybe?

There were no guarantees he'd want to see her.

Still, she steered the car down another road, closer to his home. She wasn't going to let fear win.

He hadn't been in touch since the day he walked out of the Florence house. It's obvious he didn't want to see her.

But Elle gave her the address. Her old friend wasn't a bitch and Gem had seconded that. There was no way she'd set her up for heartache.

Payback is Elle's specialty and you hurt her.

Maybe.

'Feck, feck, feck.' She squeezed her eyes shut, remembered she was driving, then opened them to narrowly avoid a pothole.

She kept going through the green Irish countryside that never failed to relax her. Everything was always so peaceful out here, reminding her of weekend hikes with her da.

The last turn took her down a dirt road and she started to get a bad feeling. There weren't any turning points on the bends and as driving in reverse could topple her and the car into the burn running parallel to the road, her only option was to keep going.

What she saw gave her a second dose of the oh-shits. There was a little cottage surrounded by acres of land but that's not what caught her attention. The massive frame of a house behind it was what took her breath away.

Nothing but foundations, walls and a roof, yet she'd recognise the structure anywhere. It was Zack's dream house, becoming very much a reality way out here in the sticks. Tears welled in her eyes until she had to blink to make sure it didn't disappear.

'You did it,' she whispered to no one. 'You really did it.'

But then she snapped back to her senses. There wasn't anyone around that she could see but they could be behind the cottage. Bumping into him with her emotions in flux would be worse than embarrassing so she turned the car until she was facing the way she came – she could come back after the weekend. That way she'd have time to calm down.

There was another car making its way down the road, and no way could she get around it – the road was far too narrow. The evening sun reflected off the windshield so she couldn't identify the driver, but the fact it was a 2010 plate Mazda gave her hope it wasn't Zack. Surely he'd be in nothing less than a brand new Merc.

The car stopped at the edge of the road, blocking her escape. She swallowed hard and took a deep breath, but it didn't calm her heart.

Next the door opened and a figure she knew only too well climbed out.

Zack.

It felt like she was stuck in both her best dream and her worst nightmare all at the same time.

He was more gorgeous than she remembered, and the stubble dusting his jaw only highlighted his features. His hair was longer, but it suited him better now and he'd lost some of the muscles, making him look slimmer but she couldn't blame him. He must be crazy busy with all his projects which meant the gym would be out.

Short of sitting there gawping like an eejit, she had two options. Force his car off the road with hers in an attempt to escape or get out and say hello.

She went with the latter.

When she was out, he froze a foot away from the bonnet of her car and used a hand to shade his eyes from the sun. 'Ciara, is that you?'

Hearing his voice made her eyes sting, her blood warm and her heart stutter – it had been far too long.

She cleared her throat. 'Hi.'

'What are you doing here?' he asked and if it wasn't for the stunned joy of his tone, the question would have shattered her.

She opened her mouth and nerves made it run ten miles a minute. 'Elle text me yesterday for the first time in forever and gave me the address. I didn't know if I should come, or if you'd want me to, but I couldn't not. Then I saw the flats on the way. They were your flats, the ones you were planning to renovate in Florence! So I asked a workman if you were there and he said you weren't so I asked if this really was your address. And… here I am.'

He treated her to that knee melting half-grin. 'Even after six weeks in Ireland I struggled to catch all that. But I'm glad you're here. Elle might be stubborn, but she forwarded your last few emails to me. I'm so sorry Ciara.'

Her face heated and her vision got blurry. 'Which ones?'

She'd begged in some, been pointlessly angry in another. She'd told her friends she'd loved him before she had the lady bits to do it to his face.

'The last three,' he said.

Squeezing her eyes shut, she prayed the heat in her cheeks didn't highlight her embarrassment.

'Open your eyes, Ciara. Take a look around you.' His voice was so tempting she had to obey.

There was only green fields beyond the trees secluding his little slice of the land. Everything was private and hidden – not flashy and in-ya-face like his granddad's properties.

Then her gaze fixed on the house he was having built behind the cottage. 'You're living your dream. I can't tell you how happy that makes me.'

He came so close that she could feel his body heat and longed to reach out to him. The sizzle in her belly would have shattered her reserve if her heart didn't ache like it did.

'I am, but you're still missing the most important part of the puzzle.'

She turned to him but he was looking out to the right, out past the fields and seemingly as far as the eye could see. It only took seconds for her mind to grasp what he meant.

'You're in Ireland!' She gasped. 'Why are you in Ireland?'

His smile was so sad and so beautiful that her eyes stung again.

'Remember after our first night together in LA? I told you that we weren't over, just on hold until you realised that?'

Ciara nodded. She remembered every second of their time together with perfect clarity.

'I knew in Miami that I was falling for you. In Paris I thought I might *need* you. And it took me until we got to Santorini before I realised I definitely did. When I got to Ibiza after the argument with my granddad in Munich, I couldn't believe you wanted to help me follow my dreams and that's when I figured you must have been falling for me too. If I hadn't met you, I don't think I'd have been strong enough to take this step.'

He linked his fingers through hers and squeezed lightly.

'Elle said she told you about Vanessa – I'm sorry I didn't. But they could have offered me the world on a silver platter to bribe me to do what they wanted but it'd never be enough. It was then I realised there was no point in the world without you.'

'Zack,' she said on a gasp. Tears streamed freely down her cheeks and she couldn't stop them.

He used his thumbs to wipe them away, but the torrent was so severe he missed loads. Still, to have him touch her again… It was like her nerve endings sizzled to life after being extinct for so long. Without thinking, she said, 'Kiss me.'

He did, but it was a too-brief peck on her forehead.

That shattered her more than if he threw her off his property without saying hello.

'Ireland, it's not that I don't want to! Don't cry, sweetheart, please.'

She took a few deep breaths, trying to control herself.

He peeled off his shirt and used it to dab her face dry. Gently. Lovingly?

God her head felt like it was going to implode.

'I do want to,' he said, running his thumb over her lower lip. 'But I can't lose you again. If we're giving it a shot we're doing it right. No time limits. No fling. And we take it slow.'

She didn't want a time limit, forever wasn't long enough. And if he dared even chat up another woman she was pretty sure at this point she'd use violence to make her feelings clear. Taking it slow, however, just wasn't going to work for her.

'Zack,' she gasped, grabbing his face. 'I love you, you eejit!'

His smile was breath-taking. 'In case you hadn't noticed, I love you too.'

'So why aren't we naked right now, making up for lost time?'

He took her hands in his, dropping kisses on her fingers before he lowered them to her sides. 'You've got a lot you need to work through. From your emails to Elle I can see things are going great and I'm happy for you Ciara, but I don't want to be the one to halt that progress.'

She freed her hands. Took a few steps back. 'So… what? We don't get to be together until my shrink declares me sane?'

He shook his head. 'You *are*. It's not that at all. I just don't want to give you more to worry about while you're dealing with things from your past.'

She screwed her eyes shut, trying so hard not to cry. Logically, she knew he was right. Emotionally, he was a hundred percent wrong. 'I don't understand what you mean. Do we see other people? Get together again later when you think I can handle a relationship? Do I need to prove to you I can commit first?

He shook her shoulders until her eyes snapped open.

'There's been no one else for me since I saw you in the pool that day with Gemma. You're the only woman I've ever wanted so much that I had the strength to walk away from everything I thought I needed. It would kill me if you even kissed another man, never mind shared your body with one.'

His voice was so fierce, so earnest she couldn't doubt he was telling the truth.

'Then what do you mean by slow?' Maybe she was crossing into bunny boiler territory but she honestly didn't understand what he wanted from her.

'Think about it. We practically lived together for eight weeks. I'm not saying it was too much for me – one of the things I miss most is waking up next to you. But most couples do it the other way around. A date or two a week in the beginning, then maybe more.'

'Good point,' she said half-heartedly. 'But I never said I wanted to move straight in with you.'

He laughed. 'I know. I'm not saying it wouldn't work if you did, but we're not on holiday anymore. Both of us are starting new careers and that can be a lot of pressure by itself. I still want to see you, take you out and spend time with you, if that's what you want.'

His eyes were so earnest, not like they were when he was holding back something he didn't want her to know and he was right. A holiday fling had to be different from trying this relationship stuff in the real world, with family, jobs, etc. Plus, after everything that happened, this was way more than she deserved.

'Of course I want that. But first, I owe you a massive apology.'

She squeezed her eyes shut against the sting. 'I don't regret being with you ever. Breaking up with you because I was scared was a terrible thing to do.'

'Shh, you don't have to say that. I read the emails, I get it.'

He pulled her into his arms and held on tight while she snuggled against his shoulder. His very, very naked shoulder that smelled like musk and felt as smooth as she remembered. She returned the hug, taking the chance to get in a sneaky feel of all those muscles, and though there weren't as much as before, it still had the same effect on her as always.

He still had the same effect on her and probably always would.

He pulled away after a while, but kept a hold of her hands like he couldn't bear not to touch her either. 'Do you have dinner plans tonight?'

She was about to say no when she remembered she had work. 'Sorry, I have to tutor one of my students and get ready for a course I'm teaching.'

'I should let you go then.' He sighed. 'I'm going home this weekend. Are you free Monday night?'

Sick as it may be, she was happy to see he was disappointed waiting until then to see her. 'Monday's my day off and I don't have plans.'

His full-blown grin took her breath away. 'Then let's spend the day together. I haven't seen much of the city. You can show me around?'

She nodded. 'Can't wait.'

'Me either.' He did kiss her then, but before she could get carried away he pulled back. 'Sorry, I couldn't resist.'

'You can not resist again and again if you want. I won't complain.'

'I don't think it would stop there. I've not got that much self-control when it comes to you, Ciara Bree.'

She pouted as she opened her car door. 'Spoil sport.'

Oh how she'd missed that easy grin. 'I'll see you Monday.'

'It's a date.' She winked before sliding into the car.

He leaned over and she rolled down the window. 'Do you still have the same number?'

She nodded.

'I'll give you a call, then.'

Zack jogged over to his car and she had to bite her lip to hold in the excited squeal waiting to burst free. When the road was clear she forced herself to get going and if it wasn't for the knowledge that she'd get to see him in a few days, she'd never have been able to leave him there.

But before she got back to the main road, she pulled out her phone and got texting.

Thank you so much, Elle. I really, really needed that.

Chapter Twenty-Four

Week Seven
To: Ciara Bree, Elle Muir
From: Gemma Howard

Subject: I think it's me who has a screw loose

First of all, YES. Geeks do Dublin! Elle drag yourself away from that desk and get your skinny arse on a flight next weekend. We're having a reunion even if I have to come down there, stick a gun to your head and force you to comply. The Elle Death Glare doesn't work on me.

Cia, I'm so happy that this guy is helping you with stuff. I hope it's still going great? Don't stop just because you feel better. I'm beginning to think having someone professional to talk to is a good idea for me, but more on that in a bit.

Are you still at the café? How's the teaching going? No wait, we can talk about all that next weekend – it's happening, my flight's booked so make sure you get it off work!

So, about my sanity issues. After a particularly intense session of the best-sex-of-my-life, something weird happened to me. It might have been the endorphins, it may have been the way he screwed me like I was a Goddess in need of all the pleasure the body can give, but after we were done, I opened my mouth and the worst set of words in the world came out.

'I think I'm falling in love.'

He looked so terrified I quickly added 'with your dick' but I don't think he believed it. This was last night, he's out in another lab today and hasn't so much as text me. I think I've fucked everything up.

Gem

xxx

(P.S I'm no longer using the L word. Ever!)

***

To: Ciara Bree, Gemma Howard
From: Elle Muir

Subject: What happened to the world as I know it?

Gem, I was hyperventilating on your behalf reading that. Nice save, though. I hope the silly twat comes to his senses. He was the one who wanted to date you after all! Do you love him? Honey intense sex can make emotions strong but you sound like you're trying to convince yourself that loving him is wrong.

It. Is. Not.

A bit soon maybe, but not wrong.

Cia, I don't know where to begin, but let me try.

I feel awful. I am one of your best friends and I didn't notice any of the things you've had to find out by yourself. That, without all the other crap, makes me the worst friend ever. If anything it's me who has the making up to do.

Florence was a shock. After everything, I expected you to go home and still be with Zack. Even if he stayed to work with us you'd only be an hour away and I knew he wouldn't dare cheat on you or I'd personally remove his balls and dick with a blunt (and very rusty) knife. Without anaesthetic.

He's here now and he told me you went to see him. I cried a little and threatened him a lot – I need to know he's going to treat you right. I have no doubt he will. Neither Granddad nor I have ever seen him this happy. Be warned though, Papa Muir is already mentally planning your wedding – that's just him. He gets a little carried away when it comes to me and Zack, which is why I've not told him I'm seeing Marco yet!

I'd love to come to Dublin next weekend, if I'm still welcome?

I miss you two more than I miss carbs. Lots more.

Love, Elle

xxx

***

To: Elle Muir, Gemma Howard
From: Ciara Bree

Subject: *Shocked face*

Gem, please answer your phone. It's Sunday already and you haven't replied! We're so worried about you.

Elle, thank you for that, but I fecked up too. I'm finally in a place where I know what I want and it's scarier than a tea party with Mike Myers and Freddy Kruger but that's not going to hold me back this time.

But please calm down Papa Muir. Marriage is so not on the cards right now – we're just seeing how we work in the real world now. Wedding bells are miles off – if ever. It never did anything for my parents.

I can't wait to see you both at the weekend. Can we stay in Dublin? I still have my Geeks on Tour tee-shirt. The city people haven't seen it yet...

Gem, PLEASE email or text or phone. We need to know you're alright.

Love, Cia

Xxx

⋆

Checking her phone every two seconds reminded her of the first few days in Santorini, except it wasn't Zack's name she hoped would flash up on her screen.

'Are you okay?' Zack asked, slowing his steps so he could look down at her.

'I'm worried about Gem. She usually emails from the lab when it's quiet but we've not heard from her in days.' That wouldn't be unusual either, since she met Brian her free time was usually filled by him. 'Of course it would help if my useless brick of a phone would load my inbox. First thing I do at the end of the month is replace this piece of shit.'

He led her over to a bench, pulled his iPhone from his pocket and handed it to her. 'It won't load fast out here but it might be quicker than yours.'

She smiled. 'Thank you. And I'm sorry for ruining this date.'

He kissed her nose – he'd been doing a lot of that this morning. Kissing her sweetly whenever he got the chance. Like she'd ever try to stop him.

She opened up his browser, surfed to the right page and had her user name and password in before he could say a word. Impressive.

'If you're here there isn't much that could ruin it for me. And by now you've probably shown me everything there is to see in the city.'

She looked to him instead of the screen, now dealing with more than worry. 'Does that mean the date's over?'

Zack laughed. 'I've missed your crazy assumptions. We have the rest of the day and night too, if you don't have any other plans.'

'None,' she said, smiling again. 'Let me see if she's replied.'

Gem's name flashing in her inbox was the best sight in the world. She opened the email, tearing up a little as Gem confirmed her absence was because she spent the weekend in Edinburgh with Brian. Apparently he'd been upset because she told him she loved him after sex and he thought it was an in-the-moment thing, when he was starting to feel for her for real.

'I'm guessing it's good news?' Zack asked.

'The best,' she said, wiping her tears away. 'They're coming over Friday and wondered if we could make the weekend a triple date thing. I don't mind going by myself, if you're busy.'

She didn't want to pressure him and Elle had played the fifth wheel in Santorini, surely it wouldn't kill her.

'*Triple?*' he asked, pulling his brows together.

Oops. Looked like Elle hadn't mentioned Marco to Zack either. 'Yeah, Elle's still seeing that Italian guy who bought the wine in Florence.'

He shook his head with a smile. 'She's more cunning than I thought. Did she tell you our granddad is already picturing me walking you down the aisle? If he knew about Marco he'd probably make us have a double wedding.'

Ciara's cheeks burned and her heart took off. She could barely get him into bed. Marriage felt like an unrealistic goal for a few years at least – if she ever decided she wanted to marry him. 'She mentioned it.'

'Well, I can't have you being the odd one out.' He lifted her onto his knee and wrapped his arms around her. She snuggled back into his chest, thinking this was *exactly* where she wanted to be as calm washed over her. 'Will we stay in a hotel here?'

As long as it was together, she didn't care. 'Sounds perfect. Though you might have to let things speed up a little if you plan to share a room with me. I don't have that much self-control.'

'I'm not making love to you for the first time in months in a hotel,' he said, deadly serious.

At least it felt deadly, to her overexcited imagination. 'But Zack—'

He laughed. 'Why don't you come over Thursday night after

your lesson? I'll cook us dinner and you can stay the night. We could go meet the crazy duo together.'

'Really?' She wriggled round so she could see his face. 'I can stay at yours?'

'Don't look so surprised, it makes me feel like a shit. If I'm honest when I saw you last week, an insane part of me wanted to drag you into my cottage and bolt the doors so you couldn't get away again.'

She grinned so hard her cheeks hurt. 'It would probably have worried my da, but I don't think I would've protested too much.'

'You shouldn't have told me that, it could still happen...'

This time she took the lead, kissing him full on the mouth like she'd wanted to do since what felt like forever. He cupped her face, then slid his hands into her hair to massage her now tingling scalp. The fire in her core made her forget everything, including where she was, and when Zack parted her lips with his she lost control.

Straddling him, she deepened the kiss until she wished the clothes in their way would spontaneously combust to save her the hassle of having to remove them. But now it was worse, because it was cold and their coats were too thick she couldn't run her fingers over every inch of him like she needed to.

Someone cleared their throat and she broke away from him in a daze. They were in the middle of a street now filled with people finishing work for the day. A man walked by them, tutting and shaking his head as he went.

'I thought you were the sensible one?' she asked. Why hadn't he stopped them like always?

One look in his eyes and she had her answer. They were burning for her, with more than lust. Need. Pure and simple. 'Oh.'

'Thursday.' He said the word like a curse.

Now sounded better. But they did have a few things to talk through before they headed for the bedroom. Even though they'd gone over everything that happened pre-break-up (as per her psychiatrist's suggestion), the future was still uncertain. She didn't know if he wanted all the things she did – all the things she'd been too scared to want a month ago.

'Thursday,' she agreed with a sigh.

***

Despite spending two days so desperate she almost made a trip to Anne Summers (more than once!) for something to take the ache away, it wasn't lust coursing through her as Ciara drove down the little dirt road to Zack's house.

It was the jitters again, vibrating through her muscles until she was worried she wouldn't be able to stop the car. But, like her psychiatrist taught her, she took a few deep breaths and managed to make it without totalling his cottage with her Fiesta.

Parking up next to his car, she took a few minutes to calm down. They hadn't talked much about the future but he'd assured her more than once that he was in it for the long haul with her. There were never guarantees they were going to last forever, and she was beginning to accept it, though she was still scared.

But the main thing, the most important thing, was that she loved him with all her heart and she was sure he felt the same. He'd moved to Ireland to start his business and not because land or property was cheap – it was far from it. He'd come hoping she'd be ready for more with him one day.

He'd been brave enough to take that leap knowing there was every chance she'd never change her mind.

Now it was her turn.

Mentally pulling on her big girl knickers, she got out of the car. Zack was waiting for her at the door, but he came over and helped with her bags.

'Is it just me or does it feel like a week since we were together?' he asked, cupping her cheek.

The nerves fizzled away at the words. The way he was looking at her like he was mesmerised helped a bit, too. 'It's definitely not just you.'

He took her hand and led her through his home. Even though he probably planned to knock it down when the bigger house was built, he still kept the place nice. The interior had a charming country feel, but even better were his personal touches. Family photographs lining the mantels – and he opened up with her more, explaining who they all were – a tapestry hanging on a wall that was made by his great-grandmother, and there was even a cabinet for his trophies. All of which he'd won at uni on the football team.

Dinner wasn't fancy, just good old steak and chips but she enjoyed it. More so the way they shared childhood stories, both the bad memories and the good. By the time it got late and they'd finished a bottle of wine by the fire, she felt she knew him, body mind and soul – cheesy as it sounded even to herself.

'Does your dad know where you're staying tonight?' he asked with a grin.

Ciara rolled her eyes. 'I'm not fifteen anymore, but yes he does.' She bit her lip before her da's request slipped out.

'What? Is he not happy with it?'

'It's not that.' Her hands started shaking so much she had to put the glass down on the table in case it spilled. 'He wants to meet you.'

Sucking in a breath, she waited for the swift 'no, it's too soon.'

But he was back to using the poker face. Only this time was different. His eyes were creased a little around the corners.

'I should hope so. I wouldn't want our daughter staying with a strange man, whatever age she is,' he said, then a grin broke free.

'You want to have kids with me?' she squeaked. 'I thought you wanted to take things slow?'

'Not right this second, though practising the mechanics of *making* them wouldn't be a bad idea…'

She couldn't even blink, she was so gobsmacked.

The amusement disappeared and he got serious. 'Don't you think about that stuff, Ciara? The future, us, where we go from here?'

'All the time,' she whispered.

'So kids aren't a stretch? One day, I mean. There are so many places I want to explore with you first and, call me selfish, but I've just got you back. I want to keep you to myself for a little while longer.' He linked his fingers through hers and squeezed.

'It's not a stretch. Not at all. And I know exactly what you mean.' Maybe dreams did come true, after all.

'I'm glad we're on the same page,' he said, pulling her onto his lap.

She went willingly, threading her fingers through his hair. It was even silkier now he'd let it grow out a bit, and the stubble on his chin was softer against her lips when she kissed his jaw.

'I've not had much time for grooming. Sorry.'

'Don't be. I like it. But honestly, all I can think about is how it will feel when you're, you know. Down *there*.' His grin had heat scoring her cheekbones.

'Lie down and you'll find out.'

Instead of waiting for her to move, he laid her down on the sofa and kissed her softly. She tried to pull him back for more, but he found her neck and the shivers made her heart quicken. She really, really liked the feel of his beard on her skin. Her core burned imagining how he'd feel between her legs.

The buttons on her blouse were next to go and she managed to wriggle out of it without him having to stop his nibbles and kisses down her body. Then he bit the cup of her bra, right over a straining nipple and a current ran straight between her legs.

She was on fire now, and the nearer her waistband he got the more impatient she grew. The torture his lips were wreaking on her stomach only added to the inferno. She wouldn't last long, not after all this time, but she wanted this a different way.

'Zack, the bedroom. I want you in me. Now.'

He undid her zip anyway. 'I want my mouth on you. Now.'

It was a good argument and when he managed to do just that after shuffling her jeans down to her hips, she almost forgot why she'd want to stop this.

But she didn't forget completely.

'Please, Zack. I don't want to come like this. Not the first time.'

He still spent another few seconds driving her to the edge before he stopped. 'Okay, but I can't promise the first time will last very long.'

'I don't think I'll need more than a minute,' she said between gasps.

After ditching the rest of her clothes, she ran behind him through the house. The second the bedroom door opened she attacked his shirt, tugging it off in record time. He dealt with his own jeans and pulled them off with his underwear.

They toppled onto the bed in a tangle of limbs, but it didn't take long for him to get in position.

'Two seconds,' he said, reaching into a drawer next to his bed.

She was happy to note the condom box was brand new and untouched. Not so happy with the interruption. 'Feck this. I'm going on the pill first thing Monday.'

'Ever impatient,' he said.

It took too long, but when they were safe time seemed to slow. They just stared at each other and Ciara wondered briefly if she'd wake up and this would be a crazy dream. Then he kissed her, so slowly and passionately that she knew this was real, right down to her bones.

Her body welcomed his like it had been hours instead of months and despite his concerns, they rocked together for much longer than a minute.

She squeezed her muscles to keep him there, she'd happily keep them joined like this for days if she could. And he must have felt the same, because when they'd both found ecstasy, he just rolled them over until she was lying on his chest, still connected.

Chapter Twenty-Five

Week Fifteen
To: Elle Muir, Gemma Howard
From: Ciara Bree

Subject: Meet the Muirs

For the record, Meet the Brees was uneventful. My da and Zack talked sport and then watched sport. I had been prepared for him to give Zack the third degree, but nothing.

Meet the Muirs was worse than the movie.

First, massive thank you, Elle. Your absence was so NOT appreciated this weekend.

My trip to London (on which I expected at least one familiar face to hand-hold me through the ordeal) was embarrassing – and that's putting it mildly.

Papa Muir spent Saturday showing Zack and I all the lovely places for weddings and he'd even gone to the trouble to check availability for next summer. I almost had a full scale panic attack.

But wait! It gets better!

He took us to the Ivy on Saturday night and introduced us to EVERYONE as his grandkids. I'm not sure who was more uncomfortable. Me or the waiter who really didn't want to hear the story about how he almost made Zack marry Vanessa for his own good.

And if that isn't enough to scar a girl for life, Sunday constituted a trip to his golf club where I was introduced to my boyfriend's ex as 'the one he's going to marry'.

I know he meant well, and I'm happy he's welcoming me to the family. But THAT had to be the worst two days of my life.

Zack said he will make you pay for not being there to keep the man's feet on the earth. He mentioned something about inviting Marco over.

Big difference from our weekend in Dublin! Maybe we should go see Gem and Brian one weekend soon? Despite hating Elle a little, I miss you both.

Love, Ciara

xxx

To: Gemma Howard, Ciara Bree
From: Elle Muir

Subject: We are NOT having a double wedding

Tell Zack the blunt knife is rusting up nicely – serves him right for spilling the beans about Marco!

You think your weekend was bad? All I've had is constant nagging about getting married alongside you two next year! I don't want all that yet – if ever! I'm all about the career, thank you very much.

A weekend together sounds great. Just us girls this time?

Love, Elle

xxx

***

Week Twenty
To: Elle Muir, Gemma Howard
From: Ciara Bree

Subject: EEEEEEEEEEEEEEE

I had a fab boy-free weekend. We HAVE to do that more often!

Guess what the squealing's about? Zack showed me the plans for the internal layout of the house he's having built, saying he wants to decorate it together. As in, both of us. As in, we're going to be living there. TOGETHER!

It won't be finished for months yet, but I can't help but be excited. Who knew I could get so excited over something commitment-like. Maybe marriage wouldn't be such a stretch.

Any news/goss?

Love, Cia

xxx

***

To: Ciara Bree, Elle Muir
From: Gemma Howard

Subject: News/Goss

Amazing Cia! I'm so happy for you. Papa Muir might get his wedding next year after all. Dibs on Maid of Honour – I can make us t-shirts for the hen night!

I have some news too. It's terrifying, and I haven't told Brian just yet, but I think I'm pregnant. Since yesterday I've bought twelve tests, peed on every single one, and only two were negative.

Very, very scary. But also quite exciting.

Love (because I'm now a believer)

Gem

xxx

***

To: Ciara Bree, Gemma Howard
From: Elle Muir

Subject: Tempted to swear like Ciara

I'm sitting in the fanciest restaurant in Florence, about to email you three with some of my own news and screamed full blast when I read your emails.

Oh my god we're going to be aunties! Congratulations Gem!

Cia, I'm so happy for you. Now get working on that ring. If you like you can tell Zack the blunt knife has rusted up nicely...

And I know I'm a contradicting bitch, but I'm now an engaged one. The minute he asked me to marry him I knew it's what I really wanted.

Crossing my fingers for a triple wedding next year!

Since you called dibs on Ciara's wedding, Gem, I'm pre-claiming yours. But there will be no more t-shirts.

Cia, would you like to be my maid of honour?

Love you all, even more than Marco (just)

Elle

xxx

**

To: Ciara Bree, Elle Muir
From: Gemma Howard

Subject: More EEEEEEEEEEEES

Congratulations! I knew you were a romantic deep down, Elle!

Brian took the news well. He asked me to move in to see if we'll work prior to the baby coming. I don't think it will be a problem. I'm hot for him ALL the time now my hormones are out of sync, and a lack of sex is what ends a relationship 80% of the time, isn't it? If not, don't tell me!

We need to get together to plan this wedding. Maybe at Papa Muirs? He won't want to be left out.

Cia, how are things?

Love, Gem

xxx

***

To: Gemma Howard, Elle Muir
From: Ciara Bree

Subject: Look at us, all grown up

Elle & Gem, that's amazing news. I'm so happy for you and definitely up for a get together to plan the wedding! As I'm not planning to have one anytime soon, can we change the location? Papa Muir scares me.

Zack and I have talked a lot about marriage. He's been pressured to do it before and doesn't want to ask me to marry him until his granddad stops forcing the issue. I've realised that I'd actually love to be Mrs Ciara Muir, but I'm not worried it won't happen. He showed me his mum's ring and asked if it was something I'd want to wear (it's gorgeous, really) when he proposes. So I know it's on the cards one day. I'm just thrilled to have a second chance with him. It's more than I deserve.

Really excited to be an aunt, too. I can teach the baby how to cuss properly when he or she's older ;o)

Elle, Gem's t-shirts are our thing! We have to wear them.

Now I have to go. My man has a romantic night planned for me which I'm sure Elle doesn't want to hear about.

Love you both always,

Cia

Xxx